From Brat to Bronco

Book One

HUNTER MARSHALL

FROM BRAT TO BRONCO

Copyright © 2018

From Brat to Bronco

HUNTER MARSHALL

Huntermarshall78@gmail.com

All rights reserved. Except as permitted under the U.S. Copyright Act of 2011, no part of this publication may be reproduced, distributed, or transmitted in any form or by any means, or stored in a database or retrieval system, without the prior written permission of the publisher except in the case of brief quotations embodied in critical articles and reviews.

The characters and events portrayed in this book are fictitious. Any similarity to real persons, living or dead, is coincidental and not intended by the author.

ISBN: 9798746596222

For more information visit our Facebook Fan Page:
https://www.facebook.com/huntermarshall2015

Cover Design by Jessica Ozment

Formatting by Jessica Ozment

**CONNECT WITH
AUTHOR HUNTER MARSHALL**

Facebook Fan Page:

https://www.facebook.com/huntermarshall2015

Acknowledgements

There are so many people who helped me throughout the writing of this novella. I'd like to thank Stacey Kamerer, Melissa Davison and Karen Hrdlicka for their assistance in naming the main characters. I couldn't decide on only one suggestion, so I used parts of the names that you ladies gave.

    Jessica Tahbonemah, you, my friend, have become a vital person in my small tribe. As usual, you have created a fabulous cover and been available whenever I need anything.

    Thank you to those family and friends who have cheered me on either near or far, never allowing me to throw in the towel. You guys rock!

    I want my children to know that I they are the reason I write. They are the reason I keep going. I hope you both know how much you are loved, needed and wanted.

    And, my parents, what can I say? They have always believed in my writing ability and knew long before I did what I would do with it. Thank you, momma, for yet another fantastic title and helping me come up with a storyline that is me and for convincing me to spread my wings.

**Hunter Marshall,
2018**

Prologue

"I cannot believe this!" Roxanne McCain shrieked as she repeatedly read the letter she tightly gripped in her hand. She wanted to let out a string of expletives, but she had been raised in a home where ladies did not use such foul language. She didn't think her mother, Belinda, was home, but she wasn't about to chance it. So, gritting her teeth, Roxanne coaxed herself through her state of hysteria. That was something she had learned, being reared by a mother who was a fantastic psychologist—obtaining an appointment with her took weeks. Then there was her father, Robert, who was the best psychiatrist in Los Angeles, California. Her parents owned their own counseling center, so growing up, Roxanne had been therapied more often than most.

"What in the world is going on?" A concerned Belinda rushed into Roxanne's bedroom where she found her daughter standing in the middle of the room, clutching a crumpled piece of paper.

"I'm sorry, mother; I wasn't aware you were home." She hung her head like a child who had been scolded.

"What has caused you to screech so loudly? I'm certain the neighbors have heard everything!"

Roxanne apologized again and handed the paper to Belinda. Tears leaked from her bright green eyes as she waited to hear what her mother had to say. An eternity. That was the only word Roxanne could think of to describe this waiting period.

"What did I tell you when you began applying?" Belinda questioned.

Roxanne could not believe her mother had chosen *that* moment, the single most important moment in her life, to treat her as if she was a ten-year-old again. "Yes, I remember," she mumbled.

"And?" Belinda tapped her foot, exasperated. Sometimes she wondered if her strong-willed daughter heard a word she said. She was certain that when she spoke, Roxanne's ears closed.

"You said that I should apply to more than one college. That I might not get into Vanderbilt."

"You didn't do that, did you?"

"No."

"Maybe next time you will listen to me."

Roxanne hated when Belinda made her feel like she was fifteen inches tall. *I am a grown woman,* she fumed as she listened to mother rant. She knew, though, that she couldn't refute what her mother had said, because she had learned a long time ago to stay quiet when this happened, or the tirade would continue until Roxanne was certain her ears would bleed. "Yes, mother," she breathed a sigh of relief only she could hear, grateful her mother was finished.

"We will speak with your father when he arrives and get his opinion on our best course of action."

Roxanne didn't fear her father or his lectures as much as she did her mother's. He had a way about him that, whenever life threw him a curve ball, he made it seem like it was no big deal at all. He accomplished this, most of the time, by his mere presence in a room, and this was definitely a curve ball in Roxanne's book.

Over dinner that evening—a pan seared salmon with mashed potatoes and okra—the family discussed what Roxanne should do next. Without her mother's knowledge, Roxanne had spoken to Robert about the reasons she wanted to attend an out of state school. Although she loved her mother, she felt that her father understood her better. She felt that he accepted her, no questions asked. They had discussed Vanderbilt, and the fact that her mother was the reason she wanted to attend that college over any other. She wanted to make her mother proud, and this seemed the best way to do it.

"If you are genuine about going to an out of state university, there are many to choose from, but it would be in your best interest to take courses you can transfer to Vanderbilt." Belinda mentioned, urging her daughter to be mindful of all aspects.

"That does make sense," Robert inserted. "There's always the University of Tennessee in Chattanooga," he smirked.

It took Roxanne a second to realize that was where Robert had attended college, at the same time her mother went to Vanderbilt. "Daddy, is it hard to get in there?" She at least wanted to consider it, and because he was an alumnus, maybe he could write her a letter of recommendation, if that was even allowed.

"It wasn't for me, but Johns Hopkins? Now, that's another story."

"Would you help me apply?" Roxanne felt desperate. Her confidence had waned with the rejection from Vanderbilt.

"Of course, sweetheart. Whatever you need, we are here. We love you and want you to succeed."

Later that night, after Roxanne went clubbing with her two best friends Tara and Simone, she stretched out in bed and thought about what leaving Los Angeles meant for her. She had never been anywhere else; vacations, yes, but she had never moved to another state before. She would leave behind her gal pals, though they could stay in contact easily with technology as advanced as it was.

Roxanne had been out of high school for three years. Her parents were not pleased when she told them the night of graduation that she wanted to take a year off. "To do what I want to do," she told them. In reality, college was the farthest thing from her mind and, and until last year, she hadn't thought much about it. Her parents had money; what did she need a degree for? That was where her thought process was. But, once she realized that her parents, in fact, worked extremely hard for what she took for granted, she knew it was time to grow up.

$$\Omega$$

Zachary Blaze wished for nothing more than the opportunity to further his education. There was only so much he could do with what he had learned watching his mom and dad, Susan and Darren, build their vet clinic in the small town of Cleveland, Tennessee where they lived. He had planned to go to college straight out of high school and had even been accepted into the University of Tennessee in Chattanooga. Tragically, his sixteen-year-old brother, Bryce, had been killed in a four-wheeling accident two years before and Zach needed to stay to help with the clinic. But he wanted to do much more than make appointments and put away patient files. He wanted to, one day, own Blaze Vet Clinic.

"You haven't asked them yet, have you?" Zachary's eighteen-year-old sister, Stevie, asked. Stevie was different than either of her brothers. If their parents would allow it, she would be content to not graduate high school, but instead, immediately settle down with her pothead boyfriend, Jeb.

"No. I haven't. Wouldn't it be better if I stayed?"

"You know that I can do your job with my eyes closed! You don't need to be here all the time."

He was teasing, but only a little. "So, you're sayin' you guys don't need me here anymore." He winked, trying to downplay the hurt he felt. But this was what he wanted, right? Maybe he could still pull off a part-time shift even when in school.

"Awwww. Are your feelings hurt?" Stevie teased. "You know we love having you home, but you ARE getting up there, and I think Mom and Dad would rather have grandkids sooner than later, rather than keep you tied up here filing charts and checking patients in. You need to get out there because you most definitely won't find the right woman here since you haven't already—not that you've looked all that hard."

"Okay, okay. I'll talk to them."

"When?" Stevie was eager.

"I don't know. Tonight soon enough for you?" He couldn't figure out why she pushed the issue. It wasn't like he wouldn't still be living at home. The University of Tennessee was fairly close—only about thirty minutes away. Being able to live at home would help, because college was expensive no matter where he chose to attend.

That evening, much to Susan's chagrin, Darren allowed Stevie to go on a date with Jeb. They didn't like him, for they felt that he would pull their exceptionally smart daughter down the hole he was in the process of digging for himself but Zachary saw this as an opportunity to brave the conversation he had been dreading the last couple of years, and the time was nigh. His parents were sitting on the couch in the living room, watching the evening news.

Zachary waited until a commercial came on before clearing his throat, vying for their attention. "Can I talk to you for a second?" he hedged. Once given permission, he launched into his argument.

Chapter 1

Roxanne could not believe the enormity of the buildings located on the University of Tennessee at Chattanooga site. Although she came from L.A., she hadn't expected such a large campus. It hadn't taken long to receive the admissions letter, and that was due largely to the fact that her father, Robert, was an alumnus. She wrung her hands together until they were red as she glanced around at the sea of unfamiliar faces. *I shouldn't have told them to let me come alone.* Not a lot frightened her, but this...this did.

Roxanne pushed a dark chocolate strand of chin length hair behind her ear. The wind was making it terribly difficult to see where she was going. She didn't notice him until she heard an audible "Umph."

"Oh, I—I'm dreadfully sorry," she stuttered as she peered up through her long, ebony eyelashes. The creature before her was unlike any she had seen before; and being from Los Angeles, she had seen many different types of people.

"Are you okay?" Zachary asked as he bent down to pick up the books she had dropped.

"Yes. I'm fine," she offered a smile. *Who is this fine specimen?* She had seen cowboys before, but none that looked as comfortable in their skin as the one standing before her in his denim Wranglers, white t-shirt under a navy-blue button up, and a rodeo belt buckle and brown lace up boots which completed his ensemble. He had straight, jet black hair that curled a bit at the collar. Roxanne saw it peeking out at her. His eyes...oh, those steel gray depths. She could get lost in them.

"My name's Zachary. What's yours?" His southern accent was thick. He couldn't be far from home.

"Roxanne," she croaked. She never tripped over her tongue before; she was too refined for that, but this man caused her to forget things, even something as simple as the name she was given.

"Nice to meet ya." Zachary drawled. He wasn't the type of person to put himself out there, but there was something about those green eyes and the dimple in her left cheek that prompted him to continue the conversation. "Where are you from?" It was only then that it dawned on him that they were still standing smack dab in the middle of the sidewalk.

"L. A."

"Would you like to go get a drink or somethin'?"

Roxanne had never heard a man speak like that—removing the -ing from the end of a word. Somehow, he made it sound sexy. She couldn't control the giggle that erupted from her lips when she realized why he'd asked that. "Yes. We probably should get out of the way," she watched as the throng of students and faculty, for the most part, went around them.

Zachary preferred the atmosphere of a bar, although he didn't drink, but she was too classy to take her someplace like that, so he settled on a small coffee shop not more than a stone's throw from where they were. He'd been raised a gentleman and pulled her chair out for her before taking his own. He'd never been in this particular shop, but he enjoyed the smell of coffee as it wafted through the air.

He hadn't realized he was off in his own world until he heard, "So, where are you from?"

"Scuse me?" He mentally berated himself.

She was used to being at the center of attention when she wasn't at home. To have to repeat herself was something Roxanne wasn't used to doing. It made her mad, but she bit back the retort she badly wanted to throw at him. Instead she repeated, "Where are you from?"

Zachary wasn't sure what had made her so angry, for he could sense the hostility as if it were tangible in the air. Maybe that was the way conversations took place in the big city. He chose to answer her question, instead of drawing attention to her mood. "Oh...I'm from Cleveland."

"Ohio?"

Zachary made the mistake of taking a large swing of his Cherry Coke right as she made the comment. He didn't want to spew the dark liquid all over her so he swallowed it, which caused an enormous coughing fit. Roxanne was none the wiser for the reason he choked. Her response was kind of funny, but Zach didn't want to give her a bad impression of him. Once his coughing fit was over, he replied, "No, it's about thirty minutes from here."

"Oh, well…that's something new I learned, then." He watched her smile at him, but it appeared to be forced. For some reason, it made Zach want to get to know her better.

"Do you have siblings?"

Zach knew if he was going to meet people, this subject would come up and therefore it was inevitable that the facts surrounding Bryce's accident would come out. Roxanne hadn't noticed the tension that Zach was certain everyone else in the joint had felt. He figured it would be easiest to be as vague as he could. If they became friends, he might, someday, tell her.
Taking a deep breath, he whispered, "Yes."

Why has he gotten quiet? Almost like he isn't comfortable with my question? The nosiness in her wanted to get at the answer, but before she could form a question, Zach opened his mouth.

"I have a little sister, Stevie; she's eighteen and still in high school. I had a younger brother, Bryce; he died over two years ago."

"Oh—" Roxanne gasped. "How awful!" She didn't know if she wanted the full story. She could see how crushed Zach was just uttering Bryce's name.

"We don't talk about it much."

"Who doesn't?" She pried.

"My family." Zach shredded a piece of napkin into tiny bits he'd found on the table between them, willing his anxiety to go away. Then, he asked a sure-fire question to either change the subject, or just like some of the other girls he had dated, make her run for the hills. "Because his death was so horrible, I have anxiety. Does that bother you?"

Roxanne let out a chirp, somewhere between a giggle and a full-on laugh.

What is she laughing at? "Pardon me." She was embarrassed. "It's not funny…really, it isn't. It's just that my mom is a therapist and my dad is a psychiatrist, so I know all about being psychoanalyzed. Lived through it my whole life."

"So…it doesn't bother you?" His eyebrows furrowed.

"No. In fact, I think everyone has anxiety every now and again. Who wouldn't with the world we live in?"

"I not only have anxiety, which is a constant in my life, but I have a panic disorder as well, which means I panic on top of already being anxious." Zach waited, and heaved a sigh of relief when she smiled. He didn't know Roxanne well, but he liked her. She was different from the cowboy boots, jean wearing girls he was accustomed to seeing. She was primped right down to her red, manicured nails and black stiletto heels. "We should probably be gettin' back. Tomorrow morning will be here before we know it, and I still gotta make sure I have all my supplies and know where all my classes are."

Roxanne tucked her hair behind both ears. She didn't want the day to end so she posed a question. "I have to go to the bookstore and was going to see where my first class is at. Would you like to come with me?"

Zachary wanted to get to know Roxanne better, but he had already divulged more to her in the two hours they'd spent talking, than to any of the other girls he'd been out with. Period. He felt overwhelmed by it all and needed time to decompress. How could he let her down gently without hurting her feelings? He didn't know her well enough, yet, to determine what might set her on edge. Instead of hemming and hawing over it for too long, he muttered, "Would you mind if we meet up another time?"

Roxanne was astounded. She was beautiful, and fun, and kept men's attention for hours longer than she had this hick's. *He's not much different, is he? When he tires of a woman, he makes an excuse.* She felt her blood boiling. *What should I do? Should I blow him off or play the desperate fool?* If there was one thing she had learned from her mother, it was never to settle; never let them see you hurt or desperate. "Well," Roxanne huffed "if you don't want to walk around with me, all you have to do is say so. You don't even have the gumption to come up with a good excuse."

Zach was floored at how quickly she had gone from sweet to feisty. He would even say pissy. He didn't think that he needed to give her an excuse. He didn't feel like being around people, but how could he explain that to her? Better yet, why did he even care? They'd only met a matter of minutes ago, and she was already making him uncomfortable.

"Umm…I didn't mean to offend you, and for that, I'm sorry. I just need to be alone right now." That was the best he could come up with.

A deafening silence ensued. Roxanne had nothing to say to him. She was more than angry. Thinking it better to leave, she grabbed her purse, slung it hastily over her shoulder, grumbled a "Thank you for the coffee," and briskly left the coffee shop.

Throughout the rest of the afternoon, Zach couldn't fathom why Roxanne had become so upset at his question. Knowing she could blow up that fast concerned him. Was she seriously someone he wanted to get to know better? There was one thing he was certain of—he needed someone who could handle the times when he wanted solitude—someone gentle, kind and understanding.

Ω

The morning school started, Roxanne awoke feeling good about the day that lay ahead. She'd taken time the previous day to find her first class; one she wasn't the least bit excited about attending. *Math. Bleh!* And, because it had been a few years since her last Algebra class, she was required to start at an Algebra I level. She had decided before coming to the University of Tennessee that, because she had no idea what she wanted to major in, she would complete her general education classes first. This semester she was taking Algebra, English 101, Science 100, and a sewing class—she had never touched a sewing machine, but hopefully, it would be easier than it looked. She might change it. As luck would have it, the students didn't have to have everything figured out that first day and could withdraw within the time allotted.

She looked in her full-length mirror, checking to be certain there wasn't a hair out of place, that there was no lipstick on her teeth—although she blotted her lips just as her mother had taught her—that her dark purple pencil skirt and cream colored, fringed blouse, tan pantyhose and black stiletto pumps all looked spectacular. "Not bad, if I do say so myself." The pep talk she gave herself every morning helped her begin her day on a positive note.

Ω

Zach rolled over in bed, slamming his fist down onto his alarm clock. He hated the need to get up an hour earlier just because he lived at home to save money. He knew he wanted to be a veterinarian, so getting all his general classes out of the way was essential. His first class of the day was Algebra. It was not the only math class he needed, but he was certain he had forgotten everything he had learned in high school.

Zach stayed in bed longer than he should have and had to rush to get to his Algebra class on time. Getting ready for the day was easy for him. His attire consisted of blue Wranglers, a t-shirt, his favorite dark brown lace up boots, and his baseball cap.

Arriving at the door of his first class just in the nick of time, he skidded to a halt to catch his breath. The first thing he noticed upon entering wasn't the teacher, or even the room full of students. It was the dark chocolate bob of the girl he was sure was crazy, or close to it. He couldn't obliterate their first encounter in his mind. *That* was why he hadn't slept the night before. It was not that she was ugly. Far from it, in fact, but the way she went from girlie cute to mad psycho within a matter of minutes stumped him. He would have enough on his plate trying to get into vet school. that he contemplated whether he should forge ahead with that…what was it...friendship? What if he did go ahead with it as a friendship and that wasn't good enough for her? Or if he pursued her as a romantic interest and she only wanted friendship? He blew out a deep breath and took a seat, but not one close enough could see that they were in the same math class.

The class had gotten rowdy by the time the professor, Mr. Jeffries, rapped his yardstick on the desk—hard enough to almost break it in half…almost. He was an older gentleman with thinning gray hair, wearing high water, puke green slacks held up by bright orange suspenders, paired with a navy blue and red plaid shirt. To top off the outfit, he wore a yellow and white polka dotted bow tie. He might have looked old, but the boom in his voice when he spoke blew that all to hell. "Good morning, students! My name is Ebenezer Jeffries and I am your Algebra I professor."

A dutiful chorus of, "Good morning Professor Jeffries," followed. Just then, someone piped up with, "Can we call you Ebenezer?" followed by a round of laughter. "Yeah, as in Ebenezer Scrooge?" another jokester added his two cents.

"Have you no manners?" From where Zach sat, he couldn't tell what the reaction was going to be, but the professor was excessively calm when he posed the question to the two who thought they were funny. "No, you may call me Professor Jeffries or even Professor. Are there any questions pertaining to Algebra before I hand out the syllabus for the semester?"

Silence followed as Professor Jeffries handed out stacks and stacks of paper with what appeared to be assignments and a checklist each student must do each night. Roxanne peered at the papers she held. They were required to have a study partner, someone to do homework assignments with, to talk through problems they weren't understanding—and the clincher? On test day, they were required to take the test together.

Once they had gotten through the syllabus, Professor Jeffries said, "Now, I know you are all college students, and therefore, think you're all grown up, but too many times in previous years when I allowed the students to choose their own study buddy, there was always confusion and cattiness. Because of that, I will choose who your partners are. In fact, I pair you up even before the beginning of the semester and make changes if needed."

Zach gulped. Roxanne hadn't seen him yet, but it would be his dumb luck if they ended up as study buddies. He fervently repeated, "Please don't let her be mine..." over and over. He must not have wished hard enough because the next words he heard forced a loud sigh to escape his lips. "Next, we have Zachary Blaze and Roxanne McCain."

It took Roxanne a couple of minutes for the information to register before she frantically began her search around the room for Zach. When she spotted him, she gave him a wide, toothy grin, a tiny wave and a giggle. She couldn't believe her luck. The pure deliciousness that was Zachary Blaze was to be her partner for the entire semester. She was over the moon about it but wondered why he looked as if he had been handed a death sentence.

As soon as everyone was paired up, Mr. Jeffries commanded them to sit with their partners—their best friend for that class. Zach glanced at Roxanne, hoping she would move so he wouldn't have to sit in the front row. He detested being that close to the teacher; even in high school he did his level best to stay as far away as possible. He wasn't even fond of it in elementary school. In fact, he would make a scene every single time he was forced to take a seat anywhere near the front. It didn't take him long to see that she was going to force him to make the move. Blowing out a frustrated breath again, Zach grabbed his backpack and baseball cap, which had been perched on the corner of his desk and sat near her. *Maybe she won't talk to me.* He should've known that was another wish that wasn't going to come true because, as soon as his butt hit the seat, she was talking about how cool it was that they were tutoring each other, as Mr. Jefferies called it.

"Zach, are you okay? You seem to be somewhere else." The furrow of her brow almost made him forget how cray cray he thought she was. . .almost.

"No. I'm fine. Didn't sleep well last night, that's all."

Professor Jefferies chose that exact moment to, once again, slam the yardstick on his desk at the front of the dusty room, just to shut everyone up. The class seemed to be enjoying getting to know who they were stuck with, which wasn't a bad thing, but apparently the professor thought it rude. The yardstick struck another time, garnering the professor's desired response—all eyes on him.

"Does he always have to do that?" Roxanne whispered.

Professor Jefferies must have heard her because he rapped on her desk next. "Quiet!" His dark brown eyes bored through her.

"Yes, sir." Roxanne squeaked.

The rest of the class period lasted so long that Zach was certain he would fall asleep. At least he hadn't been out of high school so long that the terms Professor Jefferies was using weren't totally foreign to him— variable, Algebraic equation, exponent, natural numbers and integers. Their homework for that night was to look each term up and write the definition, *what is this, high school?* He glanced at Roxanne, who was stifling her nervousness... He might think she was a few screws loose, but he did like her laugh. The pure childlike glee wasn't lost on him. It made him smile.

He is such a clown. Roxanne thought as she noticed the bored look plastered across Zach's face. She wasn't aware of what his real thoughts about her were, but he made no attempt at talking with her as he had the day before. She was honestly perplexed at the change in him. She wasn't the kind of person to let something go that was bothering her. *I'll have to ask him after class.* There was no way she was going to get her desk rapped on again.

Ω

Zachary had hoped that by ignoring Roxanne throughout the remainder of the class, she would get the hint and let him be. Since they now had to sit in the front of the classroom, they were required to wait until the other thirty-something students filed out before they could. Zach puffed out a breath of frustration when he realized that he wasn't going to be able to get rid of Roxanne as quickly as he wanted. He could only hope that she would get the hint if he ignored her on his way out. No such luck. He heard her calling his name, waving her arms frantically.

This wasn't going to work. He couldn't ignore her, no matter how badly he wanted to. Zach wasn't raised to disrespect women and ignoring her was a blatant form of disrespect. Resigning himself to the fact that he wasn't getting away from her, he waited until she'd caught up to him. She must've had to speak with Professor Jefferies because when he left, they were the only three left in the room.

"Oh, Zach..." Roxanne spit out between short breaths. She hated running, but she thought they should get a head start on their math homework. They were only required to work together on their math three days a week and complete the study guide together before each test.

"Are you okay?" he questioned.

Finally catching her breath, Roxanne talked...and talked...and talked. It was probably a good thing Zach had an hour break until his next class, English, or he would be late. "When do you want to get together?"

"For?" Maybe playing dumb would get rid of her faster.

She swatted his arm playfully, as if they had known each other longer than the twenty-four hours they had *been* acquainted. "Oh, you know, silly." She didn't move her hand from his arm.

"I have to work until seven every evening, so it'll have to be after that. I don't think we really need to get together tonight, do you?"

"Well..." she rocked back and forth on her heels, much like a little kid who wanted something badly. "I guess not, but I was thinking we could go back to the coffee shop."

Zach didn't want to give her his cell number, but he couldn't t see any way out of it, since they were now partners. "I'm usually tired after work, but let's do this...let's exchange numbers and I'll either text or call you when I'm done."

Feeling defeated, Roxanne finally agreed. Zach had the feeling she would have continued to argue the point if they both didn't have classes to get to.

Throughout the rest of his classes, Zach was grateful to see that the only other class he had with Roxanne was English. Although they had to write papers in that class, they weren't paired up as they had been in math.

Ω

Roxanne was exhausted by the time she arrived at her apartment after her classes were over. She wasn't sure how she would accomplish the dreaded assignments for each of her four classes, but she was elated that she had two with the tall, dark, and delicious Zach. But what was wrong with him? He acted as if she had rabies, or worse. He hadn't been like that the day before. She thought they'd hit it off well. In fact, she had hopes that they would become friends, but he wanted nothing more than to steer clear of her. She went back over the day before in her mind but couldn't pinpoint anything that was not her norm.

It was almost seven o'clock by the time Roxanne ordered Chinese food and ate dinner. She knew it might be a while yet before Zach called her, *if he* did. Roxanne only had to do her math vocabulary and her English essay on what she was in college to accomplish, but those weren't due for a couple days. She was grateful that her classes had worked out, so she had two on Monday, Wednesday and Friday, and two on Tuesday and Thursday. She wondered what other classes Zach was taking and whether she had any more with him.

Eight-thirty rolled around, and she looked sorrowfully at her cell phone once again, checking to make sure it was, at the very least, on vibrate. Nope...the volume was almost all the way up. *He's not going to call*, she thought as she sadly watched the time creep by. She'd just about given up when she heard the familiar trill of her general ringtone. "Hello?" She did her best to hide the thrill at the deep voice on the other end.

"Hey, Roxie."

Roxanne grimaced at the nickname. She absolutely hated being called Roxie, but with Zach's deep, southern drawl, it sounded almost sexy, but she still didn't like it. She would have to explain that later. "Hi, Zach. How are you? How were the rest of your classes?" She was eager to know everything about him.

"Work was busy, but then it usually is. I'm glad I only have classes three days a week. I don't know how I'd work and get all my assignments finished."

"How many classes do you have?" She was intrigued at how he worked *and* went to school. *Where do the parties fit in?*

"Five. Algebra, English, English Literature, Chemistry, and Communications."

"Wow! That's a lot! When do you find time to go to parties and stuff?" She let her inner self speak sometimes.

"I don't have time to party. I do good to get through what I have to in order to get into vet school."

Roxanne hoped she would get to see Zach that night, so she broached the subjects of Algebra and English. "Do you want to get together tonight?"

"Truth is, Roxie, I'm swamped with homework. We can do this Algebra assignment on our own. Let's see what the next one brings. I'm certain they're not *all* gonna be vocabulary."

Roxanne had a difficult time hiding her disappointment. Zach was the only person she knew here. She was lonely. After hanging up with Zach, she decided to watch her favorite movie—the live action Beauty and the Beast. Yes, she was lonely, but she also knew about several welcome parties going on that weekend, and she intended to take full advantage of every one of them. If Zach didn't want to hang out with her, that was fine; she would find others that did.

Chapter 2

Zach was never gladder that he didn't have classes than he was the next day. In between filing documents and checking in patients, he completed assignments that were due Friday. He was even more relieved that the weekend was coming, and he had two full days to do any homework that might be given out over the weekend.

He was almost finished filing for the day when the doorbell jingled. "I'm sorry, we're closed," he said.

"I know, but I thought you could use a caffeinated beverage," the feminine, high-society voice uttered.

Although he'd just met the person who belonged to that soft, sultry, silkiness and thought she was more than a little on the weird side, he couldn't deny he liked the way she spoke. Zach nervously cleared his throat and played it as cool as he could, "Oh, yeah? And what caffeinated beverage would that be? You don't know what I like."

"You sure about that?" Roxanne waited while he came around to the front desk from where he'd been filing papers.

When he saw she was holding a fifty-two-ounce cup filled with Pepsi he looked at her, questioningly. "And, before you ask…" Roxanne smiled, "yes. It has two shots of cherry in it...just like you prefer."

Zach was bewildered. "How did you know that?"

"Easy. The other day, when we went to the cafe, that's what you told the waitress you wanted."

He honestly didn't think she he'd heard that. He was wrong. "Well...thank you." He took a long swig and closed his eyes in ecstasy. "I needed that."

Watching him, Roxanne should've been embarrassed, but for reasons she didn't understand, it turned her on. The way his lips curled around the straw and the way he closed his eyes and enjoyed himself in utter bliss, like he hadn't tasted it before, was so enthralling. Even after he'd taken a breather and opened his eyes, she couldn't peel hers away.

Why is she staring at me like I'm her favorite chocolate she can't get her hands on? Because she'd been kind enough to bring him a drink, which he desperately craved after the day he'd had, he thought he should ask what she wanted, although he was certain he knew. "What can I do for you?"

"Um…have you finished your vocabulary words for Algebra yet?"

"I started them but haven't finished."

"Do you want to go back to the cafe when you're done here?"

Heaving a sigh because he was so tired, he replied, "I guess. We need to have them done by tomorrow morning, but I need to call it a night fairly early."

That appeased Roxanne. She grinned like she'd won the lottery. "You want to meet me over there? Or we could go together." The hopeful look that shone in her eyes made Zach wish he wasn't such a nice guy. It made life difficult at times.

"We can take my truck and come back for your car."

Roxanne was excited at the prospect of sitting near him in his old black Ford Bronco. There was only the bench seat in the front which meant, if she played her cards right, she would be sitting extremely close to him.

Ω

"Do these words make sense to you?" Roxanne asked once they'd been seated and ordered hot cocoa. She preferred lattes—her favorite being hazelnut-toffee, but since she wanted so badly to impress Zach, she ordered a peanut butter hot chocolate, while Zachary ordered regular milk chocolate with extra marshmallows.

Zach took a long sip of his hot chocolate, leaving a film of whipped cream on his upper lip. "Pretty much. Are you having a difficult time with it?"

Roxanne burst out laughing, "Um—" pointing at him, "you have some whipped cream on your lips." Oh, what she wouldn't give to be able to lick that off. *Focus, Roxanne! But he is so hot!* She couldn't believe what she was thinking. She melted every time she was near Zach, and to hear him speak was pure bliss.

Embarrassed, Zach quickly wiped his mouth with a napkin, although he would normally use the back of his hand. With flaming red cheeks, he replied, "Thank you." Changing the subject quickly, he reiterated, "Are you struggling with the words?"

After composing herself to be the debutante her mother wished her to be, she replied, "Only a few of them." They spent the next hour going over the vocabulary words that neither of them could believe a college professor would bother them with. When they finished, Roxanne was nowhere near ready to let Zachary take her back to her car because she'd have to return to her lonely apartment. She had the opportunity to room with others but, being an only child, she didn't think she could handle living with anyone else. Having spent the last couple of nights alone, however, she wondered if she'd decided too soon. "Would you like to get another hot chocolate? Or they have cinnamon rolls I've heard are to die for."

The only thing Zach wanted to do was go home and veg in front of the television for a bit before hitting the hay. He found it problematic to let Roxanne know he was done for the evening. His mom had raised him to be kind to the ladies, after all, and this one was all that and more. And as far as he could tell, she was spoiled. Her attire alone boasted that mom and dad were well off. He bet he could tell that even if she hadn't told him the day they met. Exhaustion won out, however. "Roxie—" he didn't know if anyone called her that, but she didn't say anything against it, so he continued— "it's been a long couple of days, and with a full school schedule and working at the clinic, I'm drained. I just need to get home." Lucky for him, he didn't live far from the clinic.

She'd always hated being called Roxie. But the way it rolled off his tongue, she thought she could get used to it—but only if *he* was the one to say it. "Oh...okay."

She acted a bit put out, but Zachary was glad he'd stood up for himself—something he wasn't used to doing. Much to his dismay, the frown didn't leave her face, nor did she stop pestering him to show her the sights of Chattanooga.

He had never been more excited to see the strip mall where the clinic was located than he was that night. "Well…" he cleared his throat, "thanks for helping me with the Algebra vocabulary."

"Actually, I think it was you helping me. I've never been good at math, and I'm not much of a school lover either. I was ecstatic to be done with high school. I took a couple years off, and now it's time to grow up and become something."

"What do you want to be?" Yes, he was tired, but Zach wasn't going to ignore her and push her out of the Bronco.

Roxanne was glad he hadn't just dropped her off, rather he acted as though he genuinely wanted to get to know her. She knew he wasn't fond of her, but she'd liked him even when she'd seen him from a distance before they ran into each other, and fervently hoped she could change his mind.

"Well, my parents want me to follow in their footsteps and become either a psychologist, like my mom, or a psychiatrist, like my dad."

"Doesn't sound as if those appeal to you much."

"It's that evident, huh?" Roxanne questioned.

"Yeah…just a little. So, what do you want to do with the rest of your life then, since it's apparent you don't want to do what your parents want?"

"I love clothes. I always have, but I want to design them. Have a say in what is done from choosing the fabric to where to market them and to what target audience each line belongs to."

"You want to sew them yourself?" This took Zachary by surprise, because she came across as entitled.

"No, silly. I want to design a clothing line and have others make the clothes." She looked at him like he'd sprouted two heads.

"Aaaahhh. Gotcha." Zach smacked his forehead. "What was I thinking?"

"Right?" Roxie giggled.

"We'd probably better call it a night. Algebra is bright and early, and tomorrow is yet another full day, between classes and work."

Roxanne wasn't pleased that he took leaving her so easily, but she kept forgetting that, for her, it was still two hours earlier. She had yet to acclimate to the time difference. "I'm not even close to being tired, but then, I'm still on California time."

Zachary got out and opened not only the Bronco door for her, but her car door as well. "Good night, Roxie."

Before Zachary could pull away, she replied, "You know, I hate that name; or rather, hated…"

"You don't anymore?" Zach chuckled.

"Not the way you say it, cowboy," she snickered. "See ya tomorrow!" Without missing a beat, she sped out of the parking space.

It wasn't extremely late in Chattanooga, but there wasn't much traffic, which was good, because just watching Roxie pull out made Zach cringe.

Zachary didn't go straight home as he had planned. He needed to think, and the best way for him to do that was to take the back roads and drive. Driving alone helped him gain perspective, and whatever was happening with Roxanne absolutely needed some thought. While she continued to annoy him, there was a sweet side to her as well. *She isn't bad lookin' either.*

He drove as fast as he dared in the pitch blackness of night. *If I have a type, she isn't it,* he tried convincing himself, but there was just something about her. If a person looked past the money, entitlement, and expensive clothes, he could see that she was only a girl, after all. It didn't matter where they came from, did it? In the grand scheme of things, she wasn't going to be at University of Tennessee, Chattanooga forever. Roxanne, herself, had told him she was headed for Vanderbilt, and *that* was a posh school if he ever heard of one. He decided that night that, no matter what happened, he knew she liked him. He was the uncertain one. He would treat her with the utmost respect as he had been taught as a child. No more hesitation when she wanted to do homework with him. He would help her in any way he could.

Ω

A couple weeks into the semester, after their first Algebra test, it was evident that Roxie needed more tutoring than Zach had the time to give, with his full school and work schedule. When she came to him devastated, he knew he should help her find a tutor.

"I want you to assist me," she was adamant. Watching her, Zach could see Roxanne as a kid, stomping her foot when she didn't get her way.

"I can't. You know how much I've got on my plate with a full course load and work." They'd been spending as much time as he could spare in helping her, not only with Algebra, but English and Science as well. She was only taking courses she knew would transfer as she continued talking nonstop about Vanderbilt.

"I know, and you've helped me tons. I just don't want to flunk out and have to go running back home to my parents with my tail between my legs."

"I'll tell you what…both my parents are excellent in all three subjects. My mom was a high school English teacher before she decided to be a stay-at- home after Stevie was born and my dad is excellent in math and science. He had to learn a lot to that to become a vet. What if I ask them if they could help, since you don't want to use a tutor the school offers?" Zach wasn't sure his parents would agree, but what would it hurt to ask?

"I don't want to impose." Roxie guessed that if Zachary could pull this one off, she would see him more and more, and she was okay with that. In a short period of time, she'd experienced feelings she'd never had before. Sure, there were guys in high school, and even some from the colleges at home who'd asked her on dates, but none of them called her *Darlin'* like Zachary did, or made her feel like she wasn't as dumb as a box of rocks, as she'd been told most of her life. Her parents were the smart ones in the family. Maybe that's why she didn't, and probably wouldn't, get into Vanderbilt; she was too stupid. Roxanne shook her head as she tried to shake the thoughts from it.

"Are you okay?" Zachary was concerned. She'd gone from her usual bubbly self-assured woman to a meek *I can't do this* girl.

"Yes…yes, I'm fine."

"You sure? Because you look like you're about to cry."

"I was just thinking."

"About?" She hadn't told Zach much about her life except she was well-off, and her parents were experts in psychiatry and psychology. He was sure that living in a home like that hadn't helped her any, and the facade she put on daily was just that—a facade, a mask—so others wouldn't want to get to know her. It was a coping mechanism, much like driving was for him.

"There's a lot about me you don't know," she hung her head, covering her face with her hair.

"Then tell me." They were both late for their next classes, but Zachary didn't care. He was concerned about his friend. Friend? When had they gone from mere acquaintances to friends? He didn't have the umph to analyze it at that moment.

"I can't right now. We'll be seriously tardy and neither of us can afford that. At least, I know I can't. Not if I'm ever going to see the inside of Vanderbilt."

Zach wouldn't push her. After spending the last few weeks with Roxanne, he wondered whether she had any friends at all, because she acted as if he was the only one she had. *That's sad. She needs female friends, not only me to fall back on.*

"Can I walk you to class?" He ventured.

"That'll make you later. I can go alone."

Zach knew she could, but there was something about the slump of her shoulders, the *I'm giving up* attitude she sported, that made him want to find out why she had all of a sudden gone from bubbly to morose. There was something bothering her and, keeping with his promise to himself to treat her with the same respect he would his mom, he'd wait. "Honestly, my next professor loves me. I'll just tell her I had a friend that needed someone to talk to, and I bet she won't even flinch."

Roxanne truly didn't want to be alone. When she plummeted this low it frightened her. Both of her parents had wanted to give her an antidepressant when she was in high school. They feared the worst—that if they didn't and let her deal with whatever came at her in ways she saw fit, she would do something stupid. They'd forced them on her when she was fifteen-years-old and she obliged them for almost two years, but when nearing her senior year, she had only pretended to take them, waiting until she was at school to discard them for fear she would be found out if she did that at home. Eventually, her parents found out she'd quit taking them and made her promise that if she ever felt the darkness threatening to envelop her, she *would* tell them. She was afraid of what Zach would think of her if he knew she had problems just like everyone else.

She watched him as they walked along, neither in a hurry to get to class. She'd decided if he was late for class and was okay with the outcome, who was she to stop him from being a gentleman? She'd never seen a cowboy like him—like it was in his blood, in his bones. Back home she'd seen several, but they looked like they were in costume. Zach wore the clothes as if they were a part of him. The way the Wranglers hugged his ass made her itch to put her hand down in the pocket; the way his biceps bulged even through the long-sleeved button up he wore drew her eyes. He wore those a lot, she noticed. Oh, and she couldn't forget that swagger. She could walk behind him all day long and never tire of watching him move.

"What are you looking at?" Zach broke through her thoughts.

Startled, she stuttered, "Oh—um...nothing." Her cheeks flamed red, and she just knew that Zach saw. *How could he miss it? It's broad daylight, for Pete's sake!* How could she be so careless? *It's because you find him attractive; admit it,* she chided herself.

Zach bit back the laugh that threatened to erupt from his lips. He knew she'd been staring at him—mostly at his ass. He really wanted to crack a joke, but they hadn't been friends long enough. Hell, it had taken him this long to get to a point where she didn't drive him batty—and not in a good way either. Instead, he changed the subject. He found out that when she was four, she'd told her parents she wanted to buy a baby brother or sister. She didn't understand why they couldn't purchase one like they would groceries. She knew the story of how she came to be, but this was the first time she'd told the story to anyone she hadn't grown up with.

Ω

When Roxanne's parents had found out they were expecting, both were ecstatic. The pregnancy went well, even after they found out they were having twins. Identical twins. Because Roxanne's parents were in their mid-thirties by the time they decided to start a family, this put Belinda and the babies in the high-risk category. Belinda was a healthy, fit thirty-seven-year-old woman which didn't concern the doctors...at first. As with a lot of similar pregnancies, Roxanne and her twin sister, Amelia, shared a placenta. During the first half of the pregnancy, the doctors took every precaution they could, keeping Belinda on bed rest for half a day, which meant she couldn't work at the office. That was the most difficult thing Belinda had to do at that point, but she found ways around it, learning to knit and crochet baby items for her precious twins.

The day the babies were born, there was no reason to believe that anything bad would take place. For reasons no one could explain, except that Roxanne received more nutrients than her much tinier sister, Amelia was born smaller than expected and had several health issues as well. The neonatal doctors told the parents that Roxanne was a healthy five pounds, and twenty inches long, but Amelia? It wasn't a question of when Amelia would leave the hospital, but if...and she passed away thirty-six hours after birth.

"That's awful." Zach put his hand on Roxanne's arm.

"I don't remember any of it, of course, but I've heard the stories enough and we have pictures showing us together, but there's a piece of me missing—like I can tangibly feel it. I think that's why they indulge my every whim. Guilt."

"Maybe. I know when my brother died my parents wouldn't let me out of their sight for long, and I was twenty, so it made it hard on me because I wasn't a kid but was treated as such. They wanted to know where I went, with whom, what time I'd be home, and as many details as I could give them. It got to the point that I felt suffocated."

"I couldn't even imagine what your parents went through. I know mine were so afraid what happened with me and my sister would happen again, that they decided against any more kids when I was a toddler."

"Boy, look at us. We have something in common." Zachary was honestly shocked he could be even a little like this self-absorbed, spoiled rotten brat. After that story though, the way he saw her changed. She wasn't only a well-off twit who received everything her heart desired, but, in her own way she was a hot mess, trying to find where she belonged in this world, just as he and every other student was doing "We've pretty much screwed all the rest of our classes for the day." Zach was stunned.

"Oh, my! That's wasn't my plan, at all! I hope my professors aren't angry with me. How did that happen, exactly? Weren't you walking me to my next class after math?" Roxanne asked.

"That's how it started out, yes, but I found myself enjoying your company so much I kinda steered us away from your class. You were too busy assessing my ass to know where we were at." He couldn't believe he allowed himself to admit how he was truly feeling.

Roxie chuckled, "I *am* sorry about that." She was lying through her perfect white teeth, but Zach was becoming accustomed to making her blush almost every time they saw each other.

"You are not. You and I both know that. You loved every minute of it! Admit it," he teased. He was relentless and wouldn't let the matter drop until Roxie confessed.

"Fine! You win! Yes, I thoroughly relished in checking out your backside. By the way, it didn't seem to bother you as I investigated, so don't even act like YOU didn't revel in it." Oh, she was getting good. Spending time with him was rubbing off on her.

"I don't deny it," he laughed. "This has been fun, but if I'm late for work, my dad won't be as lenient as my teachers are."

"That's okay, I'm scheduled at the bookstore until like nine o'clock tonight anyway and I have tons of homework, but surprisingly, no math."

"That is a great reprieve, if you ask me." They walked to her car. Zachary opened her door and waved as she pulled out. *How did I go from despising her to friend, to thinking about dating her? A month ago, I didn't even like her, and now she's the only person I hang out with outside of class.* He thought about the brown-haired beauty who was so far out of his league he didn't dare think about asking her on a date. The problem was, that's exactly what he wanted to do. How would she respond? Would she think Chattanooga too podunk, seeing as how she came from Los Angeles, California? She'd probably seen and done things he'd only had the privilege of witnessing on the movie screen.

Chapter 3

Several weeks into the first semester, Zach finally got up the nerve to ask Roxie out. If he didn't do it, and fast, she would leave for Vanderbilt and never look back, or she'd get snapped up by a prep or an athlete. They were more than likely closer to her type than he was, but she'd told him things he was positive she'd never told a soul. No holds barred.

The cafe they went to that first day—which felt longer than the six weeks since the start of the semester—was the perfect spot to ask her. He acted as if they were going there to study for the upcoming algebra test that was only a few days away, but Zach knew he couldn't concentrate on a study session until he knew whether she'd go out with him or not. Once inside, she ordered a caramel latte and he ordered a s'mores hot chocolate with extra marshmallows. She'd tried to get him to order a latte on many different occasions, but, after taking a sip of hers once, he decided those weren't his cup of tea.

"Hey, where are your books?" Roxie questioned. "I thought we were going to study." Confusion etched her brow.

"I didn't say anything about studying, did I?" Laughter danced in his eyes.

"Well, no, but what are we here for then?"

Zach took a deep breath. *If I say no, it could potentially ruin the friendship I have been developing.* He couldn't think about that or he would lose his nerve. Gulping, while his voice shook more than he would've liked, he said, "Ummm—uh…would you…" he fidgeted, picking at a stray piece of skin on his thumbnail,, "go out with me?" He heaved a huge sigh of relief, even though she hadn't responded yet.

Roxie badly wanted to say yes. She'd been waiting for this day almost as long as she'd known Zachary. She could've asked him out, but being raised the way she had been, that was a huge no-no, so she waited.

Why hasn't she answered yet? Zach watched and waited. It seemed like she was taking hours, but it was only mere minutes or even seconds.

She finally clasped his hand in hers and replied, "Zach, we've become extremely good friends these past several weeks of getting to know each other, and I don't want to ruin that," she paused. Zach's head hung, dejected. She was going to say no, he could feel it. When she continued, "But I would love to go on a date with you," it almost knocked him from his chair.

"Seriously?"

"Why do you sound so shocked that I said yes?"

"Well, as you know, when we first met, you weren't my favorite person."

Roxie's hand flew to her chest in surprise, "What?" she gasped. "You didn't like me?"

"Roxie, you knew that." Zach was hushed, not sure if she was kidding or not. It wasn't until her face split into a wide grin that he knew. Heaving a sigh of relief, he posed, "You just think you're funny."

"Nope. I *know* I am," she bubbled with laughter.

The laughter he'd become accustomed to. "So, where are we going? What are we doing?"

"That's for me to know and for you to find out. The only question I have is, are you afraid of horses?"

"No. I took lessons back home; been taking them since I was little."

"Good. But, be aware that the way you learned is, most likely, different than the way we ride. The saddles are different and the way you sit in it might be. Not to mention, by the time we are done, you'll walk bowlegged for a week,"

"You're not serious…"

"Yes, I certainly am." He couldn't help but laugh at the horrified look on her face.

"What, exactly, does that mean?" she swallowed.

"When you ride in a saddle for a long time, especially western style, it makes your butt and legs hurt so you walk with your legs kinda far apart. You know how to ride western style, don't you?"

"I think so...? I'm not sure."

"Did you sit with your rear end in the saddle when you had lessons?"

"Before I moved out here, I rode full saddle, but are we going to be riding all day? I'm not looking forward to walking funky or being in pain."

"It'll be fun, I promise." Zach was a little worried about getting her into a saddle longer than an hour. It was apparent her lessons weren't long, and she hadn't spent that much time in a saddle, even with lessons. He might have to rethink that part of the date. But it wouldn't be as much fun, and he couldn't take her to his favorite spot just above his parents' house. Although both parents were involved in caring for all kinds of animals, the Blaze kids learned at a young age how to groom, feed and care for the horses they kept in their small, but adequate, stable.

.

Ω

Roxanne was antsy as the day drew near for her first date with Zachary. She wasn't positive she wanted to get on a horse, but she was confident and knew she rode well; it worried her, however, that she had never ridden in the open and always had a riding crop and gear, not the jeans, boots and shirt she sported..

Zach packed the picnic and was finally ready to go pick Roxie up. She could've driven out herself, but he insisted on being a gentleman and picking her up at her apartment and dropping her off at the door once their date was finished. She tried imploring him to change his mind, but he wouldn't hear of it. He was raised as a man should be; he picked her up, knocking politely on the door, opened and closed doors for her, and made sure she was comfortable. He'd warned her that she needed to wear jeans and comfortable shoes, but to his surprise, when he picked her up, she sported a pair of brown lacers, like his, and a black Stetson cowboy hat. If he didn't know any better, he wouldn't know she'd come from a big city like Los Angeles.

"Well, what do you think?" Roxie twirled around so he could get a good view. She was even wearing Wranglers, with the tag attached. That made him chortle. "What's so funny?" Roxie demanded.

"Nothing. Remind me to tell you what the Wrangler patch on the back of your jeans, and, consequently, mine means. You ready to go?" He couldn't stop staring. She looked as if she fit right into his life. *All this just because she put on a pair of jeans that hugged her in all the right places and a shirt that accentuated her assets?*

"Okay, but what are you staring at? It's like you zoned out there for a bit."

"Sorry. I was just thinking." *She has no idea what looking like that does to me.* Even though they'd spent most of their time together when they weren't in class or at work, they had never officially planned and executed a date. It had been a while for him. After being dumped by the girl he'd dated on and off up until his brother's death, he'd been gun-shy about women, specifically those who showed an interest in him. They were the ones who could do the most damage. Roxie was the first girl he'd asked on a date since then.

"Well, should we get going? I'm curious about your plans."

He'd purposely made it an evening picnic, but also knew it could get chilly, so he reminded her to grab a sweatshirt or jacket. The one she grabbed was a University of Tennessee at Chattanooga sweatshirt. For some reason that stupefied him because he knew her heart was set on going to Vanderbilt. "I see you're getting into the school spirit," he teased.

"I figured, why not? I work in the bookstore and get a pretty decent discount." They'd gotten into Zachary's truck. Roxanne loved how he was such a gentleman, opening her door, helping her in and making sure the door closed before going to the driver side.

As they drove, the sun was barely going down, and the sunset was a beautiful yellow-orange color and the mountain air wafted through the windows and smelled of fire and the scent of oak and pine trees could be smelled. Zach pried, "Can I ask you something?"

"Sure." Roxie enjoyed listening to his voice. Answering his questions was a small price to pay to hear him speak.

"You said your parents are rich, right?"

"Yeah."

"Then why couldn't your mom pull strings to get you into Vanderbilt?

"She was angry with me because, instead of going straight to college right out of high school at eighteen, I chose to take a year off. It turned into two and she wasn't happy about that."

"Why two years?" He felt comfortable in pushing the envelop ever so slightly more.

"I don't know. All I knew then was that I wasn't ready. I needed a break."

"Well, what did you do during that time?"

"My friends and I decided to tour Europe."

"Backpacking?" Zach should've known the answer to that one. She was spoiled, after all.

"You're kidding, right?" Sheer astonishment written on her face. "Of course not. Have you not learned anything about me in the last couple of months?"

The conversation stalled when they arrived at Zach's house, where he still needed to saddle the horses. But first they went into the house to grab the items Zach had prepared to make this date one Roxie would never forget. His parents were home, on call from the clinic. His dad was watching a baseball game—it made him feel closer to Bryce since he was the player in the family—and his mom was reading. She did that a lot, mostly fantasy and romance. It was her escape, he guessed. He cleared his throat to let his parents know they weren't alone anymore. "Mom...Dad, I'd like you to meet Roxie...Roxie, my parents."

"Hello, Mr. and Mrs. Blaze. It's really nice to meet you." Blood rushed to her face as she spoke.

"Hello, Roxie." Mrs. Blaze shook her hand gently. "So, you're the one that our son talks about constantly."

It was Zach's turn to be flustered. "Moooom, really?"

Mrs. Blaze smiled, which wasn't something she did often, so Zach let it go. "Honey, the kids are here."

Roxie was astonished when she saw the man Zachary called Dad walk in. Because Zach was muscular and built like a brick shithouse, she was shocked to see a lanky, skinny, albeit tall man who definitely fit the doctor look. He appeared to dress much the same way as Zachary—in Wranglers—but where Zach wore mostly t-shirts, his father wore short-sleeved, snap up shirts. At least, that's what he wore that day. She could see Mr. Blaze as a nerd. "Hello, sir," she said as he clasped her clammy hand with his own warm one.

"Oh, my dear...calling me sir makes me feel old. Please, call me Darren or if you prefer, Mr. Blaze is fine. I see you've met Susan then?"

"Yes, sweetheart. Where's Stevie?" Susan asked.

"Stevie's my sister." Zach had kept silent up to this point, observing how Roxie interacted with his parents.

"She's out with Jeb, again. For the life of me, I'm not sure what to do with that situation." Susan huffed.

Zach took that as his cue to leave. Talking about Stevie hardly ever ended well, particularly where Jeb was concerned. His parents weren't fond of the tattooed wannabe *rockstar*. They'd hoped by not forcing her to attend college right out of high school, she might mellow out—that she'd rid herself of Jeb and find a nice boy—one without all the piercings and tattoos. But that had backfired horribly, so they invited him over a lot, hoping that he didn't like the added attention and would dump her. They didn't want to see her get hurt and, from what they could tell, he could hurt her badly if he broke her heart. "Well, if we're gonna get out of here before it gets too cold, we'd better go." Zach took Roxie's hand.

Roxie was taken aback by the gesture. They'd never held hands before. She'd wanted to, badly, since the day they met, but she was raised in a house where girls weren't allowed to make the first move on anything. Her mother never set up date night with her father. He did. She didn't say anything, only relished the warmth of his fingers threaded through hers. "It was nice meeting you," she said.

While they were in the stable readying the horses, they talked about how nice Zach's parents were and how different they were from Roxanne's. She didn't talk much about her family. It irritated her still that her mother had the pull to get her into Vanderbilt but refused to use her connections to help her only child.

Ω

"This is gorgeous," Roxie breathed as she took in the view from atop her horse, a gentle mare named Anna. She was the first horse Zachary had learned to ride at the age of five. He'd ridden ponies and such before that, but Anna was special.

"Isn't it?" Zachary wasn't looking at the same view as she was. He knew the picture all too well. Even before Bryce's death, he'd ride up here whenever he needed to think or decompress, but afterwards, maybe because he felt closer to heaven, he came here whenever he got the chance. He could feel Bryce's presence. But this time, he was ogling the girl next to him. She'd surprised him at how adept she was when it came to grooming and saddling Anna, and even boosted herself in the saddle without his assistance. The more time they spent together, the more enamored he was by her. He drank in the way her chocolate brown hair framed her face, how her rosy cheeks glowed against the setting sun backdrop. She no longer looked like the rich, California snob she'd come off as in the beginning. She fit right where she was.

"Hey!" Roxie snapped her fingers in front of Zach's face. "Where are you?" She'd noticed him staring at her but didn't say anything because she quite enjoyed the attention, but when his eyes glazed over, she knew it was time to pull him from the trance he'd put himself into.

"What?" Zach wasn't aware that he'd zoned out while soaking her in.

"Where'd you go? You gawked at me for a good five minutes."

"I was thinking," he fibbed, sort of. He had been thinking, but a minuscule amount was about anything but her.

"About?" she questioned as they dismounted and tied Anna and Joe, the horse Zach rode, to a nearby tree.

"This place has been my sanctuary most of my life, but since Bryce died, I feel closer to him when I come here. It's because of what this spot means to me that I wanted to share it with you." As he spoke, he built a fire to keep them warm. He didn't know whether Roxie knew how or not, but he'd planned this date down to the last detail. "You're probably used to fancy dinner dates and being escorted in limousines, huh?"

Roxanne rubbed her hands together in front of the fire. She unequivocally wasn't used to the drop-in temperature. Where she was from it rarely dropped below seventy degrees, even in the winter. "I am. But it's nice to do something totally different."

"And?" As they'd been chatting, Zach took the basket of food and the blanket, making a picnic area near enough to the fire to keep them warm, but far enough away so the blanket wouldn't catch fire.

Roxie eyed the picnic as he set it up. This ranked number one as a date she'd not seen herself attending, not in a million years. "To be honest, this is a date I've never even considered before."

Zach was afraid he'd made a grave mistake after her comment, but he kept his worries to himself. "Have a seat." He handed her a fresh cup of hot chocolate he'd been preparing on the fire in between other tasks. "This'll help keep the chilliness away." He poured himself a cup from the coffee can he'd used to heat the water, poured in a packet of milk chocolate cocoa mix—with marshmallows, of course—and stirred it with a spoon. "Sorry, this isn't as good as the cocoa at the coffee shop, and that it's not a latte, but I hope you like it, just the same."

Roxie remained quiet as Zach belittled the date he'd planned. She took a sip of her cocoa before stating, "This might be a date I'm not used to but, so far, it's the best date I've been on."

"Really?" Zach was astounded.

"Yes. And for the record, although I prefer lattes, campfire cocoa is *so* much better than the coffee shop's brew."

Relief flooded Zach's body. *Whew! You didn't totally screw yourself.* "Are you hungry?"

"As a matter of fact, yes, I am. I'm curious to see what you brought, considering there's not much you can picnic with."

"It's nothing fancy, but then again, I'm not a fancy guy."

"That is one of the many things I adore about you." Roxanne made a bold move. A bold one for her, anyway. She reached over and brushed her lips ever so lightly against Zach's cheek. She liked how the bristles felt against her lips.

She'd shocked him yet again. This was the girl who told him that her mom *never* did anything first as far as any type of intimacy, even holding hands. That responsibility fell on her father's shoulders. Zach loved that she felt comfortable and confident enough to do that, though. Her lips were soft. Feeling them against his cheek made him want to kiss her—to feel those delicate lips on his. Forgotten was the meal he prepared. He took that moment to cup her chin in his hand, warmed by the fire, and gently press his lips to hers, not sure of her reaction.

Roxie's heartrate sped up when Zach's hand met her chin. Her body grew warm, despite the cold weather. She had a sneaking suspicion that they wouldn't need the fire. She instinctively knew he would kiss her, and she knew she wanted it more than anything. This was something money couldn't buy. His lips met hers, and they weren't rough, not like she'd thought. They were smooth, but not quite as soft as hers, and although she'd not seen him use it, she guessed he used lip balm regularly. That was the only way to explain how his lips weren't chapped. She'd kissed a few guys in her day, but she'd never been kissed this tenderly before.

Roxie wasn't aware that she'd moaned until Zachary abruptly broke it off. "I'm sorry. I shouldn't have done that that. I should've asked permission first. Are you okay?"

Her answer stopped him dead in his tracks, "Why did you stop?" He expected her to be miffed or pissed off or something, but there she sat, giving him the go ahead.

"I thought you weren't okay with kissing me," he blurted.

"What in the world would give you that idea?" She delighted in it.

It didn't dawn on him until then why she had moaned. Lucky for him, it was getting dark, so she couldn't see the blush that crept up his neck. He felt sheepish, so he changed the subject to an easier topic. "We still need to eat."

Roxanne could tell he was embarrassed so, instead of harping on the idea, she went along. She could've missed the meal and kept kissing, if the truth be told, but this was their first date, and prior to that they'd done nothing, not even hand holding. "So, show me what you brought."

"Like I said, nothing fancy." Zach was grateful she went with the flow. "Just sub sandwiches. I hope turkey, ham, and roast beef are okay as far as meat is concerned."

"That's great!"

"Everything else I brought in separate containers, since I don't know what you like." As he spoke, Zach unloaded the contents of the basket.

"My, my, you came thoroughly prepared, huh? Honestly, I like almost everything, except mushrooms and onions."

"Well, I did bring onions, but you don't have to have them," Zachary grinned at her.

Teasingly, she responded, "If you eat them though, we can't kiss. That would be nasty."

"So, you liked that, did ya?" He'd mellowed out some since his fiasco a few minutes before.

"It wasn't obvious?" She had a hard time believing he couldn't feel her melting into him the more he kissed her.

"Can I tell you a secret not any girl knows?" his voice hushed.

"Okay." Roxanne wasn't sure what he would say, but what he did reveal, especially after the way he'd kissed her, was unexpected.

"I haven't kissed many girls." He ducked his head. He didn't want her to see the humiliation in his eyes. As gorgeous as Roxie was, Zach was certain she was more skilled at it than he was.

"You're not serious..." she almost laughed, until she saw what looked like shame in his eyes. "You *are*." Then she said something she never thought she'd tell a guy; she'd kissed quite a few, but she'd never divulged whether she derived any pleasure from it. "You want to know something?"

"What?" He finally looked up. He'd busied himself with making a sandwich, hoping to keep his hands from shaking. He could feel a panic attack coming on and willed it down. He didn't want to ruin this date anymore than he feared he already had.

"You probably think I've kissed a ton of guys, huh?"

"Probably beat me in that department, hands down."

"I've had more than my share, that's for sure. I don't know. Maybe I was making up for my sister, or maybe I did it because, as you know, I crave attention. Sometimes, I was aware I was doing it to piss my mother off. But, one thing I've never done until now, is tell a guy how I felt after kissing him."

"Til now?"

"Yes. Til now. All I can tell you is that I've never had my breath taken away like that. It was like you started kissing me and I couldn't breathe. And, it wasn't the bad kind of not being able to breathe. Oh my, listen to me rambling on. Am I making any sense?"

At that moment, forgotten were the sub sandwiches and hot chocolate.

Chapter 4

The semester ended as quickly as it started. Roxanne had made plans to fly back to California for her three weeks break before the next semester began because she wanted to see her parents. She and Zachary had gotten quite close in the last three months they'd been together, and she was pleased that he felt he could talk with her about anything, and vice-versa. She'd begged him to go home with her; she was dying for her parents, especially her father, to meet the boy who'd stolen her heart. Roxanne talked about Zachary whenever she spoke with her parents, and because they felt they knew him, to some extent, they extended an invitation.

"Roxie, you know I can't leave the clinic for that long. Maybe I can come out for a week. And besides, it'll be Christmas soon." He was more worried about getting on an airplane then being gone. His parents could handle things without him, he had no doubt. In fact, Stevie had taken a more active role at the clinic as of late. She'd taken over making appointments and worked daily. This helped Zach immensely as his schoolwork only got harder. Hopefully, she could take over filing too, because when he left for vet school, they'd have to hire someone anyway. Might as well keep it in the family.

"You could spend Christmas in L.A." Roxie was completely serious. They'd just finished their last final for the semester, which happened to be Algebra, and were watching *Phantom of the Opera;* one of Roxanne's favorites. It felt good to do nothing but cuddle.

"Could you imagine that? Me, a cowboy and soon to be veterinarian, in Los Angeles? If that doesn't scream tourist, nothing will." He was drawing hearts in the palm of her hand, not terribly enthralled by the movie. It hadn't taken long once he realized why Roxie acted and did things the way she did for him to come to terms with it. He was falling in love with her. He wanted to go with her, but fear and panic were the evil voices in his head telling him he couldn't step foot on an airplane, much less travel across country. Her parents had offered to buy his round-trip plane ticket to escort their daughter home. What they really wanted was to meet him. They had a difficult time seeing the daughter they had spoiled to no end, who owned hundreds of pairs of shoes and at least that many purses, dating a cowboy. An honest to goodness cowboy. Each time she spoke of him, they were positive no such young man existed.

"You'd be fine. We'd be together, so it's not as if you'll be left to your own devices the whole time you're there."

Ω

The more Roxie talked about taking him home, and the way she laid a guilt trip on him about how, once she left University of Tennessee Chattanooga to attend Vanderbilt, they wouldn't see each other every day—which they'd both become accustomed to—the closer she came to getting her way. She'd even gone so far as to speak to Zach's parents. Getting them on her side was key. They felt it would not only be good for Zachary to see a different way of life, but it would also help Stevie see that she was capable of so much more than being a groupie. Zach finally gave in after being cornered by his parents, who told him they didn't want him to settle just because a tragedy struck their family. He needed to do this; they were adamant.

"Well, I guess it's a good thing I asked Daddy to make sure that ticket was still available, huh?" Roxie questioned. They'd been sitting in the frigid Tennessee air on the porch swing his dad had built for his mom as a wedding present.

"You knew I would eventually give in, didn't you?" Zach brought the hand that he was holding and kissed her knuckles. She was sitting across his lap with one arm slung behind him.

"Let's just say I hoped you'd give in. The great thing is that the way the school schedule works out, we'll spend Christmas with my family and New Year's here, although Los Angeles has some fantastic clubs that throw the biggest New Year's Eve bashes you've ever seen. We could fly back New Year's Day and have two days to rest up before next semester."

Boy, she was throwing a lot at him, all at once. "Darlin,' do you mind if we stick to the original plan? I've never been away for Christmas or

New Year's so this is all overwhelming. Besides, could you see me, for real, in one of those clubs?"

Roxanne was so excited to show him *her* stomping grounds that she'd forgotten, for a second, his anxiety. She kissed him and apologized for rushing him. "Of course, sweetie. We'll do Christmas there and New Year's here, like we planned. I'm uber delighted to show you where I grew up!" Then, out of the blue she said, "Do you suppose we'll have to do this if we get married?"

"Do what?" Marriage wasn't something he thought about, constantly.

"Split our time between your family and mine, of course."

"Yeah, I guess we would." *Why does it feel so natural to talk to Roxie about stuff like marriage when we've only known each other three months?* His dad told him once, that when he found the right girl, everything would fall into place—college, job placement, marriage, family—all of it. He'd wondered on more than one occasion if Roxie was his person. The one he was meant to spend the rest of his life with.

Ω

When it came time to fly to Los Angeles, Zachary's parents offered to drive them to the airport, so they wouldn't have to pay for long-term parking. Zach could see it was harder on his mom to let him go, but who could blame her after losing one child already? She was more emotional and demanded more hugs than even Roxie did when she was on a spoiled kick. Of course, being the obedient son, he obliged his mom. "Okay, you'll call us when you get to Roxanne's, right?" Susan's voice was thick with emotion.

"Yes, mom, we will. I'll always have my cell on me too. And we left Mr. and Mrs. McCain's relevant phone numbers on the pad by the phone." He hugged both his parents, then his sister.

"It'll be weird, having Christmas without you. You've always been home for it, and since neither you nor Bryce are gonna be there it could get super awkward. You know, the whole me and Jeb, Mom and Dad thing?"

"I do. And, I'll tell you like I always do. You deserve better than an out of work wannabe rockstar. He's not a bad guy in the sense they feel he's gonna hurt you, but if he can't take care of himself, how would he care of you, or even kids?"

"I don't know."

"That's what Mom and Dad are tryin' to get you to see. Just promise me you'll think about it while I'm away."

"Promise."

With more hugs than Zach could keep track of, he and Roxie were finally invited to board the plane. "Wait…you mean your parents don't have their own plane?" He grinned to let Roxie know he was joking.

She caught on quickly when she retorted with, "Pardon me, but the private jet is being worked on, so we'll have to fly measly first class," Roxie rolled her eyes for effect.

"Darn. You mean we have to sit in these cushy seats, next to each other? How gross!"

"That's not even the worst of it. Throughout the entire flight the attendants bring us drinks or anything else we want. They can provide almost anything.

Seeing all the luxury and how first class looked more like a fancy movie theater made Zachary's fear of flying—not that he'd ever flown before—dissipate, as they were the only ones in first class through the entire seven-hour flight, and even after the brief layover in Chicago, Illinois.

The layover was long enough, however, for Roxie to show him all the little shops inside the airport. He loved watching how she oohed and aahed over even the tiniest of trinkets. Of course, she couldn't only window shop, she *had* to buy. He thought it sweet that she thought of gifts for his family to give at a late Christmas party they were planning when Zach and Roxie returned to Tennessee. "You don't have to purchase anything for my family. As you are aware by now, we aren't an extravagant bunch."

"I know, but I want to get them something because I appreciate the way you were raised which helped make you into the man, I'm in love with."

"Wait…" *Did she just say she loves me?* "What did you say?

"That I wanted to—"

Zachary stopped her. "The last part."

Roxie smiled, "Ahhh. The, 'I'm in love with you' part?"

44

"Yes. That..."

"You're okay with that aren't you?" They sat at the gate where they'd be called to board at any moment. Roxie wasn't sure whether Zach was happy about her declaration or not. Sometimes, he was a hard nut to crack. According to his parents, he'd been that way his whole life, but after losing Bryce, it took that much more work to gain his trust.

The last girl who told Zach she was in love with him dumped him not long after Bryce's funeral, even though they'd been together through high school. She couldn't handle the anxiety and panic attacks Zach experienced. She told him it was her, not him. *Yeah, right. How else did she expect me to take it?* He wanted, badly, to believe that his present relationship wouldn't turn out like the last one. Roxie wasn't Sheri and he knew that, but it didn't get rid of the doom he felt. "Just a little surprised. That's all."

Roxie could tell there was more to it than that, but she was learning along the way when to push him and when to back off. She wouldn't be able to broach the subject again until they were on the plane. As luck would have it, they didn't have to wait. Roxanne had hoped to speak with Zach more about her declaration, but he must've taken some Dramamine because, not long after the plane was back in the air, he slept.

When Zach finally awoke from his slumber, it was only because the captain spoke rather loudly over the intercom, thanking all passengers for a wonderful flight, and telling them it was time to disembark. They'd made it to the Los Angeles airport. As Zach took in his surroundings, he admitted that the plane ride, and even the layover, were easier to handle than all the people they had to wade through to get to baggage claim. "Watch...our luggage has disappeared," his voice wasn't quite a normal tone, but not a yell either.

Roxanne heard him, but sensed he'd be more comfortable once they got around the throng of people who'd converged on baggage claim all at once. "Are you ready to get out of here yet?" Roxanne teased.

"Don't you know it. Phew! How did you grow up in a place like this? It makes me claustrophobic—too many people at once." He'd grabbed Roxie's suitcases already. *She has a lot just for a ten day trip.* Now he watched as the carousel went around and around, and he couldn't see his one tiny duffle bag anywhere. He'd even explained that it was electric blue with black straps. He *had* to find it. It was really the only item he wanted to keep for himself after Bryce died. When he was alive, Bryce carried everything in it, from sports equipment to textbooks. And he would never leave home without it. "Do you see it?" Zach asked Roxie.

"Not yet, but I'm certain it'll show up."

It took another hour to find Zach's duffel. The sigh he let out was audible—a sigh of relief. He'd thought for sure he'd lost his precious reminder of his little brother.

By the time the duo arrived at Roxie's house, or mansion rather, it was only eight o'clock in Los Angeles, but in Tennessee it was ten o'clock. To say he was exhausted was an understatement. As the limousine pulled up in front of the place Roxie called home, Zach's eyes were the size of sand dollars when he saw the she sheer magnitude of it.

Observing him in her world, Roxanne realized exactly how different they were. They might both be American, but their cultures varied drastically. Until she met Zach, she thought most people, not counting homeless and vagrants, were exactly like her. Everyone made the kind of money her parents did and lived in houses like hers, didn't they? She noticed Zach visibly shift his position as the car pulled up.

"Whoa!" his southern drawl was much more evident here than in Tennessee.

"Is it too much?" Roxie was concerned about the anxiety he carried with him, she had spent enough time with him in the last three months to watch for triggers.

"It's immense, that's for sure."

"You think it looks big out here, wait until you see the inside."

It was obvious to Zachary that Roxie was proud of where she came from. It fascinated him to watch her in her element. When they reached the house, the servant who answered the door was unyielding when Zach insisted he could carry both his own, and most of Roxanne's, luggage. Zach wasn't used to having that kind of thing done for him and it unnerved him a bit.

"It's okay, sweetheart," Roxanne grabbed his hand, "they are servants. That's what they get paid for." Then she turned to the servant who looked as if he was about to receive a tongue lashing, and said, "It's okay, Sergio. Zachary here isn't used to having servants. It may take him some time to get used to it." Her voice dripped honey, which wasn't something she did with the help. Most of the time, she was demeaning and rude, demanding to be taken care of immediately when she called. They had to drop whatever they were working on to come to her aid. None of the servants had been sad when she left for college. In fact, unbeknownst to the Mr. and Mrs., since they were gone a lot, the help threw a party celebrating her departure. Sergio didn't know how to respond to this new version of Miss Roxanne, as they were required to call her, so he said, "Thank you, Miss Roxanne."

Zach stepped into the entryway of the biggest house he'd ever been in. "Oh, my gosh! This place is beautiful." He didn't dare touch anything. It was a good thing they were staying ten days, because it would take him that long to get through this maze of a house.

"Don't worry, sir," Sergio spoke to Zach, "it's not as intense as it looks, though I suppose it can be a bit intimidating."

Zachary took the time to talk with this man while Roxanne went off to find her parents. They'd gone to a red carpet party, but promised to be home in time to meet the young man their daughter had taken a liking to. Of course, they were running late. *Some things never change.* She allowed Zach a few minutes to speak with Sergio as it seemed to dim the scared look in Zach's eyes. He didn't need to know she was angry at her parents for not keeping their word. If there was one thing Roxanne had learned from being around Zach and his family, it was the importance of being truthful, no matter what the consequence, and keeping your promises. If you must break one, do it gently.

Roxie wasn't aware that Zach sensed the change in her emotions. He'd been enjoying talking with Sergio, learning about where his family was from, and that he grew up in this house, right alongside Roxanne. His father began driving the limousine for the McCains long before Sergio was born, but because his mother was a maid, Sergio and his two brothers were treated as part of the family, at least by Mr. and Mrs. McCain. Roxanne had never hidden her disdain for them. Once the boys were old enough to earn their keep, they were instructed to help the maids. Sergio took over driving the limo for his father just before Roxanne moved to Tennessee. Zach shook Sergio's hand and went to talk to Roxie.

"Hey baby, what's the matter?" he thought he knew, but didn't want to guess.

"My parents promised they'd be here when we got here, but they're still at that red-carpet gala thingy," she pouted.

Zach could totally see her as a little girl or even as a teenager, stomping her foot when things weren't going her way. He wondered if the girl he'd come to know and love, was an act she put on for him, because listening to her now, the entitled brat came out way too easily. "It's no biggie. That'll give you time to show me around, although I think it'll take me more than ten days to learn this place."

"Let me show you where you'll sleep and then we can go from there." Gone was Roxanne, and in her place, his Roxie was back.

"Sounds good." Zach replied. Sergio, of course, wouldn't allow him to carry any luggage, again, although there were other domestics available. Zach wondered if the man thought them friends because Zach was kind enough to talk to him as a person, not only someone who worked there.

The bedroom Roxie led him to was bigger than the living room and kitchen, put together, back home. The house Zachary grew up in wasn't anything to sneeze at, but it was nothing compared to Roxie's. He could tell the bedroom must've been decorated by a woman due to the lacy curtains and the frilly bedspread. At least it wasn't pink. This room was more of a beige-tan color. Boring. But a lot posher than he was used to. The bed was a California king, three times larger than his paltry queen bed that he was certain had belonged to his grandparents before he got it. "This is too much." Zach was concerned about Roxie's family doing too much to please him.

"Zach, honey," it still sounded weird to hear his girlfriend say it when he'd only been called honey by his mother, "trust me, there are plenty of servants to be at your beck and call. Besides, most of our time is going to be spent out and about anyway."

"Let me guess...we're gonna tour Los Angeles." The thought made his legs shaky. He wasn't sure he wanted to do that, but didn't want to come off as being a chicken either. Zach could tell Roxie wanted to say something, but she was evidently sidetracked by the sounds of a car.

"My parents are here," she squealed, excited to show her beau off. Zach hadn't heard anything, so he did the only thing he could do— follow her to the front hall where the elder McCains were met by a plump, older woman with silver, curly hair coiffed in a tight bun. She reminded Zach of Mrs. Potts from *Beauty and the Beast,* wearing the same uniform as the other women servants he'd seen, only hers was sky-blue because she was the housekeeper. The rest of the help, other than the chefs, wore black uniforms; the chefs wore white. Zach watched warily from behind Roxie as she excitedly greeted her parents.

"Mom..." she gave her mother a quick hug. "Daddy!" This one elicited a big bear hug, although her father wasn't big, not at all. She'd told him a bit about the differences in her relationships with her parents. She was closer to her father, as was visible by the way the greetings contrasted. It didn't take her long before she pulled Zach forward using the hand she continued to hold. "Mom...Daddy...this is Zachary Blaze. We met at school."

The introductions were awkward, to say the least. Although both of her parents said hello to him, and welcomed him into their home, they didn't act overly thrilled that Zach was there. It made him wonder how much they knew about him, but there was no way he was going to bring that up. Not in a first encounter. He was grateful that, by the time all was said and done, it was late, even in L.A. and he could retire to his room. That was okay with him because he needed time to decompress. Maybe see if there was a good movie on one of the many movie channels they had to have. After saying goodnight to everyone, Roxie walked him to his room and kissed him passionately. She knew her parents weren't being nice but could tell by the look in his eyes that he wasn't going to talk about it.

Chapter 5

The first day in Los Angeles, not much was said as far as what Roxie's parents thought of him. It was Saturday, and if her parents weren't helping clients they were either sleeping in, which was rare, or golfing. They'd tried, as Roxanne grew up, to teach her to play, but she wasn't interested. Shopping and spa days were more her style.

Zachary couldn't believe all the places there were to go, and that was in L.A. alone. It didn't count the surrounding areas. There was one place he had never been and swore that, whether he made it to Kissimmee, Florida to go to Disney World or Anaheim, California to Disneyland, he would go, and he would ride a roller coaster for Bryce even though just the thought of getting on one made him sick to his stomach. Worse than usual.

When they returned several hours later—with Zach having purchased some souvenirs for his family and even some for the ladies who worked at the clinic—they were met at the door by Roxanne's parents. They didn't look mad, just imposing, which automatically caused Zachary to throw his defensive walls up. The first question was asked by Belinda, "Have you had dinner?"

Zach wasn't used to calling it that, but at least he knew what she meant. Roxanne chimed in, "Yes, I took him to Superfine Pizza. He's had enough culture shock just being here that I didn't think introducing him to French cuisine was a great idea."

"Well..." Belinda sniffed and turned her nose up, "you should have let us know. As it were, Cook made enough for all of us, and now the extra has to be thrown out."

That remark shocked Zach. This was the first time he'd spoken up since the night before. "Ma'am, you don't need to do that. Midnight leftovers are some of my family's favorites."

"We don't do...what do you call them—leftovers? If something doesn't get eaten at the dinner table, that's too bad." Belinda ridiculed.

"Mother! You don't have to be so mean, do you?" Roxanne wasn't about to let her mother belittle her boyfriend.

They had migrated from the front hallway to the parlor, where Roxanne's father, Robert, was already nursing his after-dinner drink—Scotch on the rocks—and his favorite Cuban cigar. Roxanne and her mother were still locked in a battle of wills as Roxanne defended Zach.

"What in the world is going on?" Robert boomed. He didn't appreciate the interruption of his nightly ritual. "Belinda, are you harping on those kids about not being here for dinner? I thought we discussed this. We were going to allow Roxanne to be the adult she has been, out on her own for the last three months, and no micromanaging her or Zachary's time."

"Yes, Robert, we did consult on that, but I think, as adults, they should have had the courtesy to let us know. Don't you?" They'd all been seated for some time, as Robert and Belinda went back and forth.

"It might have been nice, but the reality is, we cannot continue babying our daughter. Pretty soon, she will have a home, husband and children of her own. Are we still going to dictate to her then?"

Roxanne could feel the warmth of a blush creep up her neck into her cheeks. *They are not seriously talking about marriage are they…specifically mine?* She glanced at Zach to see if he caught what they were doing. The look on his face spoke volumes, not to mention how red his neck was. She chose that moment to interrupt. "Mom,Dad…I know you mean well, but, as Daddy stated, I am an adult and should be treated as such. What Zach and I choose to do while we are visiting is entirely up to us." Changing the subject, she exclaimed, "You both should really come visit Tennessee again. I know you haven't been back in many years, and there are some gorgeous places there." As she spoke, she took Zach's hand. "And, you really should meet Susan, Darren, and Stevie. They have been kind enough to invite me into their home and treat me as if I belong there. I hope you will do that with Zachary now." Up to that point, they sat next to each other under the intense glare of Belinda. Roxanne, in her way, was making a statement to her parents—that she and Zach were together no matter what they thought. It was more for her mother's benefit than her father's.

"I wouldn't mind going for a visit," Robert stated. "It would be nice to visit my alma mater and some of my old haunts."

Belinda wasn't happy. The sneer was evident on her face. She didn't like this boy. Yes, her husband may have gone to college there, but he wasn't *from* there, so she had been able to mold him into the father and husband he was.

Although things hadn't gone her way, Belinda stayed seated, fuming. Normally, she would have left the room, but she wasn't about to leave her only child in the clutches of this—this…boy. He was older than Roxanne, but that's not the way Belinda saw him. He wasn't a man, but a boy.

With her mother already angry, Roxanne figured now was as good a time as any to tell them she wasn't going to Vanderbilt—that she wasn't going to follow in her mother's footsteps as they'd planned. She cleared her throat and took the plunge, "Um, Mother…Daddy, there's something I need to tell you both." Roxie could almost hear her mother's eye roll. She took a deep breath, "I'm not attending Vanderbilt after the new semester is over." Zach seemed to understand where she was going with this and gave her hand a squeeze. He'd encouraged her to pursue her dream, even if they couldn't be together for her to accomplish it. "I've decided I want to attend Lipscomb University and go into fashion design."

"I knew your path was different," Her father congratulated her.

Her mother, however, turned on Zach, "How dare you! First you're trying to get my husband to relive his glory days and now you're taking my daughter away from me!"

Roxie immediately came to Zach's defense, "Mother, he's doing no such thing! If he's guilty of anything it's helping me realize my dream and go for it."

"Who's going to take over the practice? That's been in the works since the day you were born!" Belinda flung herself out of her chair. Zach could tell where Roxie's entitled attitude came from.

Robert silenced his wife, explaining the children didn't need to worry about the practice. Instead, he took the time to ask Zachary questions about the college, his family, and the area in general. He wanted to know how much had changed in the twenty-something years since he'd been there. As Roxanne was growing up, he had wanted to return, but his wife was adamant about never going back. Belinda had made that decision without him. After years of trying, Robert gave up. It wasn't worth making his wife angry, because the more he asked, the madder she got.

At some point, while Zach was chatting with Robert, the subject of Bryce came up. It had been two long, hard years to endure since the accident, but somehow, knowing that this family had suffered a loss as well, made speaking about his own family's tragedy a little easier. "Bryce was the youngest of the three of us," he began. "He was always getting into more bumps and scrapes than me, so when he wanted to go four-wheeling with his friends that weekend, my parents thought nothing of it. He'd been many times before and came home unscathed."

Robert stopped him, "I bet that was difficult for your parents. I know when we lost Amelia, Roxanne's twin, I felt there was more I should and could have done to make the pregnancy run smoother, no matter what the doctor said."

"Roxie told me about that. I am truly sorry for your loss. No one should have to go through that, especially losing a baby." Zach was sympathetic.

Belinda and Roxie sat and listened, although Belinda acted as if she didn't want to be there. When she heard them bring Amelia up, she exploded, jumping to her feet and jabbing an accusing finger in Zachary's face. "How dare you talk about my baby girl like you knew her!"

Zach didn't know how to respond. He wasn't used to the tone Belinda was using on him. Roxanne chose that moment to insert herself between her mother and her love. "Mother?" She wanted badly to lose it, but she didn't. She chose the higher ground. "He's not dismissing Amelia, or anything surrounding that situation. He just wants you and Daddy to know that he feels your pain, to some extent," she said gently. That must've appeased Belinda because, without another word, she ascended the stairs, leaving the threesome alone.

"I am so sorry about my wife's outburst," Robert murmured. "It continues to haunt her as if it were yesterday. When you become a therapist, you are taught how to assist others through the grieving process. What they don't teach is how to help yourself through your own, beyond feeling the emotions and working through them."

"It's okay," Zach whispered. "I can't say I wouldn't do the same thing had our roles been reversed. I mean, look, her daughter goes off to college, one she didn't want Roxie attending in the first place, and then she brings home a boy—a cowboy, no less. I'm sure neither of you expected this, not in her first semester."

"It was a surprise, that's for sure," Robert laughed. "Never in all my years of being a doctor, or her father, did I imagine my daughter with a cowboy. She's more high-maintenance than that."

Roxanne chimed in, "Daddy, I'm not as high-maintenance as you think, am I Zach?" she smiled sweetly.

Zach knew, at that moment, what a deer must feel like when it gets caught in the headlights of an oncoming car. *Maybe if I keep my mouth shut, she won't expect me to answer. Whatever my response is could land me in hot water.* He kept quiet, hoping Robert would change the subject. In truth, Roxie was more entitled than anyone he'd previously dated. Before her, he would never have given someone of high society a second thought, but she'd been persistent from the beginning.

"Zach, sweetie?" Roxie drummed her well-manicured nails on the end table next to the loveseat where they sat.

He knew he wasn't getting out of answering her question. "To be honest, sir, when we first met, I knew she wasn't what I was used to, but we were paired as partners in our math class, and after that first study session I knew there was no way, no matter how badly I didn't want to work with her, that I was getting away from her."

"Atta girl," Robert praised his daughter for going after what she wanted.

"Well, actually, Daddy…" she paused, "…I wish mother was here to listen to how we met."

"Shall I go see if she'll come down?" Robert was aware that his daughter craved her mother's love, but, as he had feared all those years ago, Belinda blamed Roxanne for Amelia's death. It didn't matter that the doctors told her there wasn't anything that was wrong, exactly. Those things happened, with no explanation.

"You can, I suppose." The sadness at her mother's indifference to anything positive in Roxanne's life was clear, no matter how hard she tried masking it.

It didn't take long for Robert to come back alone. "She's asleep," he lied, and Roxanne knew he was keeping the truth from her. Unless her mother took one of her sleeping pills, there was no way she'd be asleep yet; it was only eight o'clock.

"It's okay, Daddy. You don't have to cover for her."

"I'm sorry, my dear. I know this wasn't the homecoming you'd hoped for. But I still want to hear about the first time you met this young man." The more Robert got to know Zachary, and the more he watched the gentleness Zach extended toward Roxie, the more he wanted to know about him. He wasn't certain yet, but he thought his daughter may have met her match in Zach.

Roxanne beamed as she began their story which had commenced a mere three months before. Her eyes shone like Zach had never seen before. "It all began on orientation day. Having never been anywhere near that part of Tennessee, I was completely turned around trying to find where my classes were to be held the next day. I had stopped in the middle of the sidewalk leading to the administration building, and, if I recall…" she looked at Zach "…I was looking down at my map when I ran into something. I wasn't even aware it was a person until I heard a low 'umph.' I looked up into those steel-grey eyes and was lost. We ended up going to a coffee shop Zach frequented when he was on campus and spent the next several hours talking. By the time we were done, I knew he thought me an entitled, spoiled, rich brat."

Zach jumped in, "She's not wrong. I honestly thought she might be a little crazy too." They laughed at that because this wasn't news to Roxie. "When I found out she was my math partner for the entire semester, I wasn't happy, to say the least. The instructor was such a stick in the mud, though, that there was nothing I could do. I was stuck. And thank goodness for that, or I would've never learned who the person was behind the rich-kid exterior she put up." He gave her hand a squeeze when all he really wanted was to kiss her, but he wasn't going to disrespect her father. "I'd hoped, at first, that if I put her off long enough, she might get the hint and ask for a new partner. Knowing what I do now, I should've known better."

"Why do you call her Roxie?" Robert inquired. Unbeknownst to all of them, Belinda had been listening the whole time from a corner where she couldn't be seen. She was curious too, as to why Roxanne allowed Zach to call her by that name when she'd hated it her entire life.

Roxanne answered that one, "Daddy, have you *heard* the way he says it?"

"Yes, I have."

"It sounds so…so…" she wasn't sure whether she should say the word she was thinking in front of her father, but it was the only one that could describe his southern drawl when he called her Roxie "…sexy."

Instead of being angry, her father laughed, "Well, okay…leave it to my daughter to not mince words."

Ω

As promised, two days before Roxanne and Zachary were to depart for Tennessee, the pair took off to Disneyland. And, as promised, he decided to go on Big Thunder Mountain, more to prove to himself that he could do it than for his brother. Roxanne was pleasantly surprised when he asked her to go with him. She thought it more for his own comfort than hers since she'd been on every ride at Disneyland more than a few times, but she wasn't about to dismiss any chance of gripping him tightly. Her mother had mellowed out some, but she still disliked Zachary. Roxanne was grateful she was tolerant of him, since there wasn't much vacation time left. I took Zach a bit to get his legs back under him; Thunder Mountain made him squeal like a little girl the whole way. Then, it was settled that, whether he felt he could or not, Zach would take a ride on one more roller coaster, the fastest of all coasters at Disneyland, called California Screamin,' which went as fast as fifty-five miles per hour.

"Roxie, I'm not sure I want to do this." The sound coming from Zach's throat was no longer the self-assured twenty-three-year-old she'd come to know but sounded more like a frightened child who needed monsters chased from his room.

"Zach, you already kept your promise to Bryce and rode a roller coaster for him. And, let's face it, Big Thunder Mountain isn't for pansies."

That caught Zach off-guard. He'd used 'pansies' plenty of times when they were talking, but Roxie was too refined to use such words. "Did you just say pansies?" He couldn't have stopped the laugh that escaped his mouth even if he'd wanted to. Of course, laughter was the best medicine, so Roxie joined in. Once i subsided Zach was resolute in going on this one last ride for Bryce. He had no idea how his and Roxie's relationship would turn out, nor did he know if he'd make it to the West Coast again. He hoped so, but just in case, he would ride California Screamin' for his little brother.

"Want me to come with you?" Roxanne wanted to go with him. She was afraid he didn't have what it took to handle such a ride alone. He was too gentle. Too soft. But these were the qualities that had drawn her to him in the first place

Boy, did he ever, but he also felt the need to go alone, half expecting Bryce to be sitting there with him. *That's not possible, is it?* "No. This is one I think I should do alone."

"Are you sure?" Roxie didn't hide her displeasure at being dismissed. Although being at school and around Zach and his family helped her to change the way she viewed many things, when it came to her wants and needs, *she* came first. "Do you realize how fast you'll be going?"

"Yes."

"And you almost threw up on Big Thunder Mountain. This one goes twice as fast."

"I need to do this. There's a part of me that feels like Bryce will be there with me, you know, along for the ride."

"Whatever you say. The line isn't excruciatingly long, but I'll be waiting over there," she pointed to a wooden bench off to the side of the pavilion the ride side beneath "…on that bench, when you're done." Roxanne's coolness spoke volumes as she flounced away.

There's the girl I met three months ago. The one who thought the world revolved around her. She's changed so much in such a short amount of time. I wish Bryce could meet her Zach. Once he sat in a seat, he felt the hairs on his arms stand up. He wasn't so sure he'd made the right decision to do this by himself until he heard, "Hey, bro!"

"Bryce?" Zach was confused. "How are you here? I mean, how can I see you?" Zach wasn't sure what to think about what was taking place.

He wasn't a huge believer in ghosts, but he did believe the dead walked among the living, as spirits.

"First, your girlfriend is *hot,* but quite spoiled, if I do say so myself. Second, I'm here because you asked me to come."

"I've asked for you to come back several times in the last two years. Why now? Have you been around the whole time?"

"Yes, I've been watching, and the only reason you can see me is because you're open to it. You wanted badly for me to know you kept your promise about the ride and I was allowed one last visit to enjoy it with you." Bryce smiled a wide, toothy grin. Oh, how Zach missed that face.

Skeptical, Zach asked, "Who can see us?"

"You? Everyone. Me? Just you." Bryce laughed; a sound Zach had missed dearly.

"You're telling me I look like I'm sitting here talking to myself?" The conductor chose that moment to start the ascent to what, Zach was positive, was his death. "Don't leave me, Bryce!"

"Hang on tight and enjoy the ride," Bryce instructed, "Honestly, I never thought you'd make it out this way. Remember when we were kids and talked about the roller coasters and how *this* was the one I thought was the coolest?"

"I do," Zach stuttered, still not believing what he saw. He had to blink several times just to make sure this was not a dream. His brother was truly sitting next to him, "You know, I planned on doing this *for* you but this? This is unreal."

"Just hang on brother, I can make this cart do things you'd never imagine." Even before Zach could come to terms with the fact that he could see Bryce, they were twirling around in circles. Then, before he knew what was happening, Bryce made them fly. "How the...?" Zach couldn't form the words.

"The perks of being immortal, brother." They enjoyed what felt like hours, but at the same time seconds together., "As they ride came to a stop slowly, Bryce piped up, "*That* was fun!"

"Will I ever see you again?" Zach wondered.

"I can't say, but will you do me a favor and give mom, dad and Stevie an extra hug for me?" Before Bryce disappeared, as quickly as he'd come; no smoke, no fanfare, he left with these simple words, "By the way, she's a hottie!" Referring to Roxie. Zach's next awareness was the conductor instructing him to get out of the car, as there were other patrons waiting for their turn. "Oh—I'm so sorry!" He stood and his legs buckled beneath him without warning.

It was a good thing Roxanne wasn't far away, as she came to help him find somewhere to regain his strength. He wanted badly to tell her of his encounter but was afraid she wouldn't see it as sacred as he did, but he couldn't help it. Roxie didn't say a word until he was finished with his story. At first, her mouth hung open in disbelief, but then she said, "*Now* I get why you wanted to go by yourself." She asked questions about where Bryce was in his resting place, and whether Zach thought she might get the chance to contact Amelia if he were able to contact him again. Zach had no answers for her, which she wasn't happy about, but by the time they arrived back at Roxie's parents' house they were discussing flight plans and getting home the next day.

Roxanne had surprised herself while she was home when she only saw her girlfriends, whom she'd been inseparable from prior to her move south, a couple times for lunch and a shopping day. It was good for her because she was able to purchase Christmas presents for her parents and Zach, although he would receive a gift from her at his parents' house as well. They would celebrate Christmas and have their annual Christmas party. The only reason she could pull that off was because her father insisted on taking Zach golfing, although the only kind of golfing Zach had ever done was of the miniature variety. She enjoyed her time with her friends, but she'd grown up a lot in their time apart. She hoped she hadn't been as shallow as they now seemed, but the few times she'd let her old self—whom she'd decided she didn't like all that much—come out, she could see why Zachary thought less of her when they met.

Because it was their last night in Los Angeles, and Christmas too, Mrs. McCain insisted on throwing a huge party, and invited everyone who was anyone. This meant almost everyone were either clients or friends of Roxanne's parents.

Zach was extremely uncomfortable about the whole Christmas party thing. "You know I won't fit in."

"I don't care. They'll either love you because you're mine or they won't. Doesn't matter to me-- I love you." They were alone, one of the few times they had been the whole trip, and Roxie took advantage of it. She kissed Zach's neck, little, tiny pecks, and nibbles at his earlobes before settling on his lips—oh, so soft. What she hadn't expected was her mom to barge in just as they were locked in a passionate embrace.

"Roxanne Gillian! What on earth do you think you're doing?"

Instead of being embarrassed, Roxie was mad, but calmed herself before speaking politely, "Mother, this is my room, my space, and when I am home, I would appreciate it if you would knock first."

Zach was humiliated enough for both and apologized profusely. They might be adults, but he was in someone else's home. He knew better, even though he thought Roxie had a point. "I'm sorry, ma'am."

"Well!" Mrs. McCain was disgusted, but several people were expected to show up at any moment and knew she couldn't let her emotions run wild. "Your guests will be arriving in about thirty minutes for the Christmas party. Both of you, get cleaned up and come downstairs!" Neither Zach nor Roxie missed the glare Belinda gave them.

The party wasn't as bad as Zach thought it would be, although he was beyond grateful when he could make himself scarce. Alone, in the solitude of the bedroom he'd occupied for almost two weeks, he went through and packed the Christmas gifts he'd received from Roxie's parents as well as gifts from Roxie, so that everything would fit nicely in his bags. Roxanne was able to leave some of her stuff there, which helped the hordes of luggage situation. After kissing his beautiful girlfriend Merry Christmas and thanking her parents for their generous gift—a thousand dollars toward his graduate degree--given to him secretly by Roxie's dad—he lay in bed, glad he'd be home the next day.

Chapter 6

Zach couldn't believe how much he'd missed home. The smells, the sounds, the intimacy of it. He never thought he'd say he was glad he hadn't been born into money. His parents weren't poor by any means, but they'd taught their children from an early age how to earn their keep. They didn't believe in allowances just for doing chores around the house but paid them for extra things like helping to clean out the animal cages and feeding animals who had to stay overnight at the clinic. Zachary remembered being three-years-old and helping his dad. He wasn't quite big enough then, but looking back, especially after spending the last several days in a mansion, he never thought he'd be so grateful to come from such humble beginnings.

Due to the lateness of the hour they returned, they made plans to take an Uber to get home. Zach's parents weren't overly happy about it but were also aware that he was no longer a child, and just because a terrible disaster had struck their family didn't mean that he would die as Bryce had.

Ω

They arrived at Roxanne's apartment, where Zachary paid the Uber driver extra to wait while he kissed his girlfriend properly.

"Man, just make it quick. I don't have all night!" The driver blew out a frustrated breath.

"Dude, I just paid you an extra fifty bucks! I'll take whatever time I feel necessary." Zach wanted to be mad at the guy, but he couldn't. "Be right back," he laughed. He walked Roxie to her door, wishing he could hold her hand, but being the gentleman he'd been raised to be, his arms and hands were full of luggage and gifts Roxie had purchased for Zach's family as Christmas gifts, even though he told her she didn't have to. But she'd insisted, and if there was one thing he'd learned by dating someone of Roxie's caliber, it was that arguing once her mind was set on doing something, would get him nowhere.

Once they were inside Roxie's apartment, Zachary wasted no time in pulling her to him. They'd been able to hold hands and hug in her parents' presence, but after her mom caught them kissing and had such a hissy fit about it, they didn't do that while still in L.A. *Boy, am I glad we're home!* Zach lowered his head, lips meeting lips. It was almost like they'd never kissed before. Like this was the first time. He hated feeling that inept, especially when he'd kissed those lips quite a lot prior to their travels. "I've missed this," he breathed when they came up for air.

"I know, me too! I was horrified when my mom walked in on us."

"Right? I noticed it's easy for her to make you feel like a little kid again—like you're not almost twenty-one. By the way, you've never told me how far away from it you are. A man needs to know these things." Zach knew he'd veered off topic, but he couldn't help it. If he'd have thought about it while in L.A., he would've asked her father. If she wouldn't tell him, he might just have to do that anyway.

"It's soon. Can we get through New Year's first? This vacation was anything, but…I'm not surprised by the way my mother reacted to some things on this trip, but the way she treated you, like you had the plague or something, was uncalled for." Roxie wrapped her arms around Zach's neck signaling she wanted less talking and more kissing.

He was more than happy to oblige. Obviously, she didn't recognize the incompetence he felt. It was another hour before Zach finally stumbled into his own bed. Being on two different time zones sucked. It had taken most of his time in California to acclimate to Pacific Time and now, here he was back in Eastern, and would have to get used to it again. He was so tired so, after waking his parents just long enough to let them know he was safe, he fell into bed. He didn't even bother changing into pajamas. He knew the next few days would be busy getting ready for the Christmas/New Year's party he promised his parents they could have upon his and Roxie's return. Not only that, but he and Roxie needed to go get their schedules for the next semester too. However, that would have to wait, since the school was closed.

Even though Zach had spoken regularly with his parents while he was gone, it didn't stop them or Stevie from bombarding him with hugs and claps on the back, letting him know they were glad he made it home safely. As he watched his family interact that morning during breakfast, the only thing he could think about was how thankful he was for them— for the fact that they were so much different than where Roxie came from. After spending time in her home, though, it put her brattitude into perspective. For people who counselled families on ways to be closer, they had issues in their own. Robert wasn't bad, as far as Zach could tell. He loved his daughter, but from Zach's standpoint, he was more afraid of his wife and the repercussions he might experience than anything, so he was more apt to do whatever she desired. Zach didn't blame him. He had seen some of Belinda's volatility, but was certain she was watching herself because she didn't want to come off in a bad light to Zach. There wasn't much love lost between mother and daughter.

Later that afternoon, after giving his family the rundown on the trip, Zach and Roxie decided they would see what was playing at the theater and if there wasn't anything they wanted to watch, they'd go back to the solitude of her place after picking up movies from Redbox. That's what Zach preferred, and since he was so bad at party planning, his mom and sister were more than happy to hand him over to Roxie, so they could work. As luck would have it, the theater was sold out. *Guess everyone had the same idea. Not that I'm complaining. I'd rather cuddle up on Roxie's couch watching chick flicks because she loves them anyway.* Zach knew they were going to have to talk about where they wanted their relationship to go, since she was transferring to Lipscomb University in Nashville after the next semester was over and he to the University of Tennessee College of Veterinary Medicine in Knoxville, which would make seeing each other difficult, being almost three hours apart. He'd had a few friends try the long-distance relationship thing; some were even shorter distances than the three hours, but they didn't work out after only a few weeks.

"Roxie," he whispered as they lay bundled on her couch, sharing a blanket. Although it hadn't been too cold in L. A. as it was in the Golden State, in Tennessee it was quite a bit colder.

"Yes?" she inquired sleepily.

That was okay with Zach. He loved that she felt comfortable enough with him to fall asleep. He hated to ruin that, and debated on waiting, but knew they only had four months left to be together before they either tried long distance or didn't. Zack, personally, was wary of doing it, but he wasn't prepared to lose her either. "We need to talk."

That immediately threw Roxie's defenses up. "What?"

"You realize we only have four months until we head in different directions, right?"

"Yes, but what does that matter?" she knew why it was significant but didn't want to have this conversation; not today, not ever. *What if he dumps me? Why can't we live the next few months in bliss?*

"You know just as well as I do that a three-hour drive to see each other won't leave much time together. I'm concerned that, without the ability to see one another whenever we want, we'll drift apart. You'll have your hands full with your class load, as will I."

"Can we talk about this after your family's Christmas/New Year's party? I don't want to put a damper on it."

"I guess." The only thing Zach was sure of was that, in a short amount of time, this woman had become extremely important to him and he wanted more than anything to do whatever he needed to make their relationship work. But at the same time, he was realistic. For the remainder of their chick flick marathon he pushed all thoughts of that discussion out of his mind.

Ω

Two days later, the night before classes began, the Blaze clan had their party. Since most of the friends Zach had in high school had moved away and the only person, other than family that he saw on a regular basis was Roxie, Zach invited the few friends who'd either moved back to town or were visiting for semester break. Most of them had graduated, and in a way, it made him feel inferior because he'd started college at the same time as most of them and he was far from being done. They were all taken with Roxie and wondered how a simple cowboy could land someone of her stature. Coming from money and all, they joked.

"He didn't 'land' me, as you so eloquently put it," Roxanne had listened to these people who claimed to be friends of the family degrade Zachary enough, "if you must know, I *chose* him." That shut them up real fast. She couldn't believe that the—most of the time—self-assured man she'd fallen in love with was even associated with these goons. Luckily, it was getting late and she and Zach had early classes the next day. She, being raised the way she'd been, couldn't ignore them and leave as she wanted. Besides, that wouldn't be fair to the host and hostess who had been nothing but kind since they had met. While Zach dealt with the neanderthals, she went to bid Darren, Susan and Stevie a good night and thank them for the gifts she received from them.

"Well, guys, thanks for coming, but I have early classes in the morning and want to make sure I get there in plenty of time." Zach had enough of these people he'd once called friends. Looking at them through different eyes, the ones Roxie had given him, made him wonder how and why he'd ever been friends with them. Of course, said friends couldn't let him go without a sneer or two about what Zach and Roxie were really going to do.

Zach chose to ignore it until one of them piped up with, "I wouldn't mind gettin' that little filly under the sheets."

Zachary whirled around, and with gritted teeth and clenched fists, said, "Don't ever talk about Roxie or any woman like that! You guys weren't so crude in high school. What happened?" Zach held his anger in but wasn't certain what would set it off.

"Oh, Zachary, my fairweather friend, we've always been this way! We were just careful because we weren't sure your virgin ears could take it."

"And it appears we were right! You're probably still a virgin, huh?" another guy jeered.

"Give me a little of that high society sass! Come on, you know how to share, don't you?" The three who were bad mouthing him, and, in turn, Roxie, knew Zach couldn't take them on, but that didn't mean he didn't want to. Somewhere, somehow, he gained the strength to remove them from his house without having to fight.

"I would have if I had to, you know," Zach said.

"I know, but it's done, it's over. Just think about this…did any of them that were making demeaning remarks toward me have a date?"

"One did, but he stayed silent most of the time."

"Now, think about how jealous those boys are because I didn't give any of them the time of day. I can almost guarantee they ran home like puppies with their tails between their legs because you put them in their place." Roxie swiftly and stealthily maneuvered onto Zach's lap as she was talking. And as she talked, she kissed, nipped and licked at his lips, to his neck, to his cheeks.

Zach was so enthralled with Roxie's actions there was no way he could respond, even if he knew what to say. It wasn't long, however, before he took the reins and, he hoped, helped her sense how powerful they were together. Neither knew nor cared how long the intense make-out session lasted, but by the time they came up for air, the windows were fogged up and they no longer needed the heater on. "Holy Moses!" Zach breathed. "What was that?"

Once Roxie recovered, she said, "I wanted you to have zero doubts about how I feel about you."

"I didn't have doubts before." Zach scrubbed his hand over his face.

"Really? Then, why the talk about possibly breaking up just because some people have long distance relationships that don't work?"

"I'm just afraid in the end, you'll get hurt if we try this and we don't work out." The tenderness not only came through Zach's voice, but could be seen in the depths of the steel grayness of his eyes.

"Don't you think that breaking up prematurely might cause just as much pain, or even more? And we aren't every other couple," Roxie sighed. "I don't want to talk about this right now, okay?"

"We will sooner or later, but for now, let's get outta here."

"Why? Your 'friends' won't be bothering you for a long, long time, if they ever do again."

They ended up staying until the end of the party, which was full of a bunch of people getting drunk and eating too much before having to get a taxi called. It was definitely not the kind of party Roxie was used to. These people, for the most part, were friendly, not counting the nimrods who called themselves Zachary's friends. The adult friends of his parents included both her and Zach in conversation. Most of them were clientele from the pet clinic. *Is it weird that I feel more at home here, among complete strangers than in my own house?*

"What did you say, Darlin'?" Zach questioned.

"Did I say that out loud?" Embarrassment washed over Roxie.

"Well, not that anyone could understand much of what you said, but yeah, ya did. It's okay though. What's on your mind?" Zach stroked her cheek with his knuckles. He was glad his parents didn't freak out at their public displays of affection. He'd grown up watching his parents portray what a husband and wife were supposed to be like, and although it grossed him out as a kid, he was grateful for that knowledge now. The knowledge that spouses needed to be each other's rocks. The ability to pick up the slack when the other wasn't able.

"Nothing."

"Yes, there is. It doesn't have to do with the conversation we need to have eventually, does it?"

"No, I was just thinking about how more at home I feel here than in my own."

"That's a good thing, isn't it?"

"I guess so."

"What's wrong then?"

"To be honest, the fact that you act like you want to go to Knoxville with a clean slate, with no girlfriend to worry about, bothers me more than I've let on."

"Whoa…wait...I didn't say that!"

"But it was implied."

"What do ya say we blow this popsicle stand and go to our favorite cafe?"

"Sounds good to me." The couple thanked Susan, Darren and Stevie for the great party, said good-bye to the guests who were left, and went out into the chilly night.

Ω

Roxie surprised Zach when she ordered a hot chocolate with extra marshmallows—exactly what he ordered. "I see I've rubbed off on you." His laughter permeated her soul.

"Well, since we only have about four months to enjoy our daily outings, I decided to step out of my box."

He sat, just watching as she fidgeted with a napkin, much like what she'd done the first time they came to their favorite spot. In some ways, Zach felt he'd known her in a previous life or something, and maybe he had. Who was he to say?

"Why are you staring at me?" Roxie asked.

"When we first met, did you feel like we'd met before?"

"Like, in a previous life or something?" Skepticism mixed in her eyes, but there had always been a pull toward him that she didn't have an answer for.

"Maybe. I can't think that there isn't some other place. Otherwise, how could I have seen Bryce. I mean, we had to have come from somewhere, right?""That makes sense, but can we talk about the elephant in the room? Let's get it out of the way so we don't ruin what's left of our time together."

"I think…" Zach began.

"Wait…can I go first?" Roxie felt she needed to plead her case of pursuing a long-distance relationship.

"Sure." Zach wasn't sure of what he would say or where he was leaning. Not anymore, not after the way she put those guys in their places for him. And what she'd said about feeling more at home in his family than in her own got him thinking differently. He'd thought, for certain, he would be the one to break it off, but…

"I know long distance doesn't work for some people," Roxie began. "But think back to what you just said about knowing each other before…what if we had, and we chose this time to meet? I feel like we are soulmates. Our differences complement each other, and we've found some similarities, but the fact that you have opened my eyes to new and wonderful things—places and people I never dreamed I would see—tells me that you are good for me. My Daddy swore he wouldn't let someone take his daughter, but Zach, even though my mother is indifferent, my father loves you. Almost as much as I do," she paused.

"Does this make you change your mind, even a little?" Hope shone in her eyes.

"To tell you the truth…" he made her wait, watching as she bit her bottom lip. He'd come to love that part of her, "I was prepared to break it off now, thinking it would hurt less. Even when we were at my parents' house, that was my plan, until I talked with my mom. I felt she needed to know about my experience with Bryce, and I was confused about what to do about us. She didn't have a single doubt about us and told me if I didn't keep you, I was making the worst decision of my life. That's when she gave me the promise ring my dad gave her when they were dating, before they got engaged. But I think you're right. We are soulmates and I don't want to mess that up out of fear. I'm sorry I made you worry. One day, I'm going to ask you to marry me, but for now…" he pulled a ring from his pocket, "will you wear my mom's promise ring?"

The tears which cascaded down Roxie's cheeks gave Zachary his answer. Through hiccupping between bouts of crying, Roxie managed to ask, "So, before we left the house, you *knew* what you were going to do?"

"Yes, Darlin' I did." And with that, he slipped the ring on her finger and kissed her with all the passion he felt. They were soulmates. Of that, he was positive.

The next installment of
the From Brat to Bronco Series:

CAPTURED HEARTS

Captured Hearts

Book Two

HUNTER MARSHALL

CAPTURED HEARTS

Copyright © 2021

Captured Hearts

HUNTER MARSHALL

Huntermarshall78@gmail.com

All rights reserved. Except as permitted under the U.S. Copyright Act of 2011, no part of this publication may be reproduced, distributed, or transmitted in any form or by any means, or stored in a database or retrieval system, without the prior written permission of the publisher except in the case of brief quotations embodied in critical articles and reviews.

The characters and events portrayed in this book are fictitious. Any similarity to real persons, living or dead, is coincidental and not intended by the author.

For more information visit our Facebook Fan Page:
https://www.facebook.com/huntermarshall2015

Cover Design by Jessica Ozment

Formatting by Jessica Ozment

**CONNECT WITH
AUTHOR HUNTER MARSHALL**

Facebook Fan Page:
https://www.facebook.com/huntermarshall2015

Acknowledgments

I could not have been happier when asked by a reviewer who'd read From Brat to Bronco what was going to happen with Roxie and Zach. They know they are engaged, but does it work out, does something awful happen? So, I decided to make this a trilogy. This is the second book. I do not know who that reader is, but I would like to thank them because I have never written a series before and this makes me stretch farther as an author.

Thank you so much Jessica Tahbonemah for not only creating fantastic covers, as usual, but taking my story and making it the greatest story it could be. Thank you for being there whenever I need a listening ear or to rant and rave with. You are truly one of my best friends.

I'd like my best friend to know how much his reading and soaking up my words; begging me to write more so he has more to read means to me. He believes that I have several stories to tell and helps me hash out different scenes as I'm working. You are truly one of the best men I know!

My family! Mom and dad especially for getting excited for me whenever I reach a new milestone or publish a new book. They realize this is not just a hobby for me. They know that it's vital to my wellbeing to write. Thanks to my kids for allowing me the time to write. And, for at least acknowledging when I get ecstatic about where I'm at in a story. I have the best kids on the planet. Okay. I might be a tiny bit biased. My daughter is the bomb! She came up with the twist in the story that was better than the one I had planned. Love ya bunches mini-me!

Last, but definitely not least. Thank you to my readers and fans who take a chance on my work every time they decide to read any of my books. Y'all rock!

**Hunter Marshall,
2021**

Prologue

Roxanne McCain and Zachary Blaze had attended the University of Tennessee at Chattanooga for a year together, as intended. They'd quickly, in most peoples' eyes, gotten serious and became engaged only three months into the first semester. For Roxanne, or Roxie as only Zach could call her, she'd felt a connection to her gentle, but sturdy cowboy the day she'd all but knocked him over when the wind threatened to blur her vision, blowing her dark, chin-length hair every which way. Thinking about it, even now, made her cheeks warm with embarrassment.

Now, here she sat, waiting for the airplane that would take her from her home in Los Angeles, California to Lipscomb University in Nashville, Tennessee where she would begin her degree in fashion design. It felt like a lifetime ago when she had insisted, with the assistance of Zach's parents, that he go to L.A. with her for Christmas, where, after returning to Tennessee, Zach had asked for her hand. They were now miles and miles apart because she decided to spend much of her summer break with her parents, still doing her level best to soften the blow with her mother about the fact that she was attending, and doing, somewhere and something vastly different from her mom's psychology degree. That was what her parents wanted her to become; following in their footsteps, but she was interested in fashion design more than listening to others' issues. Roxanne had been therapied and questioned enough being raised by her parents that it turned her against wanting anything to do with it. It was not until she met Zach and learned she could stand on her own two feet; that she could become whatever she wanted. As she waited to board the plane, heading back to see the love of her life, the one she hadn't seen in almost a month, Roxanne envisioned what their reunion would be like. Zach was meeting her in Nashville to help move her into her new apartment. She fell asleep waiting for the boarding call…

▶▶ ▶▶ ▶▶ ▶▶

As Zach drove from Chattanooga to Nashville, all he could think about was Roxie. They'd been apart nearly the entire summer because she had insisted on returning to Los Angeles to repair her relationship with her mother; or at the very least, try and see friends she hadn't seen since Christmas. He'd flown there once to see her and she did the same, but he wasn't rich by any means, so it was a good thing they could FaceTime and Skype or he would have gone crazy. He hated that she was going to be over two hours away once she began classes as a fashion designer, while he had a few more years before he would head to Veterinarian school in Knoxville. He wanted to take over the family business when his father retired. Zach hoped to be done with school in time, but, in the meantime, he worked as an assistant, filing and transcribing notes on each patient. He wasn't particularly fond of this part of the work, but he would make do until he went to Knoxville. No matter what, he would be too far away from her for the next few years, and he feared with their vast differences, she might find someone else who was more her speed.

Zach was a down to earth guy, a tell it like it was, work your butt off until you achieved your goals, but then keep going, kind of guy. Although Roxanne had changed over the last year, there were times when the arrogance she grew up with reared its ugly head, especially when she was impatient about wanting something. Zachary hoped, that with his love, and being around his family, this sort of behavior might eventually, stop altogether. Throughout their time together, however, she learned that working for what she received yielded a much higher reward than having mommy and daddy foot the bill for everything. She was forced to work part-time during her two semesters at U of TN-Chattanooga, which she did at the school bookstore because anything she wanted as an extra, she had to pay for. Her mom was no longer happy about Roxie's choice of schools or degree, and literally forbade her husband to assist their daughter with anything more than tuition, so Roxanne would have to work while attending design school as well.

Zach wasn't sure she could work more than part-time because he saw what her curriculum entailed and there was *a lot*. She clearly wasn't used to pushing herself very hard, and she'd have to if she was going to make a go of her lifelong dream. She wanted to be the next Top Designer all over the world, like Alexander McQueen or Coco Chanel. He hoped and prayed she would accomplish her dreams. He loved her that much. Even the spoiled parts.

Once arriving at the airport in Nashville, Roxie sat on pins and needles as she waited for her beloved to show up. A month didn't seem long to some, but for her, it was an eternity to wait. She had come to an arrangement with her mother to agree to disagree on Roxanne's choices. She knew she was on her own, mostly, with these next steps. Roxie was grateful for the man who had come into her life at a time when she felt she was not worth much more than the *brat* title she had earned throughout her life. As she waited for Zach, she couldn't help but look at her watch. *He should have been here by now.* She watched as people eagerly met loved ones as they exited the gates from the planes. *Where is he?* He promised to be there to pick her up, and to take her to her new apartment. As she mulled over all these details, her mind wandered to the worst possible outcomes. *What if he is hurt? Or worse?*

Chapter 1

Zachary couldn't believe his eyes. The vision he took in as he walked toward Roxanne while she sat oblivious to the fact that he was at the airport, was something that would be forever ingrained in his mind. There she sat, dressed in cut-offs, which hiked up her lengthy thigh. *I wonder if she feels that*, he licked his lips. Zach knew, if she had, she would've yanked them down so fast his head would spin. He gawked, loving the view and the fact that she seemed unaware of it. Her denim shorts were paired with sandals, high-heeled, of course. That was one thing she would never change, not unless she was wearing jeans, then, she wore cowboy boots. Because it was so hot and humid in Tennessee in mid-July, the usual button-up over her red tank top was missing. If her mother were aware of all the rules she was breaking when she wasn't in LA, she would spit bullets.

Roxie felt his presence more than saw Zach. She sprung from her chair when she spotted his familiar figure and thought nothing of jumping straight into his arms.

"Whoa, sweetheart! You're gonna knock me over," Zach couldn't help the laugh that erupted from his stomach.

Roxie loved that deep, baritone laugh of his. "Are you saying I'm fat?" She teased. That was an inside joke between the two of them. Roxie punched him in the arm, "It's a good thing I love you, ya know?"

"Oh, yeah? Why's that?" He quipped. "And, no, you're anything but…"

"You just might find yourself in the emergency room."

"Darlin,' you're tiny and all legs. There's no way you could hurt me bad enough to put me in the hospital. Besides, it's like you said, you love me." With that, he kissed her senseless. Boy, he sure missed those lips of hers. And her smell—familiar and welcoming. Her favorite cologne since being in Tennessee was Cody Musk. The light scent of it paired with the shampoo and conditioner she used that smelled like strawberries, could cause a man to lose all his senses. What he didn't know, was Roxie was thinking pretty much the same thing. The Stetson he wore, along with the woodsy scent of his shampoo and Irish Spring made her mouth water.

Once the two parted, Roxie asked, "Have you been to my apartment yet? We still need to get the keys so we can get everything moved in."

"I haven't. Came straight here from work. Hit traffic like you wouldn't believe."

"It's quite a drive to your mom and dad's just to have to come back in the morning. Let's get a motel, order some dinner, and maybe junk food and a couple of videos or something. Besides, I need a shower, like pronto. All this grime and sweat? Ugh," Roxie groaned.

Zach thought she looked ravenous, not grimy at all, but he wasn't about to turn her down. "Okay, let's get your luggage and see where there might be a vacancy." He knew she could afford a fancy-schmancy hotel, but he wasn't going to stoop to bringing that up. "While you get your luggage, I'll google places in the area." His Roxie might have come from money, but he was well aware of the newly imposed stipend from her parents, though that wouldn't even kick in until after school began which wasn't for a couple of weeks. This meant she was almost as broke as he was. Almost.

⏭ ⏭ ⏭ ⏭

Boy, am I grateful for that hot shower!" Roxie had on her dark purple, silk robe overtop her dark purple shorts and nightie. She believed that, even though she and Zach had never slept together, a woman needed to look her best, especially when there she didn't have any makeup to hide all the blemishes marring her face. Zach had told her on numerous occasions that he didn't care whether she wore makeup or not; in fact, he preferred her without it. That didn't stop Roxie from feeling inferior. Oh, she knew she wasn't, far from it actually, but she always wanted to look her best for the man she was going to spend the rest of her life with.

Zach watched as Roxie appeared. Her dark hair had gotten longer than it had been when they first met. He preferred the longer hair over the chin-length bob she had then. *More to run my fingers through!* He would never, even when they were old and gray, understand why a woman of her status and beauty chose to be with someone so—so—middle-class. His family, compared to Roxie's, wasn't as well off as hers, but they held their own. He'd asked Roxie many times in the last several months if she was certain she could live in Chattanooga or Cleveland so he could take over his family's vet clinic once he was finished with school. That way his dad could retire and get what he wanted too. He still wasn't aware that she'd been searching for houses for them near where his parents lived. She loved him, and his family that much.
"Feel better," he peered at her from under the baseball cap he wore.

He took in the silky clothing she was wearing, hoping his cap kept his staring hidden. He should have known better when she giggled, "Getting an eyeful, are we? "Zach was never one to blush, but he could feel his cheeks warming up as he tried stuttering his way through an answer, "I—uh…" he rubbed the back of his neck nervously, knowing he was caught. Throwing his hands up in the air, he valiantly did his best to sound stoic, and replied, "Yes! Okay, you got me. I was lookin' at that purple robe that barely conceals anything, but just enough to make a man drool."

Roxie tee-heed as she watched him backpedal himself out of the situation. *Boy, he certainly is sexy when he's embarrassed.* "You know, I should catch you more often. The red of your cheek matches your shirt. It's very cute!" She bent and kissed him before he could respond.

Damn, he missed those lips! He knew that thought would stay with him forever. The smell of the strawberry shampoo and conditioner she used. The lavender lotion: just the scent that was *her*. It was intoxicating. Before either one could utter another word, they found themselves cuddled up on one of the queen-sized beds the hotel provided, having a full-on make-out session, minus the boundaries they'd set. Oh, but it was hard to keep that promise; for the both of them.

"Okay, okay...we have to stop now before I throw all our rules out the window and have my way with you," Roxie commented through bouts of breathlessness.

Zach did his best to stifle the guffaw that he knew was coming ass he listened to her. As she rolled off him, rubbing all her body on him on the way off, he chuckled, "Ya think?"

"Why are you laughing?" Roxie feigned hurt.

"You and I both know which of us would be likelier to break the rules," Zach grinned.

"Yeah...me." Roxie couldn't help it as a snicker burst from her lips. "You really think you'd break them before me? You *do* know that I'm not a goody-goody two shoes, right?"

Zachary wasn't sure whether she was serious or not, but usually when they were together, there was more laughter than somberness. That was unless of course, they were at her parents' house. There was only one time in the last three months since the semester's end that he'd made it to California. It wasn't even that money was an issue; L.A. felt weird. Although Roxie's father was nice to him and treated him as if he belonged there, going as far as giving his blessing when he asked Roxie to marry him, he still felt like an outsider. As for Roxie? She learned fast how to 'fit in' in Tennessee; almost like she was born to be there. He watched as she snuggled against him, her dark hair was damp, partially from her shower, but also because Tennessee was humid, especially in July. He observed her as her eyes began to droop, having no idea what movie they were watching. He was more enthralled by the sleeping beauty next to him than anything on tv. He knew she'd be exhausted, not only from jet lag, but also from the two-hour time difference. *How am I? To be the fiancé of such a fantastically gorgeous, smart and yes, sometimes infuriating woman?*

It being much later than he anticipated, he knew he needed to move to the other queen-sized bed at some point, but as Roxie started snoring, those little, almost non-existent ones that he found so endearing, she despised. Zach remembered the first time he had brought it up.

It was during the Christmas Break. She had begged him to fly home with her for it. To Zack that would mean spending Christmas away from his family, which he had never done. She went so far as getting his sister and parents involved, too. This was, of course, after they'd gotten to know her a bit more. He finally succumbed to the incessant badgering and agreed because they'd made a deal that Roxie would return to Tennessee in time for New Year's Eve. While they were at her parents' house, after her parents had gone to bed, either Roxie would sneak to Zach's room or vice versa. Neither cared whether her parents found out or not, though they truly didn't want to explain anything to them; not that they were doing anything immoral anyway, but she was certain that at least her mother would think otherwise. Zach was not about to out his girlfriend to the people he was working on getting to know. That first night, they talked well past the two-hour time limit they'd set for themselves, and as he spoke, she got drowsy. Up to that point, they'd never been together when the other got tired. When the soft snoring began, Zachary could not help the grin that lifted the corners of his mouth. Part of him wanted to wake her up and tell her she needed sleep, but the other part of him would be okay with holding her all night if only to hear that sound. He knew he couldn't.

Zach didn't realize how long he'd been reminiscing about the gorgeous, yet jet-lagged woman he held, until he glanced at the hotel alarm clock sitting on the night table next to him. It was after three in the morning. The sitcom playing on the television was one he hadn't seen in a long time, but one he knew Roxie loved. Full House was a show he was forced by his little sister to watch when they were growing up. They'd begun the marathon on TV Land once Roxanne was out of the shower. He should be exhausted after working all day at the vet clinic, and then the drive to the airport, but since, for him, filing paperwork and taking appointments was not hard, he found he couldn't sleep.
Boy, I'll be glad once I can work with the animals.

Maybe if he could get his arm out from under Roxie and lay on the other bed, he could will himself to sleep. Deciding to take action, he gently removed his arm out from under her, careful not to wake his beauty, laid her more comfortably on the mattress, and covered her before removing his shirt and stretching out on the other bed. He should have known he wouldn't be able to stop his brain or even fight watching the rise and fall of Roxie's chest. Zach could still smell the strawberry of her shampoo, even though he wasn't holding her any longer. Finally, he forced his eyes shut, tearing them away from her, and his brain off, because he would never be able to help Roxie get moved in over the weekend if he didn't.

The next morning, Roxanne awoke early because her body was still on California time, even though it was eight o'clock in Tennessee, it was only six in Los Angeles. They still had a while before they needed to check out, so she took the time to observe the man she would marry. He wasn't wearing a shirt, and in the Tennessee heat, who could blame him? He'd developed his biceps more while she was away, that she could easily see. His sexy six-pack was ever-present, and boy was he tan! Roxie felt her mouth watering and jaw dropping. She was so happy to be back with him. The few months they were apart were a lot more difficult for her than she thought they would be. She'd had boyfriends before, but she'd never felt the same kind of connection with any of them that she did with the man sleeping soundly on the other bed in the room with her. *I must've been incredibly tired! I don't even remember him laying me down or covering me,* she thought as she continued her perusal of the chiseled man's torso. She knew that he worked with the horses on his family's ranch when he wasn't working the long hours he usually put in at the family-owned veterinarian clinic, getting a head start on his vet degree. Roxie could definitely see that the time he'd put in outside during the summer had undeniably done him justice. As she watched, she debated on waking him up, knowing how tired he must be.

At nine, she thought it best to wake him from his deep sleep. She didn't want to do it, but they needed to get on the road. The pair only had today to get her stuff moved into her new apartment before the movers her father had hired, much to her mother's displeasure, left. "Hey, sleepyhead," she whispered as she kissed his ear lobe. "It's time to get a move on."

"Ugh," was Zach's labored response. He stretched out his body, making his washboard stomach more pronounced. "You can wipe the drool off your chin now, Darlin," he grinned, feeling her eyes peel off him somehow.

"I...uh—" Roxie fumbled. Eventually, with no apologies, she added, "Fine. Yes, I looked. In fact, I've been ogling you for quite a while now," she crossed her arms in a 'so there' stance, trying to act stoic, but couldn't stop the giggle that escaped. A giggle which ruined her whole macho ideal.

"Oh, really?" Zach leaned over and gave her a soft kiss on his girl's rosy lips. "We better hurry if we want to catch the free breakfast before they close at ten." Zach could see the cogs moving inside Roxie's head. "What are you thinking?"

"Well. We could go down right now, then come get dressed before check out."

"*You* want to go into the lobby dressed like that?" he eyed her silk nightie and nightgown. He would not have been able to see all of that but the ribbon that held her robe closed had slipped undone. He wasn't going to lie, he liked what he saw *a lot.*

Flustered that she'd been caught, Roxie didn't know what to say, "Umm...sorry, you weren't supposed to see that," she replied, discombobulated.

"Don't tie it shut on my account," Zach could not help but chuckle.

Befuddled that he would say so, Roxie remained silent. Secretly though, it made her feel powerful that he did; that she was the woman who made him feel all dumbfounded. After a few seconds of waiting in silence, she exclaimed, 'No, silly. By the time you get out of that bed and put a shirt on, I'll be dressed enough to go down." True to her word, by the time he'd thrown on a black t-shirt from the bag he brought in the night before, Roxanne had changed into pink sweats with 'Babe' written across the backside in black lettering, and a black t-shirt. She figured since they would be moving stuff all day, she didn't need to look spectacular. Besides, she already had the attention of the only man she wanted it from.

"Nice sweats," Zachary teased when he saw the ones she had put on. They were his favorite and he loved making her entire face turn beet red whenever he mentioned them.

Trying to downplay her embarrassment, she chimed, "Oh, these ratty old things? I decided since we're going to be sweaty and filthy today, there's no need to get all dressed up."

"Mmm... sweaty...and dirty! Question is, what kind of dirty?" Zachary usually didn't talk to Roxie like that. They came from two completely different worlds and he was generally careful with what he said, but he couldn't help it this time. She looked darned sexy in her attire, even with her dark hair piled in a messy bun on top of her head.

Swatting his arm, Roxie tried playing mad, but looking at the face he donned, she just couldn't. Instead, she busted up laughing, "Is this what I get to look forward to for the next eighty years?"

"With any sort of luck, love, and communication, you bet your pink sweats we will! Let's get out to the lobby. I'm suddenly ravenous."

Roxanne didn't miss the glint in his eyes at his words. How did she get so lucky? Although they had yet to decide on a wedding day; they were hoping to get some schooling under their belts first. Roxie was aware that she might have to put her career aspirations on hold so Zachary could finish his, and she was okay with that, seeing that his taking over of the family's business his top priority. She understood neither of them could wait the three years she had left to finish her degree, nor did they want to. They hadn't talked much about setting a date yet, even though they'd known each other for over a year. Roxie was afraid Zach didn't bring it up because he knew she wanted to finish her degree. Though, at the same time, couldn't wait to marry him.

▶▶ ▶▶ ▶▶ ▶▶

The waffles and maple syrup with bacon and eggs they wolfed down was delectable. "Man, I'm not going to be able to eat anything else for the rest of the day after that meal." Roxie sighed, feeling content as ever.

"You might after all the work we have ahead of us today. We need to get checked out. The movers will beat us there if we don't put some metal to the pedal. They do know where they are going, don't they?"

"Yes, sweetheart, they do…" Roxie batted her eyelashes at him, "I'm almost smart enough to give them directions *and* my cell number in case they get lost," she only half teased.

"I didn't mean to offend you," Zachary apologized. "I keep forgetting you've lived here long enough to take care of yourself. That you're not the little rich city girl I met this time last year."

"I know you didn't. I get grumpy when I'm tired. You know that." She smiled to show him all was forgiven.

It took them less than thirty minutes to get everything together to check out, as neither of them opted to change clothes. When they arrived at Roxanne's new apartment, Zach was amazed at the grandeur of it all. It floored him how well off her family was; that although they put a cap on how much they gave her, she was not living in a hole. Not like a lot of the other college sophomores he knew. He hadn't seen it yet because she refused to take him to see it the couple of times she'd flown out during the summer break. "You can close your mouth now, sweets," she poked him.

"What?" Zach feigned complete innocence. "It's impressive. Is that okay?" He grinned at her; that lopsided grin she had learned to love in an extremely short amount of time.

"Would you like a tour or are you just going to stand there with your tongue hanging out? It's not a two-story like my apartment in Chattanooga, but I think I like this one better." They started in the entryway, which led directly into the living room. The one thing Zachary noticed was that there wasn't any carpet, not in the bedroom, not in the bathroom. There was authentic hardwood flooring, mahogany coloring throughout the whole place. "Don't you just love the hardwood floors?" Roxie gushed.

"It's really nice." Zachary mumbled, not knowing what to do or say. The flooring was flooring to him. *I'm a guy for Pete's sake!* He could care less what it looked like. He might pay more attention when they get around to building their own house, but not yet. He decided he liked that the living room was smaller than her old apartment. Even the kitchen seemed smaller to him. That was a positive thing because he had yet to teach his future wife how to cook anything that couldn't be popped into the microwave.

She'd said in the past that she wanted to learn her way around the kitchen because she knew he wanted kids, and to raise them more like he was, was an important milestone to her. Above all, she realized being the wife he deserved was crucial to her. There were times she was afraid she would never be the wife he craved, but she was bound and determined to try.

By the time the tour was finished, a larger-than-life moving truck had pulled up outside. "They're here," Roxanne hollered, loving the sound of her voice as it resonated in the empty rooms and bounced off the walls.

"Okay!" Zach yelled back, enjoying the fact that he was aware of the game she was playing. It wasn't like they'd done this before. She had already moved into her old apartment before he knew her. It was as if they were in sync at this point. Or he was, at least. Without anyone else in the apartment, he snuck up behind Roxie as she looked out the window, watching the moving van back up as close to the front door as they possibly could. It was pure luck Roxie had gotten a bottom floor because when she applied, most of what was left was the second and third level. "Boo!" Zach boomed as he wrapped his arms around her waist at the same time. It probably wasn't the best combination, but he loved to see her jump.

Roxanne let out a blood-curdling scream. "Zachary Blaze! What are you trying to do? Give me a heart attack or see exactly how hard a girl from L.A. can punch?"

"I'd apologize, but then I'd be lying, and you know as well as I do that I cannot." He held up two fingers at his side above his head as if to say, 'scouts honor'.

"Ooohhh… it's a good thing I love you or I'd give you a black eye, a bloody nose and a 'what for.'" Roxie shook her fist at him but couldn't stay mad for very long when he looked at her with that sheepish, lopsided grin of his.

The conversation halted when there was a heavy knock at the door. The men Roxanne greeted were both over six feet tall, bulky and appeared as if they could have been bouncers at a nightclub. "We're here to deliver furniture for a Miss Roxanne McCain?" The larger of the two might have been big but didn't have the booming voice either Roxie or Zach expected.

Roxanne hid the giggle as best as she could as she listened to the bulky man with a tiny voice. "Yes, that's me," she claimed. "This is my fiancé, Zach," She held onto Zach's hand tightly as if to signify he was hers.

"Nice to meet you," Zach offered. Hopefully, with the assistance of the movers they could, at least get everything into the house and the heavier stuff like the couch, bed, and table put where Roxanne wanted them to go before they had to leave. "Shall we get started?" Zach asked pointedly at the movers.

"Yes, sir," they replied in unison. "Y'all just tell us where you want things to go, and we'll deliver them no problem. The smaller one answered. Interestingly enough he might have been the smaller of the two, but he possessed a roar much larger than anyone expected.

"We'll help," Roxie explained. "I can get some of the boxes that aren't exceptionally heavy." She'd never moved a thing in her life. Being raised as a rich brat there were always maids and servants to do her hard labor, but since moving down to Tennessee, she learned with the help of Zach and his family that being self-sufficient and doing stuff for oneself was much more gratifying. When she got the chance, Roxanne did her best to rid herself of the 'L.A. Brat' persona she had grown up with.

As it turned out, it was easiest and best if Roxie supervised. After taking in a couple of boxes, not being inside where the movers could ask where she wanted things to go slowed moving in up considerably. It was determined that she would direct traffic, so-to-speak, which definitely assisted in the process.

By eight o'clock that evening, both Zach and Roxie flopped on the couch and huffed. "I'm so pooped," Roxie said exasperated.

"It's been a long day but look at the bright side; most everything is done so you can stay here from now on."

Roxie was quiet. It had not dawned on her until now that she would be living in Nashville alone, two hours away from her love. Zach sensed her apprehension. He thought he knew what was bothering her, but he wasn't sure she would tell him. Instead of saying anything, he wrapped his arms around her, pulling her close, and lifted her chin with the pad of his thumb. He held her gaze for several minutes before kissing her softly. "Darlin,' we will be fine. Two hours isn't that far away, and besides, we always have weekends together."

"How did you know that's how I felt?" Roxie should not have been surprised that he knew what she'd been thinking. They were growing closer by the day.

"Sweetheart, you're so much like me." Zach kissed her nose. "You wear your heart on your sleeve and if anyone, even an animal gets to know you, they can read you like a book."

"I'm just afraid we'll break up. Distance doesn't always work out," Roxie whispered, trying to stem the tears that were thick in her throat.

"Don't cry," Zach spoke softly. "We'll make it work. Hey, we made it all through the entire summer."

"Yeah, but that was a few months, not years."

"Hon, you can't worry about the 'might-have-been's.' We'll take every day as they come; spend as many weekends together as we can. If we want this to, it will work."

Kissing him soundly on the mouth, Roxanne responded, "Thank you."

"What for?"

"For being you; putting my mind at ease like you do. I love you." She leaned her suddenly heavy head on his shoulder. "You feel like watching a movie since I don't have cable yet? You're not planning on going home tonight, are you?"

"To your first question, yes, let's watch a movie. To your second, I'll sleep out here on the couch since we were able to get your bedroom put together, for the most part, so you can sleep there."

She blinked hard and answered him quickly. "Of course, you can stay! I was hoping you would. What movie do you think we should watch?"

"Are you hungry? We could order a pizza or Chinese. That's the nice thing about living here; you can get almost anything delivered."

"I could eat. Do you want to order a pizza from Pizza Hut since we haven't found any good mom and pop places yet?"

"Sure, while I do that, why don't you choose a movie to watch."

Chapter 2

The weekend came to an end way too fast for both Zachary and Roxanne. As they stood on her front stoop in a warm embrace; it didn't matter to either of them that it was the end of July, one of the hottest months of the year in Tennessee, neither could let go. "I don't want you to go," Roxie said matter-of-factly.

"I know, Darlin,' but I have to work. You know that. You have your car. I wouldn't say no to a surprise visit since we've got about a month until school starts." They did not start the same day, but they did the same week.

"I really need to look for a job; someplace retail maybe? What do you think?"

"Since you're going into fashion design, that wouldn't be a bad thing. It will give you some much-needed experience in the clothing industry. That's why I keep workin' for my dad. Because, without that experience, I wouldn't know as much as I do about being a veterinarian. Although, all I do right now is make appointments, file papers and calm the animals down."

"I wish you could stay and help me. Do you seriously think we can make a long-distance relationship work?" Roxanne repeated her fear of divulging it the night before.

"Are you sincerely worried about us?" concern etched Zach's brow.

Hating that she let that doubt slip again, Roxie tried backtracking. "I mean…" she cleared her throat, "...sometimes I think about it; wondering if we'll survive this. It's not like we knew each other long before we became engaged."

Zachary hadn't had that same kind of fear. When he proposed to Roxie, he knew without a doubt she was his person; the one he was supposed to spend forever with. He did understand the long-distance thing, though. "We can make most anything work if we strive for it. Don't you think?" He didn't like the questioning in her chocolate brown eyes, eyes that were deep pools he'd fallen into rather quickly. There was something about her that drew him to her after he got over her spoiled brat persona.

Roxie sighed heavily, "If you think we can survive this, I will do my best not to let it get the best of me." She gave him a timid smile, "You'd better get out of here before it gets dark. I don't want you hitting any animals on your drive home." She kissed him softly on the lips, begging the tears that threatened to flow not to fall.

Zach knew Roxie was nearly in tears just by the way she clung to him, as if for dear life. He didn't want to leave her here in a city she wasn't familiar with all by herself, but he also knew his parents counted on him to be at work the next day. "I gotta go." He kissed her passionately, then waited until she went back inside to pull away. He made her a promise that he would call her when he was safely home.

As he drove the two hours to his parents' house where he lived, this time seemed to go by quicker than when he picked Roxie up at the airport. He thought about her fears and how he could make her understand, that no matter what, he was all in. He hadn't forgotten about the vast differences in their upbringings, but he saw so much change in her than the first day he met her, that sometimes she seemed like she'd grown up in the south. Zach's thoughts returned to their first date. He was so afraid she'd say no that he almost didn't ask her.

Zachary remembered back on that day as if it were yesterday, not nearly almost a year ago. It had taken him the first half of the first semester to get over the fact that Roxie was born with a silver spoon in her mouth and was given most of what she needed from her parents. Having been forced by their math professor to be partners in helping each other learn where they might need assistance or a tutor, was not his choice. He was stuck. And…she was ecstatic. He recalled her coming by the vet clinic that first night wanting to get a jump on their homework before their next class. Zach couldn't come up with a good enough reason which could get him out of having to do it so they'd gone to the coffee shop for that first tutoring session; the same coffee shop that had changed both of their lives.

The day that he planned on asking her on an official date, Zachary made certain it wasn't on a day that they had a class or had planned on meeting at their usual spot anyway. He'd met with the manager earlier in the day to set everything in motion. Then, all he had to do was wait. He met her outside the door of the English class they shared, along with the math class they had together. On the pretense that he needed help with studying for the upcoming math test. They went to 'their cafe'. Once there, Roxanne could tell it had absolutely nothing to do with homework. He remembered the confused look on her face and the nerves he thought he'd grown past made themselves known. Wiping his sweaty palms on his wranglers he pulled out her chair, something he had done even during the times he could not stand being around her. He was a gentleman, regardless of his feelings. He recollected the look on her face when he asked his question. One would think that he was asking her to marry him with her response. Although he had been afraid, she would say, "No," he remained silent waiting on her answer. When he thought he could not wait any longer, she finally gave him what he was looking for. To say he was eager was an understatement.

That date was the first of many more to come in a relationship Zach hoped would last forever. Hadn't realized he was already to the Cleveland exit until he was right upon it. *Wow, that time went fast!* Zach made excellent timing getting home. It was a little after nine o'clock in the evening when he walked through the door. "Zachary? That you?" his mother hollered from her recliner in the living room. Zach was sure his dad was in the other one or sprawled out on the couch.

"Yes, mom. I'm here," Zach called back, walking into the living room after taking his shoes off at the door. He stooped low to kiss his mom on the cheek and shake his dad's hand.

"Did you and Roxie have a good weekend?" his mom inquired.

"A lot of hard work, but we got everything unloaded and most of the pertinent stuff put in its place."

"We're glad you were able to help her," his dad chimed in.

"I'm worried about her, though," Zach was abrupt.

"Why's that?" his dad questioned.

"Well, first of all, she's in a place she's never been before, all by herself; not knowing anyone."

His mom interjected and added, "It was like that for her here too, remember?"

"Yeah, but I was *here*." Zach countered.

"Son," his father jumped in, "You can't always be there to hold her hand. She's a strong, brilliant woman and she will be just fine." His father could sense that was not the only thing bothering Zach and wanting to get to the bottom of the issue, he struggled when he asked, "That's not the only thing that's on your mind, now is it son?"

After a moment's hesitation, Zach sighed. He knew he couldn't get anything passed his father's intuition. "She's afraid we won't be able to make our relationship work with our schools being two hours apart and my needing to work at the clinic. Then, there's always vet school which is tacking on even more time."

"What do you think about all this?" Zach's mom probed, knowing full well what his answer would be.

"I told her that we can make anything work if we both want it badly enough. I explained about how technology makes it easier to stay in touch than it did when her dad was going to Chattanooga and her mom was at Vanderbilt, but they made it work."

"Well…" his dad trailed, "That sounds like good advice. The question is, do *you* believe what you told her?"

"Yeah, but it worries me, just the same. Look, I better go call her and get some sleep before work tomorrow. I'm bushed."

"'Night son,'" both parents offered in unison.

Zach's call to Roxanne was longer than he expected, but he was able to let her know he had returned home safely and explain to her what he had discussed with his parents, hoping she would not get angry that he went to them with his concerns. He should have known better, though. From the time she had met them, she loved them and they loved her. It wasn't like that when Zachary met Roxanne's parents. Her father was fairly easy-going, but didn't dare cross his wife… about anything. When Zach had asked Roxie's father for her hand, he didn't hesitate, but even now, after spending more time with her family, Roxie's mom still gave him the cold shoulder. Maybe when she met his parents, things would be different. The plan was for them to come out to Tennessee for Christmas so they could make it back to Los Angeles in time for their big New Year's Eve party they throw every year. Zachary thought that might be part of the reason Roxie's mother had such hard feelings toward him, because he had taken Roxie back to Tennessee for New Years.

"I'm so glad you made it back safely," Roxie's sweet-as-honey voice couldn't hide the tears she kept swallowing, hoping Zach wouldn't catch on.

Too late, he heard it loud and clear. "Darlin', please try not to cry. Just think, tomorrow, while I'm toiling away at the clinic, you'll be out looking for a job doing what you enjoy."

Roxie endeavored to smile through the thickness in her voice, wishing Zach could at least see her attempt at not letting this distance thing get to her. "I'll try. I've been looking on-line since you left and came across three postings that look promising."

"Oh, yeah? Where?"

"Bella Boutique, Scarlett Begonia, and Vinnie Louise."

"Ohhh. Those are pretty high end, aren't they?"

"Yeah. That's why I want to apply to them first."

"There…see? We've got this no matter what," Zach affirmed, hoping his words help put her on the right path for the next morning's job search.

Roxie felt marginally better after talking to her cowboy. She loved that, even when she did her best to hide her feelings so he would not worry, he still managed to pick up on it; especially when they were not in the same room. "I guess we better call it a night," she claimed, although she wanted nothing more than to talk to Zach all night.

"We probably should. Six o'clock comes awfully early." Like Roxie, Zach could have listened to her all night. The sound of her voice was soothing to his very core. He couldn't wait for the day he could call her his for real and never have to leave her, again. "Goodnight, Darlin,'" he told her smoothly. "I'll talk to you tomorrow. Good luck with the job hunting."

"I love you," was Roxie's reply.

"I love you more than the moon and stars combined." He hung up, but sleep would not come. He had worked many days on little sleep, and it looked as if the next day would be no different. He had gotten used to it when he was in school.

▶▶ ▶▶ ▶▶ ▶▶

Roxanne did not sleep well the night before, although she was in her own bed this time. All she could think about was every little noise as she was not used to the sounds of her new place yet. The next morning, she sluggishly slinked straight to her coffee pot, grateful to Zachary for finding and setting it up before he left the day before. Zach did not drink coffee and she knew he wanted her to quit, but she couldn't. If she were honest, which she was, she was a hard lined coffee addict. As she savored the warm liquid, she glanced at her phone and noticed Zach was at the clinic. Knowing Mondays were their busiest days, she would have to wait to call him until later in the day. She hoped she would be able to wish him a good day before he went in, but she had slept in having been kept up most of the night by the weird sounds of her new surroundings. It was after three in the morning before she fell into a fitful slumber with dreams of the day, where she wouldn't be apart from her man.

After her normal breakfast of coffee and toast, she did her best not to dip into the small stipend her parents´ had left her every month, knowing full well she would need as much of that as possible when she began school. Roxie took a hot shower and dressed in her best interviewing outfit. Having lived in Tennessee for the better part of a year, she wore her cowboy boots most of the time and her other black ones, complete with a Turquoise necklace and earrings. The ensemble made the white skirt and black vest over a white tank top, pop. She hoped when she ambled into all three places, they would take her seriously. As she put the Scarlett Boutique in the GPS of her silver Porsche, Roxanne's stomach revolted and the toast and coffee she had eaten threatened to come back up. It took all the willpower she possessed not to puke right there in the parking lot. It was a good thing today was not about interviews because if that were the case, she would most certainly be late and her nerves would be far worse.

Stepping into the Scarlett Boutique was like going home for Roxanne, reminding her of her favorite store back home called, *Misa*. It took every bit of strength she had not to go crazy and spend money she knew she had to save for tuition and fees. She hadn't even paid those yet or bought any of her books either. She wasn't sure why and knew school started soon, so she couldn't put it off much longer.

"Hello! How may I help you?" a woman with a deep southern drawl asked from behind a counter.

The woman reminded Roxanne of Zachary's mom. She had kind eyes and a beautiful smile. "Yes," Roxie returned, "My name is Roxanne McCain, and I saw online that you are hiring."

"We are. Are you interested in filling out an application?"

"Yes! I am, thank you so much." The nerves Roxie felt not ten minutes before had dissipated.

When the clerk came back with an application, she asked about a resume. Roxie explained to her that she came from a well-to-do family from Los Angeles, and it was not until she moved to Tennessee to attend college the year before that she had ever held a job. She promised to put her previous employer from the University of Tennessee-Chattanooga as a reference. She also chose to put two of her professors from there as reference, too. Once, she'd finished filling out the application, she handed it back to the clerk, whom she found out during a chat earlier, was also the manager of the store and the one doing the actual hiring. "Well, thank you for letting me come to peruse your store and apply for a job."

"Y'all are most welcome," the manager, whose name was Lauren, replied, "I should be conducting interviews here in the next few days. I have your phone number and email on the application, correct?"

"Yes, ma'am. I hope to hear from you soon," Roxie commented as she left the store. The other two places went much the same way, but she had an exceptionally good feeling about *Scarlett Boutique*. She decided to treat herself to her favorite caramel latte and a Bacon/Ranch salad from McDonalds. It was not her usual go-to lunch or snack, but she had to be as conservative as possible. She blamed Zachary for her taste in the less expensive places. It was only two o'clock pm by the time she arrived back at her apartment. What would she do with the rest of her day? Then an idea dawned on her. She wanted to surprise Zach.

⏩ ⏩ ⏩ ⏩

"Please, sign in," Zachary directed the client who had walked in without looking up from the computer. The day had been a busy one and he'd barely had time to breathe. He hadn't had much free time to think about how Roxie was doing, although she was always at the forefront of his mind.

"If I must," a familiar soothing voice responded back.

"Wha—" was the only response Zach could give. His jaw dropped when he saw his beautiful fiancé walk through the door. He was definitely not expecting this! Once recovered he asked, "What're you doing up here?"

"Well…I visited those three stores I told you about last night and filled out applications, grabbed some lunch and when I got home, realized how stupid it was for me to stay there when I have like three weeks left before classes begin, and none of those places will be holding interviews for the next couple of days. Besides, I missed you." She winked her right eye leaned in close over the counter.

"You sure you don't need to get your books and everything yet?"

"Sweetheart, I have plenty of time to do all that. Besides, I haven't seen your family in a while. How's your sister? Is she still with Jeb?" They hadn't spent much time when they were together talking about his family.

Zach hadn't realized that until now, "Yes, she…is but he's cleaned up his act more in the last few months. Since you've been gone anyway." Just then, the phone sitting next to him rang. "Hang on a second, Darlin.'"

A few minutes later, he returned the phone on the receiver and turned his attention back to Roxie. "I don't get off for a couple more hours. You think you might want to go catch a movie when I'm done for the day?"

She didn't even have to think about it. "That would be fantastic! The new Lion King is out. How does that sound? We could even go to our coffee shop beforehand. It's been a long time since I have been there."

"Sounds good. You wanna come and hang back here with me or I can ask my parents if you can go to the house. My sister should be there."

"It's completely up to you." What Roxanne did not tell him was that she had planned on staying a few days anyway. At least until she heard back about one of the positions she'd applied for. "Wouldn't I be in the way?"

"No. Why would you think something like that?"

"I don't know how to do what you're doing, and I don't want you to feel as if you must entertain me when you should be working. I know how important it is to you."

With a smirk, Zach gave Roxie an endearing look. "Entertaining you is, by far, my favorite thing to do." He wiggled his eyebrows at her, but first making sure there wasn't anyone around. Not that it bothered him per se, but he knew it might bother his dad if he happened by.

"Are you flirting with me, Zachary Blaze?" Roxie knew he was, but since there weren't any patients in the waiting room, she wanted to keep it going. This was the best part of their relationship.

"What would give you such an idea?" Innocence crossed his face, but she did not miss the glint in his eye.

"Oh, I don't know. The twinkle in your eye is a dead giveaway." At this point, Roxanne had taken up residence in the secretary's chair Zach usually sat in. He'd made the mistake of getting up to file a patient's paperwork and she quietly snuck behind him and stole it fair and square.

"Hey!" Zach pretended to be put out, "Who said you could have my chair?"

"You weren't using it." Roxie bit her bottom lip, pretending to turn this flirting fiasco into something more. Something she *knew* drove him nuts. "I thought maybe you could teach me what you do, *and* I could help so I don't feel so useless waiting for you to get done."

Just then, Zach's dad stepped into the receptionist area, giving Zach instructions for a patient and their file. "Oh, hi Roxanne. I didn't know you would be here," he gave her a fatherly hug. "How are you liking Nashville?"

"It gets kind of lonely, but I'm hoping one of the boutiques I applied at will hire me. Once school starts, I'm certain to be busy."

"Are you planning on driving back tonight?" Zach's father was concerned.

"I hadn't thought that far ahead to be honest with you." She *had,* but wasn't going to tell Zach's dad.

"Well…why don't you plan on staying in the guest room (that used to be Zach's brother's room before he passed away from a 4-wheeling accident the year before Roxanne and Zachary met). You know, the same one you've stayed in before?"

"Yes, I remember it. Thank you."

"Zachary, call your mother and tell her we have a guest." Then Zach's father turned back to Roxanne, "How long are you planning on staying up here?"

"I don't know just yet. I guess a couple of days. I'm hoping to hear from the places I applied to for an interview soon," she repeated.

"Sounds good." Then Mr. Blaze to Zach, "Son, are you and your beautiful fiancé going to be home in time for supper?"

"No. I thought I'd treat her to our favorite coffee shop since she hasn't been in it for a while and then we planned to go see the live-action Lion King."

"That's a fantastic film! Remember, I took your mom a few weeks ago?"

"Yep." After that, there were patients to see and Zach called his mom who was all too happy to have a guest, especially one that was part of the family. It was good, because at first, Roxanne felt out of her element, but the Blaze family made her acclimation into the southern way of living quite easy.

The rest of the workday went by quickly. Zach showed Roxanne how to enter appointments on the computer, where to find customers that needed reminder appointments, and how to file their paperwork. In fact, he set her in charge of calling the patients who had appointments the next day to remind them.

As Zach watched her move around the office, so at ease with confirming appointments and even making a couple herself, Zach's thoughts drifted to how nice it would be to work together every day; much like his parents did when Zach and his siblings became school age and his mom would work until her children were out of school and then she would be at home helping with homework, handing out snacks, just being at home so her children had security. Zach was fully aware not all families could be like his own. He realized that Roxie just might want to work instead of being a stay-at-home mom and would rather work at building a career in fashion design. He was fully prepared to support her, whatever her decision but having her there, with him, during this moment could not have been any better.

Chapter 3

Finally, closing time had come, and around six o'clock the last patient, happy as a clam, was led out by the owner. "Do you want to go to the house and freshen up?" Zachary questioned, pointing passed his truck toward his family's house.

Mortified that she might stink, Roxanne frantically replied, "Do I need to? I stink, don't I?" *Why else would he offer*?

Zach knew he probably should have prefaced with reassuring Roxie she did not smell bad at all. In fact, far from it. He loved her smell and did not think she could have body odor even if she tried. "No, sweetheart, you're gorgeous!"

"I would have to take my car to your parents' house, so maybe I will freshen up just a bit. I'll meet you there, okay?" She kissed him softly and stepped out of the door before Zach locked up for the night. He, like all other employees, parked in the back as that was the first door opened in the morning and the last one locked at night. By the time Zach reached his house, Roxie had already taken up residence in the guest bedroom and was in the kitchen stirring a pot for his mother.

"Hey! How are my two favorite women?" Zach made himself known after watching the scene for a few minutes. He loved that his family treated Roxie as if she belonged there, even at the beginning when they were nothing more than friends. Zach wondered if his parents knew after that first visit that they would be engaged?

Both women squealed at the same time. "Zachary Blaze! It's probably a good thing I have this spoon in a pot of homemade chili or I would smack you with it!" was his mother's reaction.

"Oh, you love me, and you know it!" Zachary continued to tease her while stealing a mouthful of chili. "Mmm…that's so good! Mom, it's fantastic!"

"You aren't trying to butter me up, now are you?" his mom quipped.

"Moi? I would never." Zach batted his eyelashes at her. Then, promptly sauntered up to his fiancé, "Are you angry too?"

She squinted hard. "No. You'll get yours when the time is right."

Zachary believed Roxie would make good on her promise, but the anticipation would kill him, he was sure. Kissing her soundly on the lips, he asked, "Ready to go?"

"I'm thinking we should stay for this disgusting chili and cornbread your momma made. Then go to the movie after," Roxie teased.

"We can do that. It is pretty gross, isn't it? Always is when she makes it." Zach needled his mom.

▶▶ ▶▶ ▶▶ ▶▶

Zach was glad they'd stayed for supper because he was able to talk to his baby sister and Jeb, which he did not get to do often because they spent most of the time at his house. Zach's mom didn't approve because he lived alone, and they didn't like the two being alone in the same room together. They weren't ready to be grandparents but there was nothing they could do. She was twenty-one, after all. It was nice too, for Roxie because she got to talk about wedding plans, even though they hadn't set a date just yet. They weren't sure what their best course of action was since their schools were so far apart.

"That was fun." Roxie cuddled next to Zach in the theater seats where they waited for the movie to start. Roxie had a rule she stuck by that meant they would not touch the popcorn or snacks until the actual movie began, not even during the previews. Zach hated the rule and even tried talking her out of it once. He'd lost that argument quickly. So, there he sat while the soft, buttery goodness goaded him. He hadn't eaten much supper just for this occasion. He was oh-so-tempted to steal a kernel or two but knew she was watching it even if it did not look like it. Finally, the movie began. More often than not, they both reached for the bucket at the exact same time. In unison they laughed softly as to not disturb the other guests. "We usually do this, huh?" Roxie whispered.

"Ya think?"

"You think you're cute, don't you?" she could not help the giggle that bubbled up.

Zach responded with his lopsided grin, "You know it. Why else would you love me?"

"What makes you think that?" Roxanne played.
     "Oh, I don't know. Maybe it's the fact that you keep coming back when you know your mom is bent out of shape about your choice of, not only a career but fiancé as well."

"She likes you more now than she did at Christmas." She had worked on her relationship with her mother in both regards all summer and hoped that her feelings had changed enough that Zach would feel more welcome in Roxanne's world. It was harder for him, she knew.

Zach did not respond. He was engrossed in the movie at that point and he didn't like talking about their different worlds. She fit into his much better than he did hers.

⏩ ⏩ ⏩ ⏩

It was almost midnight by the time the movie was over, and they had made it back to Zachary's truck. Even though Roxanne had her Porsche, she loved the feel of his truck. She loved being able to sit as close to him as she could without sitting in his lap and enjoyed how the vehicle roared to life as he started the engine. It made her feel powerful for some odd reason. As they drove the twenty minutes to Zach's house, the warmth of the evening, the softness of the seat, the smell of her man, and the lull of soft country music put Roxie straight to sleep.

She wasn't aware that she had fallen asleep until a quiet, "Hey, we're here," jostled her awake.

"I didn't conk out, did I?" Every time she fell unexpectedly fell asleep when Zachary was around, it mortified her. She was always afraid she drooled or worse, snored.

"You did, but you have to remember, you're still on Pacific time and getting over jet-lag. Let's get you inside." He wished they were married so he would have an excuse to carry her into the house and his bedroom. "I'm honestly surprised you stayed awake for the movie."

Once inside, they said their, "Good nights" at the doorway to the spare room. Zach had not realized how tired he was until he crawled into his own bed. In no time at all, he was asleep like Roxie most likely already was, too. It usually took him a couple hours of reading or something that wouldn't make his brain run full steam. He thought it might be because his soulmate wasn't two hours away, but instead, only a couple of doors down from his own. That made it easier not to worry about how she was doing.

The next morning, everyone was up before Zachary was. "Hello, did you have a good night's rest?" Roxie asked as she kissed him. He noticed she was already showered and made up for the day. She was one of those women who did not believe in going out in public without all the bells and whistles. Unless of course, she was ill.

"Yes, I did, actually. How did you sleep?" He inquired, kissing her back.

"Better than I would have had I been in Nashville. I'm still not used to the unusual sounds in my apartment. The only night I've been there by myself, noises kept me up most of the night. You know me and my fear of being robbed, living alone."

Unfortunately, he did know. He wished more than anything she had stayed at the University of Tennessee-Chattanooga because she would live closer should she need anything, but Zach wasn't one to stomp on a dream as her mother had so eloquently done. "What's up for you today?" He asked Roxie.

"I'm hoping one of those boutiques will call me for an interview."

"Did they give you any idea as to when they would?" Zach's mom piped up.

"They said two or three days, but the first one. Scarlett Boutique said it could be as early as today."

"That means you can't stay until the weekend when I can go back with you," Zach responded a hint us sadness laced his words.

Much to his surprise, Gerald hopped into the conversation, voicing, "Well...your mom and I were both young once and know what a toll long distances can take on a relationship. I think we could do without you for a few days. We'll have to when you go to vet school anyway, son."

Zach had heard the story a million times but wanted Roxie to hear it.

"I was in Knoxville going to vet school when Clara decided she wanted to see what life in New York City was like. So, being the sweet boyfriend I was, and seeing that we weren't engaged yet, I did not stand in her way."

Just then, Clara interjected, "Pardon me," she said with a smile, "If we are going to tell the story, let's tell it correctly, shall we? You fought me tooth and nail up until I got on the plane."

"Oh... yeah. Forgot about that," Gerald replied. Roxanne didn't miss the roll of Clara's eyes that followed. She couldn't help herself and snickered. "Well, so yeah, I did my level best to talk her out of going up there until they called for her plane. She kissed me, told me she loved me, then disappeared."

Roxanne was intrigued, "Then what happened? Were you able to stay away?" she pointed her question at Clara.

"When I arrived, I was completely overtaken by the grandeur of the city. Before I went, I had already secured a loft apartment on the cheaper side of the city. Not the slums, but the middle-class area. I had one roommate whose name was Dawna. She was a true born and bred New Yorker, so I had my very own tour guide."

"What she's not telling you is that every night we would talk, she greeted me in tears. She thought she had fooled me, but no dice," Gerald proclaimed.

"Moving on…" Clara smirked at her husband. "At first, I loved everything about New York. It was big, new and there was *a lot* to see. I missed my man terribly but couldn't get Gerald to come up to visit; he had no desire to see a big city. Like father—like son." she smiled at Zachary, recalling how much talking and cajoling it took for him to spend Christmas in Los Angeles with Roxanne and her parents, Robert and Belinda. "Anyway, I lost the newness of it all fairly quickly. I think I was there about three months when, without saying anything to Gerald, I jumped on the next plane and showed up on his doorstep just before he graduated."

"She didn't tell you?" Roxanne asked Zach's dad in surprise.

"No. I was dazed when I saw her standing there. She said nothing to me about being home early. I knew she would be there on the day of graduation, but a week early? Don't get me wrong…I was never happier than that day to see my love. My fear was that she'd get to where she loved New York and try to convince me to start my practice up there. Luckily for me, she loved it here too much."

As Zach listened to the story he'd heard a million times in his twenty-three years, it dawned on him how closely his story was to his parents'. He knew the best places for Roxie to jump-start her career would be either Los Angeles or New York. That was one of the huge differences between their story and his parents' story; both of his parents were from the Chattanooga area, not separate sides of the United States like he and Roxie were. Deciding to change the subject because it was on one he wasn't ready to face yet, he asked, "Shouldn't we get to work? It's getting time to open."

Roxie could tell there was something bothering Zach, but she doubted she could get him to talk about it. Not right now anyway. They rode in silence to the vet clinic where she would learn more about how the filing system worked. It wasn't like it fascinated her, but it allowed her to spend time with Zach so there was a plus side.

⏩ ⏩ ⏩ ⏩

The morning went by fast, but by afternoon, Roxie was beginning to think she wasn't going to get a call for an interview from any of the places she had applied to. Maybe she was thinking prematurely, but the part of her that was used to getting what she wanted, when she wanted, came out sometimes and this was one of those times. "Should I call Scarlett Boutique?" she wanted to know Zach's opinion.

"Getting antsy, aren't we?" he teased playfully.

Roxie slugged him in the arm, something she did not do often but realized sometimes she needed to give him a 'what for;' to show him that his Tennessee roots had taught her a few things. Like, don't let your boyfriend tease you without letting him know who's boss.

"Ouch! You beat me!" Zachary kept up the needling. Roxanne gave back as good as she got, though and it took a lot for him not to burst out laughing. It was a good thing the day had slowed down because otherwise, they couldn't play around if there were patients in the waiting room.

By the time closing time, all Zach wanted to do was veg out in front of the television with Roxie snuggled up next to him. He preferred to watch sports but knew he probably wasn't going to win that battle. He and Roxie cooked corn on the cob and barbecued spareribs and insisted on the clean up as well, giving his parents some much needed time together. After everything was done, they ended the night in the den. Clara and Gerald had retired to the living room, but that was okay with Zach because the den was cozier, in his opinion. The brown, faux leather overstuffed couch and loveseat were the most comfortable spots in the house. The loveseat was just large enough for the two lovebirds, though the couch was great if they wanted to lay together and nap. Then there was the big-screen television with surround sound. This was usually the place that, when everyone was home, they hosted movie marathons. "Should we see what's on television?" he asked Roxie. He hadn't seen that while he was finishing up on the kitchen, she had gone into the den, lit some candles, ones that smelled like vanilla and chestnut. He loved that combination. She had also put on some slow country music. When she had come to Tennessee, she had never even thought to listen to it, but after spending time with Zachary and that being the only other music besides heavy metal he listened to, it rubbed off on her. Roxie found herself listening to it more and more.

"Mr. Blaze," Roxanne said playfully, "if you will please come with me, I have something much better than watching sports."

The seductiveness of her voice was not lost on Zachary. He liked it when she let her hair down, so-to-speak. "Why, yes ma'am. What would you like me to do?"

"Sit down on the couch and put your feet in my lap," she instructed.

Zach noticed she had a bottle of Hemp lotion next to her. He knew she either used coconut and watermelon or pomegranate, but with how dark it was, he couldn't tell since both bottles were the same color and the words were not visible.

"A foot massage, perhaps?" he asked.

"Possibly. Now, please remove your boots and socks," she commanded once he has taken a seat. "Now, I need both of your feet in my lap."

"Yes, ma'am." He did not get his feet rubbed often, but it was something she did to show she loved him. He recalled the first time she did it. He had thought that, because of her entitled status, she would have balked at it; been totally grossed out by the idea even, but once he'd given her one and she realized how good they felt (they were much better by someone you're close to rather than going to a salon), she asked if he had ever gotten one. When he responded in the negative, Roxie didn't hesitate.

Now, here she was. Offering a foot rub when she had been on her feet as much as he had that day. It took her about forty-five minutes, paying special attention to his arches since they were the part that bothered him the most. When she was finished, Zach wouldn't allow her to get away without one herself. "I didn't do that just to have the favor returned, you know," she stated defiantly.

"I know that, but you don't get the privilege of watching the pure ecstasy crossing your face when I do that. And…I'll tell you a little secret…*that* is a major turn on," he uttered softly. Of course, that made Roxanne blush, so much so that Zachary could see her cheeks glowing in the candlelight. "You're blushing, Darlin,'" out came the lopsided grin, again.

Although she knew she was, as she could feel the warmth of her cheeks, she denied it vehemently. She also knew if he chose to, Zach could argue this point late into the night if she kept denying it, so she closed her mouth and relished in the calloused but softness of his deft fingers as they worked the kinks out of her feet.

Once they were finished, they compromised on a romantic comedy in lieu of sports. She promised he could choose whatever he wanted the next time. They both must have fallen asleep because Roxie's next awareness was the credits rolling on *My Best Friend's Wedding*. She gently nudged Zach awake. "Did you enjoy the movie as much as I did?" she teased. "I watched most of it with the back of my eyelids. How about you?"

"I think I got to the part where Julia Roberts met Cameron Diaz. After that, it's all blank. See? Foot rubs cause drowsiness," he chuckled, "maybe we should call it a night," as they untangled their legs where they had laid cuddled on the couch to watch the movie.

"That might be a good idea. What time do you want to leave tomorrow?" The next day was Thursday and, true to his word, Zach's dad let him have the rest of the weekend off.

"Whenever you want," they kissed goodnight at the doorway of Roxie's bedroom. "All depends on when we get up since I don't have to work again until Monday"

⏵⏵ ⏵⏵ ⏵⏵ ⏵⏵

It had been a long time since Zach had been able to sleep in past 6:00 am. He was surprised when he looked at his phone and it was after ten. There wasn't any noise in the house. He assumed his mom was doing something quietly and Roxie was still asleep. He snuck out of his room because he didn't want to wake her. The sight that met him though, made his heart melt. Clara and Roxie were sitting at the kitchen table with Zach's parents' wedding album and wedding paraphernalia sprawled out on the kitchen table, and his mom was showing her their album. He could still see the love she had for his father by the way she lovingly touched each photo as she told Roxie the significance of each one. Zach did not want to interrupt them by barging in, so he cleared his throat, making himself known.

"Good morning, my boy," Clara noted first.

"Hello, my love. We were beginning to think you were going to sleep in all day." Zach traveled over to where Roxanne sat and planted a kiss on her lips. When they first started dating, it troubled Roxanne to kiss in public, but more so in front of her parents or his. But, as she began to stand on her own two feet more and more, it wasn't as disconcerting, not even in her parents' presence.

Zach knew what they were doing, but decided to play dumb anyway, "What are you two doing?"

"Your mom has been so kind as to show me your parents' wedding album. She was telling me about the story behind each picture, especially the candid ones."

"What's the rest of the stuff sprawled all over the table?"

"Oh, we were just looking at dresses and invitations and stuff. Just to get a feel for what Roxie might like," Clara said.

"It looks like tons of fun. Y'all continue while I go shower."

"Oh, sweetheart, before I forget…I have an interview at Scarlett Boutique at 3:00 pm today." Roxie jumped in.

"Well, it's a good thing I got up then, huh?" Zach jested.

"I would have woken you up by 10:30 am had you not gotten up. Go get your stinky self in the shower. I'm already packed up, but if you're planning on staying the weekend with me, you'll need to pack," she cajoled.

As soon as Zach was showered and packed, it was decided that they would go together in Roxie's Porsche and he'd catch a bus back sometime on Sunday. They made it to Nashville in enough time for Roxanne to choose the perfect interview outfit, adjust her existing makeup, and get there with fifteen minutes to spare. One thing she had learned from being around Zach's family was that it was better to be early. It showed the manager she was serious about taking on the job. At three o'clock, right on the dot, the manager came to grab Roxie from the front of the department store.

A middle-aged woman greeted her with a warm smile and reached for her hand to shake it. "Nice to see you again, Roxanne. I'm glad you could make the interview today. You're the last person I have on my list and I should have something to tell you by Monday, either by phone or email. Whether you get the job or not, I will let you know either way. Oh yeah…my name is Margie, by the way. Please don't hesitate to use my name. It makes things more personable; don't you think?"

"Yes, ma'am." They entered Margie's quant office; pristine and clean. Not what Roxie had expected of a manager's office with all the paperwork that needed to be done every day.

"Have a seat and we'll get started." Margie extended an arm to signal Roxie could sit in the armchair before her own desk. "Well, I understand you don't have much work experience, but I spoke to your previous employer from the university as well as your professors, and they all had nothing but glowing recommendations for you."

"That's good to hear." Roxanne had worked extremely hard at both her job and her studies. She was tired of being known as a rich brat and knew if she applied herself, she could lose that name altogether. After only ten minutes, and a few questions later, the interview was over. Margie asked a few extra general questions at the end of their conversation and assured her that she would be in touch. They shook hands and Roxie left.

▶▶ ▶▶ ▶▶ ▶▶

The weekend went by just as quickly as the one before. Roxie and Zach spent the weekend sightseeing and soaking in each other's presence. Roxie's favorite place was The Grand Ole' Opry which was funny since she hadn't listened to a lick of country music until she'd met her cowboy. This time though, Roxanne was not afraid to be alone in her new home, 'the big city'. She was overly excited about the prospect of a job in a place she really wanted. As they said, "See ya later," Zachary sensed that Roxie felt more at ease with their situation. It scared him because, in a way, with her gaining independence, he feared she would not need him anymore. He feared she would choose not to marry him, and he loved her so much that if that were the choice she made, although it would break his heart into a million little pieces, he would let her go. He knew her best bet to making a career was not in Tennessee and it worried him fiercely. Would she be content to stay around Chattanooga once he was finished with veterinarian school? He did his best not to let that issue gnaw at him as he boarded the bus to take him home. But, as he waved at Roxie, he realized his home was where she was. *Maybe this far away thing won't work*, he thought as the bus pulled out of the terminal. There *had* to be a way they could both finish college and still be together. Zach decided that, once he was home and talking to Roxie, he would bring up his concerns; concerns he did not really know he possessed until they'd spent an entire week together.

Chapter 4

Once Zach returned home, the first thing he did was talk to his parents to get a feel for what he needed. "Hey mom, dad? Can I talk to you for a second?" He wanted to make sure he was doing the right thing before talking to Roxanne about it.

"Sure, son. What's up?" Gerald asked, uneasily.

"As you know, once I finish my bachelor's degree, I've always planned to go to Veterinarian school in Knoxville, but the more time I spend with Roxie, the more I realize that I don't want to wait until we're both finished with school to be married. I haven't spoken with Roxie about this yet, because I wanted to run it by you guys first."

"Well, what would you do instead of what you've planned to do?" Gerald questioned, the uneasiness clear.

"I was thinking that even though I'm taking over the clinic when you both retire, I thought about getting my business degree, so I have all the business stuff out of the way. By then, Roxie will be done with her degree."

"Where do you plan on getting your business degree from?" Clara jumped in.

"I looked into Lipscomb University where Roxie is going, and they have what looks like a decent bachelor's degree in business."

"It sounds like you pretty much have your mind made up," Zach's dad divulged.

"Does it sound like I'm jumping the gun? You can be honest with me."

"Not as long as you're both aware of the difficulties that could arise should you get married before one of you graduates. I know that Roxie really wants to get married as soon as humanly possible," Clara replied.

"She doesn't know that I have been thinking about this pretty much this entire last week, spending almost every day with her. It makes me realize that I need her closer to me now. I didn't realize it before and couldn't have until we got into this situation for real. She's not comfortable staying in Nashville alone and if I lived in the vicinity, at least if something happened or she got scared, I would be closer than a phone call and almost three hours."

"You have a rational argument there, so I don't see why it wouldn't work," Zach's dad reiterated, "My only concern is that you can't apply at Lipscombe until next semester. Unless you can go and plead your case."

"Let me talk to Roxie first. Then I'll decide what my next steps will be."

"Is it possible that where she began her associates degree at Chattanooga, that she could get in late there? That way you can both go to the same school, work at the clinic; yes, I was watching how quickly she was picking things up at the receptionist's desk. If she were to take over in that area, you could be more hands-on in the back; learning the ropes of a vet."

"That's great, but with the interview she just had, everything looks like it may pan out there. I don't want to take that away from her. I probably should go call her before she starts blowing my phone up with text messages."

"Son," Clara stopped him dead in his tracks, "whatever you decide, we support the both of you. You know that we love Roxie. Just as much as if she were our own daughter."

"I know. Thanks, you guys." Hearing it, even though he'd known all along, made his heart flutter just thinking about how Roxie had been accepted by his own tribe.

A few minutes later, Zachary found himself almost too scared to phone Roxanne knowing how much she lived for fashion. Whatever he did, he didn't want to put a damper on her plans. "Hey, Darlin,' what are you up to?"

"I was beginning to think you forgot about me," Roxie sighed.

"You're not serious?"

"No, silly. What took you so long?"

"I needed to run something by my parents before I brought it out with you. You know, get their opinion first?"

"Zachary Blaze, what on earth is going on?" worry caked Roxie's voice.

"Darlin,' it's nothing bad. At least, I don't think it is."

"Would you mind filling me in, please?" the irritation was evident in her voice.

"I was thinking on the way home about how I hate being so far away from you, and I know you don't like being away from things and people you were just barely getting to know over this last year."

"Okay," she drew it out.

"What would you think about coming back to Cleveland, or Chattanooga, going back to the university and possibly working at the vet clinic with me?"

"That would mean moving again."

"I know, but you haven't finished unpacking so it wouldn't really take much to load it into one of our horse trailers and find you a place here."

"What about the positions I applied for here?"

"They haven't made a decision yet. And, about school...you could call your dad and see if he could give you the recommendation you needed to start in the next few weeks with me."

"So, what? I'd get my bachelor's degree there and then what...move with you to Knoxville?"

"Or I could move there and get my business degree from Lipscomb. The only issue we run into is getting someone to take over my job at the clinic. Mom and dad are hoping you'll take the position. Dad was quite impressed with what you learned in the few days you were here. Besides, we would be working together. I was doing some looking, and you can get your degree in fashion design right at the University of Tennessee-Chattanooga."

"What? Why did we not know that before? I didn't even look there because I was sure they wouldn't have what I wanted. I see you've been doing your homework." Roxie had been trying to find an easier way to closer to Zach. She didn't like living so far away from the only people she knew in Tennessee.

"We just assumed you'd have to go somewhere else, as I did, once I get my BS."

Roxanne was giddy. She had not spent that much time in Nashville, and now she wouldn't have to be that city alone. She'd worried and wondered how they would handle the next several years with them both attending different colleges. She had shared her concerns with Clara but made her swear she would not bring Zach into it until Roxie was ready. That's what they had been discussing while pouring over their wedding album and looking at wedding dresses and invitations. "We could get married whenever we wanted instead of having to figure out how to do it around our schooling, work and just getting to spend time together without one of us having to pack a bag all the time. We could even set a date if I move back here."

"Well...it's too late to call my dad tonight, but first thing in the morning I will. I'm certain my mother will demand we come out there for the wedding, especially since she's still sour at me for not becoming a psychologist."

"Even if you couldn't start this semester, you could apply for winter. That would give us time to get you settled here without rushing it.

"True. Well, it's getting late. We'd better call it a night. Before we do though, I want you to know I am so glad that you feel the same way as I do."

"What do you mean?"

"Remember the last day we were at your house and I was looking at your parents' wedding album with your mom?"

"Yeah?"

"I was talking to her about how hard it's going to be being at different schools and having to possibly wait a few years for us to be married. I asked her not to say anything to you because I didn't want any more stress added on you."

"Darlin,' you shouldn't have worried so much about what I would think or feel. I should have come to me with your concerns."

Roxanne's stomach butterflied again at the term of endearment Zachary used for her. "I know. I just didn't want to make things more difficult for you," she yawned, "I think we better call it a night before I fall asleep sitting here listening to your voice." She knew that if he wanted, Zach would keep her awake even longer because of her comment.

"You love it…you know you do," he teased. "Goodnight, Darlin.' Let me know what happens. I know you wanted that job at *Scarlett Boutique* badly, but you want to be near me even more, right?"

How could he even ask a question like that? Of course, I want that job, but the idea of being able to get my degree where he'll be and being able to run the receptionist's desk at the vet clinic so he can learn more than secretarial duties, is even better.

"Of course, babe. Goodnight. I'll keep you posted on what my father says, although he's not the one I have to worry about." With that said, Roxanne hung up before Zachary. He was usually the one to hang up first because he knew that if he continued talking, they would never get any sleep.

⏩ ⏩ ⏩ ⏩

It took Roxanne nearly two weeks to get ahold of her father, Robert. It was a good thing she hadn't purchased any of her books for Lipscombe and it was easy to call and drop out. The administration's office did not even ask why or what they could do to keep her. Roxie guessed it was the turnaround rate. It was so high that they wouldn't have a problem filling her spot. By the time Robert returned her call after several messages; she understood he was a busy man, she had made the decision to move to Cleveland. She had only lived in Chattanooga that first year at the university she was determined to hate and never return to. Now, she wanted a place closer to Zach.

"Hi, daddy. How are you?" Roxanne inquired.

"I'm doing well. Your mother is fine. How do you like living in Nashville?"

"Well...daddy. That's actually why I have been trying to reach you."

"Oh?" Robert was worried. The Roxanne he knew did not complete a task before getting bored and moving on to the next thing. He hoped this was not one of them, but he didn't say a word to her.

"I've been in Nashville for a short time and while I like the city, it's too far away from Zachary. We have come to a decision that we can both receive our bachelor's degrees from Chattanooga and his father has offered me a receptionist position at the vet clinic. I do have to say, it's not too bad. When I was there a couple of weeks ago, Zach showed me how to file charts, set up appointments and even coached me on what to say to a disgruntled customer. I got the hang of it quite fast, so Gerald gave me a position should I decide to move."

"What do you need from me? I can't change your mind, it looks like." Robert clearers his throat.

"You're still on the board of trustees at the university, aren't you?"

"Yes."

"Is there any way you can pull some strings to get me in this semester? It would be a late admission, and I would have to catch up, but Zach will help me. And, if I need a tutor, I'll get one."

"Haven't you started at Lipscombe though?"

"I dropped all my classes."

"Oh, your mother will have a heyday with this one. But honey, you know I will do whatever I can to help you whenever you need it. What is your plan if you cannot start this semester?"

"I can work at the vet clinic until the winter semester starts. That puts me a semester behind Zachary, but as I said, I'll catch up."

"I am certainly grateful to Zachary's parents for giving you a job, but that is not in fashion as you wanted."

"I did receive a job offer at a boutique called Scarletts, and although that would be my ideal choice, I believe I will be much happier being able to actually plan my wedding not just wonder when we might set a date."

"Have you set a date yet?"

"No. Zachary and I both feel that you and mother and his parents should meet first. Are you still planning on coming down here for Christmas?"

"I believe so. Your mother isn't looking forward to it, but I think if I pester her, possibly lure her with our old haunts even at Vanderbilt, she will give in."

"You won't mind if I don't hold my breath that she will come willingly, will you? Remember Christmas last year? How she bad mouthed the entire state of Tennessee? I only hope and pray she will come, if only for my sake and the sake of my fiancé.

"Well, dear…my next client is waiting. I will call the board and see what I can do, and I will call you as soon as I hear something."

"Thank you, daddy. I love you."

"I love you too, honey. Talk to you soon."

The only other thing Roxie had left was to find someone to take over her lease. The manager said it wouldn't be too awfully difficult to find someone, since there was an actual waiting list a mile long with people waiting for a downstairs apartment. No one liked climbing flights of stairs, especially when first moving in.

⏭ ⏭ ⏭ ⏭

Two weeks after Zach and Roxie made their life-altering decision, Zach brought one of the family's horse trailers to her apartment. "Seems like we've been here before," Zachary jokingly teased, putting his arms around his sweetheart. "Darlin,' you sure want to do this? I mean, you still have that other job offer at Scarlett Boutique?"

It didn't take long for Roxie to shut him up with a sensually soft kiss. "Well…if all I have to do is ask you questions like that in order to be smooched the way you just did there, well, I'd have asked a long time ago!"

"Zachary are you not aware kissing you is one of my top five favorite things to do? It ranks right up there with shopping." The horrified look on Zach's face caused Roxie to burst out laughing and she couldn't stop, which made her stomach muscles ache.

"That's right, baby. Just yuck it up." He did his best to hold a scowl but couldn't because her laugh was so contagious. "Okay—okay, we have to stop goofing around and get to work. I'd like to at least get back to Cleveland tonight. Then we can unpack your stuff tomorrow. Zach had taken Friday off, knowing Roxie hadn't unpacked most of her belongings. He figured they could get everything placed in the trailer in no time since nothing had to be cleaned out and everything was still in boxes for the most part. Luckily, her couch was light enough they did not need extra help from paid movers. Zach was afraid they might because Roxie wasn't used to any kind of general or manual labor. He was proud of how hard she worked, never complaining, not even for a second.

By the time everything was loaded, it was dark and late. Neither of them felt like driving back. Three hours was a long time to drive after pushing it so hard all day. "Should we grab a hotel for the evening?"

Roxie asked, pushing away a wry strand of hair that insisted on making hanging low down over her jade green eyes.

"That's hilarious," Zach chuckled.

"What?" He wouldn't laugh at her would he? He never had before.

"Didn't you notice my mouth opened just as you were about to speak?"

"Yes…so—?"

"I was going to ask you the exact same thing. I guess we can read each other's thoughts now," Zach grinned.

"Oh my…we are turning into your parents, aren't we?"

"That wouldn't be such a bad thing, would it?"

"No! I love your mom and dad! They treat me as if I belong in your family, although I'm not part of it yet. Hey, can you put that last box in while I find us a place to stay? We're both grungy but I am starving! Should we stop and eat somewhere or grab something and take it to the motel with us?" Roxanne *had* changed a bunch by being around his down-to-earth family. Normally, she would have insisted on getting showered and dolled up before even considering going into an eating establishment but tonight, she would be good with a Wendy's Jr. Bacon Cheeseburger or nuggets. Her stomach growled loudly, and she had another thought, o*r maybe a McDonald's Bacon-Ranch salad or maybe I'll be so bold as to go with a Big Mac*!

Chapter 5

As luck would or wouldn't have it, Robert was unable to get Roxanne into the University of Tennessee-Chattanooga for the current semester. That did not deter her plans, however. She was already moved into her new apartment, only a stone's throw from Zach's house. Most days, he dropped her off at work, went to classes, then came back.

Roxanne became more and more comfortable with her job as a receptionist for Blaze Family Veterinarian Clinic. Eventually, she felt she could do her job in her sleep. She was annoyed she would be a semester behind Zach. That would mean, should they marry while in college, he would have to work while she finished. Married. Roxie liked the sound of that. She insisted they get married during their spring break if their parents met during Christmas, as planned. They could have a winter wedding, which, in Tennessee would be gorgeous. They didn't have to wait until *after* they met, did they? Couldn't they get married the same two weeks her parents would be here? She knew her mother had already demanded on helping with planning of it. It did not matter that Roxanne wanted a small, intimate wedding; Belinda, her mother, wanted extravagant. Maybe Roxanne could convince her less was more, but she highly doubted it.

By mid-October, everything was running smoothly, until one day, Belinda called Roxie and stipulated that, since she had screwed up her schooling plans so much, she should fly out to Los Angeles and see her parents whom she hadn't seen since the beginning of August. This was code for, "We need to start wedding plans—NOW!"

"Mother, I cannot up and leave for three weeks. I have a job and they count on me to be there every day."

"It's Zachary's family. Can you not ask his father for a few weeks off? Tell him something terrible has happened at home?"

"Mother, I am not going to lie to my soon-to-be father-in-law but, I will see if I can take some time off and come home."

It turned out that it wasn't as difficult as Roxanne thought to get the time off she needed, especially when she was going home to see her parents. Both Clara and Gerald were aware of the strained relationship between her father and her mother but understood why her parents wanted to see her. The thing that bothered Roxie the most was that she hadn't gone home between August and December the year before, and it didn't seem to disturb her mother...why now?

Roxanne caught a flight two days later to Los Angeles, the place she once called 'home.' As she sat back to relax, she realized that her home was no longer in Los Angeles but wherever Zach was. As the flight grew closer and closer to the airport where her parents were to meet her, for reasons she did not understand, nerves began building the closer she got. Both of her parents were waiting at the end of the terminal. Her father dressed in a black Armani suit and her mother dressed to the nines in a white blouse and black pencil skirt with a matching black blazer, her hair done up tightly in a bun; the way her mother usually dressed. All business. There was no casual in her mother's attire.

Robert was the first to extend affection to his daughter, "Hello, sweetheart. How was your flight?"

"Uneventful," she turned to her mother who had yet to acknowledge her, "How are you, mother?"

"Fine, dear. Shall we go? This place is too crowded for my liking." And that was it. All the way to their mansion, as Roxie had come to call it; it felt more like a museum than a home, all Roxanne could think about was how long the next two weeks were going to be. She wanted nothing more than to go home but still couldn't tell her mother 'no' when she demanded Roxanne do something.

Once at the mansion, the butler took Roxanne's bags to her room. She had gotten used to packing her own things that she smirked when she realized how accustomed she'd grown to handling her own bags.

"Is everything okay, miss?" the butler inquired, he too seemed to be worried about Roxie.

"Oh. I'm fine. Thank you, John. I've just gotten used to taking care of things myself, but I know you have a job to do, and I must not anger mother." They both snickered quietly at her saying that. Roxanne felt as if she had turned a corner with the butler; more as a friend than someone who worked for her parents. She hoped the rest of the servants might see she wasn't the same person they had known her to be all her life. She wanted them to see her as Roxie, the hard-working college student, not the uptight, entitled brat they knew.

"Well, Miss... would you like me to help you get settled?"

"No, thank you, John. I've got it." With another thank you and a kiss on his cheek, Roxie was left to her own vices. She did not bring her entire arsenal as she had during her previous visits. She decided upon leaving them home. As she looked around what was once her bedroom, it felt strange. Yes, all the items she left when she moved to Tennessee were still there, but she did not feel as if she belonged in this space anymore. She slowly unpacked her suitcase and put her makeup in her bathroom.

Once she was finished settling in, she called Zach. "Hey, Darlin,' I was beginning to think you met some hot celebrity up there and decided I wasn't your cup of tea," he heckled.

"Oh, my poor man. Do you not know yet that I wouldn't trade you in for all the celebrities in the world? I much prefer my cowboy, thank you very much."

"I love you more. How are your parents?" He knew not to use the word 'folks;' he'd made that mistake once before during the Christmas break and boy did he get a comeuppance from Belinda.

"Oh, my mother is just as icy cold as ever; dressed as if everything, even my visit, is all business. Daddy is a little warmer, but I think they're going to leave me to do my own thing while I'm here. I'm not sure why mother wanted me to come to visit now."

"Maybe she'll surprise you."

"You're not serious?"

"Completely. She might not go to work and want to help you look at wedding dresses. I heard L.A. and New York are the best places to go for that kind of thing. What if she plans on taking your family's private jet on a shopping trip to New York City?"

"I've been there many, many times, remember?"

"Yeah, but not for wedding dress shopping. It might be fun."

"I hope you're right, though my mother wouldn't change that quickly, if at all."

"Darlin,' give her the benefit of the doubt."

"I will try, but I'm not going to count on it. Well, it's getting late here, so we better hang up. But hey, before we do, I need to ask you something. My father asked if we have set a wedding date yet." Roxie added.

"We can set one whenever you want, now that we know what we're doing over the next few years."

"I don't want to wait until spring, I want a small wedding, but I'm certain Mother will insist on getting married here, regardless of when we choose to tie the knot."

"When do you want to get married then?"

"I was thinking on the flight here, that if we can convince my parents, we could get married in Tennessee while they're there for Christmas."

"That's pretty quick, isn't it?"

"I know but…think about it, and I'll see what my parents think."

"Mine won't care, so give me a heads up when you have your mom's yay or nay at the idea."

"Ok. I love you, babe. Goodnight."

"I love you, too. Sweet dreams."

It wasn't even nine o'clock in Los Angeles, and, because the nights were cooling down, Roxanne decided to take a walk. She felt she should get in touch with some of her new and old friends, but her desire to act like a rich brat did not appeal to her any longer. She walked by a lot of the places she had taken Zachary when they had come out less than a year ago. Seeing these places through different colored lenses made her appreciate them so much more. By the time she had arrived back at the mansion, her parents were already in bed. She had never been allowed to bother them, especially after they retired to their room for the night. No one ever explained why, but she was aware after watching other people, especially in the south, most families were not like hers; not even those that were well-off. They all seemed as if they liked being together, where her parents counted her being under their 'roof' as family time. Roxanne wandered around this place that she once called 'home,' but never realized how cold it was. It was definitely not the warm place the Blaze's home had been to her. This was not a home; it was just a house. Once Roxanne decided to call it a night, there was a note taped to her door which read:

Roxanne,
In the morning, be prepared to speak to me about your wedding plans. I thought we could go to Vivienne Atelier and try on some wedding dresses; to get a feel for what you might like. Be up and ready by ten o'clock...no later, because I have appointments from two until quite late.

                Mother

The note should not have surprised Roxanne, but if truth be told, she would much rather look through magazines with Clara. She knew they wouldn't be looking for what Roxie wanted. It was whatever her mother was pleased with, and would most likely be something frilly.

⏩ ⏩ ⏩ ⏩

"Mother, this has more bells and whistles than I would like." The dress was white but had faux feathers on the bottom which Roxanne hated. If that was not horrid enough, the thing had long, lacy sleeves and silver bling covering the bodice. The only thing it was missing was going clean up to her throat.

"It looks lovely, dear," Her mother defended her first choice but then became angry. "Well…I never…if you think you can pick out a dress better than that one, be my guest." Belinda sounded like a defiant, spoiled child who had not gotten her way.

The dress that Roxanne picked was a simple, white, sleeveless, sweetheart neck with a tiny silver belt around her waist which hugged where it should and flared out a bit at the bottom. "This is gorgeous," she gushed as she saw herself in the mirror.

"That is one of our best sellers," the clerk injected into the conversation. "And right now you're in luck! It's on sale! What kind of vail were you thinking?" For some reason, the clerk directed the question to Belinda.

It's because she looks like she would have no qualms in biting a snake's head off, Roxanne thought.

"Well," Belinda replied snootily. "I would choose a lacy one to go with the first four gowns we tried on that I approve of, but since my daughter seems to know better, maybe you should consult with her first. She's not paying for this farce anyway."

Farce? Where had that come from? She thought she and her mom had made strides over the summer regarding her God given right to make her own choices, but apparently, she was wrong. Or her mother was angry because Roxanne stood her ground when she wanted to choose her own wedding dress. She was still getting used to defying her mother when she wanted something different. The clerk, embarrassed for Roxanne, turned to her, "Do you know what kind of a veil you want?"

"I was thinking about daisies in my hair if we get married in spring, but maybe one with a tiara built in if we get married around Christmas."

At that comment, Belinda's head jerked up, "What do you mean 'around Christmas'?" she demanded.

"Mother, that's something I must talk with you and father about, but can we at least wait until you're both in the same room so I only have to explain the idea once, okay?"

With a huff and a turn of a heel, her mother replied, "Are you getting that plain and simple thing or what? If we are to have lunch before I have to go to work, we must hurry."

Roxanne could see that, once again, she had disappointed her mother, but she couldn't see herself walking down the aisle to her cowboy in that frilly, blinged up mess. Even if it meant her mother spent the next two weeks staring daggers at her in hopes that being mean would make her point. In the past, Roxie would have given in just to make her mother happy, but the more of an adult she became, the more she realized her mother would be unhappy no matter what anyone did. Belinda thought that by controlling her daughter's life, knowing every part of it, choosing her friends, her school and even her career, it would make her satisfied. Roxanne realized she would have to sit down for a heart-to-heart with her mother sooner or later, but she didn't think her mother was ready yet. She might never be.

There was not much talk as Roxanne's mother hailed their driver. "Where shall we have lunch?" Roxanne asked in hopes of softening the idea of the dress and getting married at Christmas in Tennessee; she *could* warm to the idea, couldn't she?

"You seem to know everything. You choose." Belinda bit out.

"Well, you're not a big steak eater. What about that Italian restaurant, *Angelini's*? Is that satisfactory?"

Belinda waved her hand as her response. All Roxanne could do was hope she meant yes. After a silent lunch, the town car dropped Belinda off at her office and took Roxie back to the mansion to spend the rest of the day alone. Instead, she decided to talk with the servants. Her entire life, she referred to them as employees and, although they were paid by her father, they were still people and some even had families they only saw on the weekends because it was mandatory, per Belinda, that they stay in close proximity just in case she or Robert needed anything. Roxanne thought that bit a little excessive. If either of them wanted a sandwich in the middle of the night, they weren't invalids; they could fix it themselves. As Roxie spent the day assisting the servants with the chores her mother demanded to be done daily, she learned things about them and their families she would not have known otherwise. *If my mother saw me now, she would be spitting bullets; cleaning with one of the hired help.* Roxanne enjoyed her day of assisting and helping, immensely.

She should have known that her mother would not allow her to bring up the wedding in her own time. Her parents came home at seven o'clock that evening and, like clockwork, dinner was ready and in place waiting for them to partake. Before Roxanne could get a word in edgewise Belinda cried, "Robert! Do you know what kind of day I have had with this child?"

"It was not a lot of fun, at all?"

"Well—" Belinda scoffed, "First of all, she didn't love the dress I was prepared to purchase today, neither did she like any of the other four contenders," she glared at her daughter as if she didn't know that she was missing out.

"Belinda, darling. She is not you. Roxanne is entitled to her own opinions about things and besides, this *is* her wedding," Robert did what he could to lessen the impact of Belinda's anger.

"*That* was not even the worst of it!"

"What else happened?" he inquired calmly, hoping his demeanor would rub off on his frazzled wife.

"Well, we purchased the dress she wanted and then she said something about being married at Christmas time! Is she really so dense that she does not realize there is no way we can get the biggest wedding in this city put together in such a short amount of time?"

It was then that Robert let his daughter speak after he said, "Sweetheart, that *is* awfully short notice. Why Christmas time?"

"I don't want a big Los Angeles wedding. I never have. A small, intimate gathering with a few family and friends is what both Zach and I want. We could hold the wedding and a small reception in Tennessee when you come for Christmas and then mother can plan a huge reception here for a later time."

"That doesn't sound too bad," Robert answered.

"The Blazes have this gorgeous backyard with a waterfall in the backdrop of the landscaping. I was thinking we could put an arched trellis there to get married under in the backyard. Only have a few friends and family. That way, those from L.A. wouldn't have to come out since we'll most likely be doing an open house here for all of them."

"Have you spoken to Zachary about any of this?" Belinda sneered. She didn't like the idea one bit and once she made up her mind, there was nothing anyone could do to change it.

Robert stopped her right in her tracks. "Belinda," he spoke sternly, "Do not ruin our daughter's wedding plans." He seldom stood up to his wife, "I realize this was not what you had planned for your daughter, but she is an adult and should be treated as such. She can choose whatever she pleases." And, with that, the subject was dropped for the time being.

Chapter 6

The two weeks that Roxie spent in Los Angeles were the longest of her life; even longer than the summer had been if that was even possible. Her mother gave her the silent treatment the rest of the time just because her choices did not coincide with what her mother thought was etiquette. It did, however, give Roxanne time with her father, whom she felt much closer to. This time she had with her father now was something she considered he had not taken when she was much younger. They spent time talking about her childhood and Robert apologized for not being around more—for the fact that she spent more time with the nannies than her parents. He tried justifying it, at first, by telling Roxanne that when Amelia was stillborn, they were afraid to parent her out of the fear that they would do something terribly wrong. Instead, they hired nannies to care of her while they buried themselves in their work. As she listened, she began to understand her father more. Why he was at times, like most fathers, listening to her, and making her feel loved but at others, held her at arm's length, especially as she grew older. "You see, my dear daughter. It was not because I did not love you; far from it. I was so afraid to show you too much love and attention because I dreaded the idea of losing you, so it was easier for me to show love and affection sparingly."

"I know you aren't justifying it anymore and I'm grateful for that, but it still hurts that my formative years were spent with virtual strangers than with my actual parents. Why wouldn't mother be a stay-at-home mom for me? It was not like we didn't have enough money coming in with you working where you do."

"I cannot speak fully for your mother, but I will tell you that she was more fearful than I. When we found out we were having not only one, but two babies, the plan was for your mother to stay at home, and we were going to hire help during the day, of course. But, as I said, when we lost Amelia, I think your mother couldn't handle seeing you every day as you were her reminder of the child that did not get to come home with us."

"It wasn't my fault, but I grew up thinking I had done something wrong because the both of you were so cold toward me when you were home. I thought that maybe I should have died too, because then neither of you would have to look at me anymore. Do you remember when I asked nanny June if I could call her 'mommy' because I was only allowed to call Belinda, mother?"

"Yes. I do."

"It didn't seem to bother mother, and that hurt as I got older because I *knew* who she was. Then again, I knew she'd always been more concerned about the outward appearance of our family than being an actual family. I do know my children, your grandchildren, will have a parent at home at one time or another. I will never make my children feel unwanted or worse—unloved.

"I'm so sorry for making you feel that way. That was never my intention."

"Thank you for helping me see both you and mother in a different light. Do you think she will come around about a Tennessee Christmas wedding?"

"I do not know, but whether she comes around or not…*I* will be there. I only get to give my daughter away once. By the way, we haven't talked much about how you and Zachary are doing."

"Honestly, it wasn't unequivocally difficult of a choice to make once the realization of how a long-distance relationship meant and what we would have to sacrifice. Don't get me wrong, I know there must be sacrifices made in every relationship; I feel I know what sacrifice I'm going to have to make. Although, talking with Clara makes it more like a blessing than sacrifice. Once we both made the decision to continue at the University of Tennessee-Chattanooga, it was as if a huge weight had been lifted from our shoulders."

"What sacrifice do you think you will have to make after you're married—the one you said you think you already know?"

"Children. I know Zach wants me to be a stay-at-home mom like his mom was. They feel it's important that one parent stays home when the kids are home and being raised by nannies then watching the closeness Zach's family has. However, his brother passed away and it makes me want that even if it means that I run my fashion design business from home or wait until the children are in school to start my journey. I made Zach promise we would put having children on hold until I get my degree in three years."

"Well..." Robert said with a chuckle, "Don't be too surprised if that one doesn't happen as you have planned. These things generally don't work out the way we expect them to."

"So, you're saying, be prepared for the baby hungriness that could accompany being married?" Roxanne was aware of that pitfall because she had discussed it at length with the only 'mommy' she knew, on several different occasions.

"That's exactly what I'm saying."

That long talk occurred as Robert was driving Roxanne to the airport. During her time in L.A., she found the guts to work up the nerve to call some of her old friends and they went out shopping and grabbed some lunch as they usually did when they were in high school. Roxanne realized that although they had not changed much, she had changed leaps and bounds since her move to Tennessee. As was usual, their conversation was surrounded by questions about Zachary, about how she could see herself married to a cowboy and living in the country, of all places. She reassured them that she felt more at home there than she did in L.A. and it took her two-week visit to confirm where she belonged.

Roxanne reminisced about her visit home this time, on the airplane ride home. *Home—that has a nice ring to it.* There were parts about her parents she never knew and it, in a way, bolstered her drive to be a better parent than they had been. But, at the same time, it aided her in getting to know them as people now that she was an adult and not a child. Quite possibly, the dynamics of their relationship would change—in time. Roxie felt she'd made strides with her father, if only because he felt bad that her mother refused to speak with her for the remainder of her stay. It saddened Roxie, but after talking about Amelia and the different ways each of them handled her loss, she cut her mother some slack and even received a hug goodbye. Roxanne also realized her L.A. friends were no longer really friends, if they ever were because she saw them as moochers—why work if mom and dad would buy you anything and everything you wanted? And to top *that* off, with your own credit card and no limit? Roxie pondered on the fact that she used to be like those girls. She realized in her own case, she didn't know that she wanted to be a better person until *someone* came along to show her she could be.

▸▸ ▸▸ ▸▸ ▸▸

Roxie was coming home today! Zachary could not contain his excitement! It had been two of the longest weeks in his life, but no more. They had decided, after talking at length with both sets of parents, that Belinda and Robert would be all right with a small wedding in Tennessee, but Belinda was adamant they wait until at least spring even though Roxie grudgingly gave her okay for Christmas when they would meet Gerald and Clara for the first time. This way, at Christmas they could all get acquainted and there would not be any wedding stress going on at the same time. Christmas was a stressful time without the added bonus of a wedding. Belinda was even okay with two receptions, one right after the wedding and then once spring semester was over, Zachary and Roxanne and their parents would fly to Los Angeles. All were aware that party would be a lot more expensive than the middle-class one they were planning for Tennessee.

Roxanne was flying into the Chattanooga airport and would call him when they landed so it would give her time to go to baggage claim. She had insisted that she should rent a car and drive home, but she knew why Zach wanted to pick her up. The poor guy missed her almost as much as she missed him. Her flight was scheduled to land at 6:15 pm, Central Standard Time, which meant it was 4:15 pm in Los Angeles.

As the time drew closer and closer and Roxie still hadn't shown up, Zach's stomach grew into tight knots. He could sense that something wasn't right. He felt it in his bones. He asked his father if there had been any news reports about airlines, planes or anything that might help him understand why he felt the way he did. Usually, his gut instinct was correct. Suddenly, on the television he heard a news anchor's voice pipe up and read from his teleprompter, *"...flight 264 from Los Angeles to Tennessee has crashed, somewhere in the Colorado mountains. It was supposed to land at the Denver airport for a layover, but the pilot had to execute an emergency landing. We're not certain at this time where the flight landed or if it crashed, and we do not know yet whether there are any injured passengers or survivors. We have been in contact with emergency responders near the area where they lost contact with the tower. We will keep you updated as we know more..."* Zach listened with a trained ear, at the same time, itching to do something—anything. "Dad," he called with hurt in his heart to Gerald between gulps of air as his dad held onto him. Zach crumpled to the ground with little effort. "That's Roxie's flight," his voice shook, "Oh, dad...what should I do? I can't lose her."

Gerald was just as astonished as his son. Clara was out running errands, but he was sure she had heard what was on the news. "Son don't borrow trouble. We don't even know how or why they had to land, so let's just wait until we hear more," he reached down and searched for Zach's worried, wandering eyes, "okay?"

"Should I call Belinda and Robert to see if they've heard anything?" Zachary wrung his hands until they were red from the friction.

"That might be a good idea. They may know even more than we do, but you need to make sure that they are aware of what is going on either way. Be gentle, son."

Zach did not want to make the call, but he knew that if he were in their shoes, that he hoped they would call him to let him know before he saw it on TV. His hands shook as he dialed Robert's cell number. As he listened to the ringing, he pondered on what exactly he would say. Robert picked up on the second ring, "Hello, Zachary. I suppose you have heard the terrible news."

"Yes." It was all Zach could do not to sob into the phone's receiver. He was so alarmed at the whole situation. "I just wanted to call and see how you and Mrs. McCain are doing. Have you heard anything more? Do they know if there are any survivors yet?"

"I do not know. I've only heard what the news has divulged, which isn't much. But, we must keep hope and faith that she is still alive. Are you religious, Zachary?"

"Yes, sir. I am."

"We're Christian here and think praying is a good idea."

"I've been doing that since I knew she boarded the plane this morning. I pray every time she gets on a plane."

"The more I get to know you, the more I'm convinced you're the right man for my daughter. You care for her very much, don't you?"

With the thickness of tears clogging his throat, Zach found it difficult to respond but he managed to choke, "Yes, I love Roxie with everything I have."

"Why do you call her that? I've heard you say it like that before, but never asked."

"When we started our first semester at the University of Tennessee-Chattanooga, I wasn't exceptionally fond of her. She and I butted heads often, but the more time we spent together, the more I realized she wasn't the shallow person I thought she was. I mean no offense by that, Robert."

"She has changed so much since meeting you, that much is true Zachary. She realizes the value of a hard day's work and that money doesn't come easily; that you must earn it. I think the reason we spoiled her at such a young age was due to the fact that, in a way, we tried to not only make up for Amelia's absence but our absence in her life as well," Robert was near tears. He only wanted to do right by his daughter.

"She *has* changed, and I like to think I had something to do with that."

"She's much more levelheaded since being with you. I appreciate how you love and care for her. If you hear anything more would you keep us posted and I will be certain to do the same?"

"Of course."

"I don't care what time of day it is. Understand?"

"Okay. Pray we hear something soon." Just as he was about to hang up the phone, Robert stopped him, "Thank you for calling. You didn't have to, you know?"

"I did though. There is someone we both love and hold dear on that flight; for different reasons, but love just the same," Zach replied, his voice cracking with every word. "And…before I forget, would you please let Mrs. McCain know I called? And that you both are in my prayers as we deal with whatever comes?"

"I will. Thank you. She may learn to like you yet." With that, the two men hung up. While Zach was conversing with his soon-to-be father-in-law, they had read the manifest over the news; sure enough, Roxie's name was on it.

"Oh mama," Zach bellowed. He could no longer stem the tears. "What am I going to do? What if she's hurt or worse?" His mom had returned from running errands as he was talking with Robert.

"My dear, Zach. You cannot think like that or it will drive you crazy." She held him close, much like she'd done when he was a kid.

Chapter 7

As that first day without her turned into two and then three, Zach began to lose hope Roxie or anyone else, for that matter, had survived. The airplane had gone down somewhere in the Rocky Mountain National Forest. They had not found the wreckage yet and sending out search parties was difficult due to how cold the temperatures were during the day and how far the temperature dropped at night. Zach prayed for all those onboard, as any normal person would do, but mostly begged for Roxanne to be okay. She was not the kind of person to know what to do in the wilderness and he was afraid for her. She had no idea what to do to keep warm. He hadn't taught her that kind of survival stuff yet.

After the third day of no news regarding any of the passengers, to Zachary's absolute dread, plane debris had been located in the mountains and they were now actively searching for survivors. His worst fears had been realized and it tore him up inside to even think about his love being helpless. By day five, Zach was going crazy. The plane crash had been on almost every news station all day, every day, but never anything about Roxie. It was always the same, *"Of the one hundred and fifty passengers aboard flight 265...we have found one hundred and forty-seven who did not survive, including the pilot, co-pilot and three of the stewardesses. We will not be releasing names until the families of all the victims have been notified. There are still three passengers unaccounted for, and we have yet to find the full wreckage.* Zachary was completely freaked out because he hadn't heard anything from the proper authorities. He couldn't concentrate on anything and, at the same time, he jumped every time the telephone rang in fear it was about her. He spoke almost daily with Robert and Belinda, hoping that keeping them close would, in some small way, keep them from thinking the worst, too.

After the first week had passed and there had been no news of Roxanne, Robert decided he would fly to Denver, Colorado and join the search parties, but he had no qualms about searching by himself, even though that wasn't the brightest of ideas. His baby girl was out there somewhere, in freezing temperatures but he felt in his heart that she was still alive. When he made his plans known to Zachary, Zach insisted on going along with him.

"Zachary," his mom pinned, "You can't go out there. What if something happens to you, too?" She was crying into her hands.

"Mom, I'll be fine. I promise I won't do anything stupid, but I *need* to do something. She's out there. What if she's alive and no one finds her? I mean, there were dead bodies scattered everywhere, but there is still no sight of the full plane hull? What if she's with the rest of the wreckage?"

Clara knew there was no way she was going to stop her son. She'd been young and in love once, too. She understood his situation was much different, though, and although she and Gerald had been married almost thirty years, she knew that if it were Gerald out there, lost, scared and possibly hurt, she would do the exact same thing. "Son, at least wait until Roxie's dad gets here. Do that much for me, okay?"

"Okay, mom. He packed his gear, some food, and a proper first aid kit they taught him to always have handy when in the wilderness and waited on bated breath for Robert to arrive.

It surprised everyone in the Blaze household that Belinda had accompanied Robert to Tennessee. "I could not sit in that big house alone, pondering the worst."

"I know this wasn't the way we had planned to meet, but it's nice to meet you both," Gerald shook both their hands, but Clara, seeing the anguish showing up in Belinda's eyes, hugged her. She knew the heartache Belinda felt. When Chase passed away, she thought her life was over, but Belinda had already lost one daughter. She couldn't stand it if she lost Roxanne, too.

Clara was astonished when the hug was returned. "Robert," she shook the man's hand. "We'll take good care of your wife. Please bring both kids home safely."

"I plan on it," Robert affirmed. "I won't let anything happen to Zachary, and with faith and the Lord's guidance on our side, we *will* find Roxanne and bring her home."

He and Belinda had flown to Tennessee in their private jet. The same jet they had tried convincing their daughter to fly back to Tennessee on when she left a few days prier, but she was adamant that she lived like a normal fiancé and fly coach. "You ready to go, son?" Robert motioned to Zach.

"Yes, sir." He gave his mom a hug and a kiss on the cheek, then hugged his dad. "Don't worry. We'll be careful."

⏩ ⏩ ⏩ ⏩

They landed at the Denver airport about five hours later. The flight, although posh, seemed to take forever. Neither family had slept much over the last week, so Zach and Robert tried to sleep during the flight but realized after about an hour that it was a futile attempt. Instead of sleeping, they spent their time poring over a map of the area where the survivors should have been, and most of the dead were found, trying to see if there was something that the search and rescue teams had missed. "What about this small area here?" Zach pointed to an area that was kind of off the beaten path. "Where it's out of the way a little bit, do you think they searched it?"

"I don't know, but when we land, we will talk to the person in charge."

"There's not any way to take the jet up and look at it from the air, is there?"

"I'm sure they have done that already, but I let them know that my daughter was on that plane when I called the number the newscast provided, and so far, she is not one of the dead or the surviving. In fact, she has not been found yet."

"What did he say?"

"He told me they were still looking; that they had done several aerial searches, but money does have its perks. I rented a helicopter and pilot so if the need should arise, you and I can go up. We might even be able to see what area you were speaking about from the helicopter."

Once they landed, they rented a Chevy 4x4 and headed in the direction of the search and rescue team. *I guess it really does pay to have money,* Zachary supposed. It was as if Robert could say, "Jump," and the other person would only replied with, "How high?" That's exactly how things had gone for them up to that point.

When they arrived at the mobile search and rescue station that had been set up at the edge of where the police thought the plane went down due to the body count, Robert immediately went to speak with the chief of police. "How many of the hundred and fifty people have been found?"

"Excuse me," the Chief asked, "May I ask who you are?"

"I am Robert McCain. My daughter was on that plane, and her name was Roxanne McCain. Now, how many have been found either dead or alive?" His commanding voice, which Zachary had rarely ever heard, came out so easily. He had only heard it a little bit when he was at their mansion the Christmas before, but for the most part, Robert was an extremely soft-spoken man.

"We have found all, but the three that we've given to reporters," the Chief responded.

"One of those has *got* to be my daughter. We have not received word and it's been a week!"

"Mr. McCain. We're still searching for and through the wreckage. There may still be survivors to be found. We just don't know at the moment."

"Look, my son-in-law has a worthwhile idea I think you should hear." Upon hearing Robert call him his son-in-law, when he and Roxanne were not even married yet, made him tear up, which he explained away with as the cold making his eyes water. Robert knew different, though. He knew Zachary was afraid he would never be accepted into the McCain family because of his status in life. Having spent time with the young man, especially under such horrible circumstances, just reiterated how much his daughter meant to the young man.

"With all due respect, sir—we're expertly trained in this sort of thing. I don't think your son-in-law is," the Chief quipped. He did not have the patience or the time for this. Every minute that passed meant they would find more bodies. They needed to keep at it until the last three were found.

⏩ ⏩ ⏩ ⏩

"We're never going to get out of here," Joshua, one of the survivors moaned.

"You can't think like that." Vivienne, a record producer from Hollywood stated, "I'm worried about Roxanne here, though. She can't move, and we don't have many more nights left to keep this fire going."

Roxanne could hear them, and there were times when she was lucid enough to talk with them, but she was mostly in and out of consciousness. She was so cold, and the icy bitter wind made it so that she could not feel anything. Her arms were even numb, although the two strangers she only knew by name did their best to make certain she was as warm as they could make her. She cracked her eyes open and whispered hoarsely, "Zach will find us. There is no way he is sitting at home right now." And with that, blackness overtook her, again. Whenever she awoke after each blackout, Roxie wondered if it would be the last time, she opened her eyes. She wanted...no, needed to live! She had many amends to make to her mother and she had a wedding to plan. She thought a lot about that during her lucid moments, just because it helped her hang on. As the days and nights came and went, she wondered if they would ever be found.

"Who's Zach?" Joshua asked.

"I don't know, but he must be fairly important to her because she keeps saying his name over and over," Vivienne replied, her teeth frigidly chattering all the while.

"Maybe he'll be the one to rescue us," Joshua was once again filled with hope.

Little did they know, that's exactly where Zach was. And determined as ever to find the remaining three, even if it only meant closure for their families. He wanted to find them alive, but as the eighth day got darker and colder than ever, he worried his Roxie was in huge trouble.

"...just listen to the boy." Robert was urging. Zachary had not heard the rest of that conversation being lost in his own thoughts.

"Fine," the Chief caved. He knew he was never going to hear the end of it until he heard the kid out. He was not from Los Angeles, but he knew who Robert McCain was and the influence he held. He was known all over the United States.

"Zachary, show the chief what we discussed." Robert let Zach take the lead.

"As we were flying here," Zach laid out the map, "I wondered if you thought to search this area right here," he pointed to the place on the map which he had previously circled during their brainstorming sessions earlier. "Have you been over this area yet?"

The Chief sighed, "We've been as close as we can get and haven't found anything."

"Have you tried using a helicopter?" Robert inserted.

"We do not have funding for that kind of thing. Look, we're doing the best we possibly can with all of the resources we have."

"It's a good thing I didn't listen to my wife and stay at home, waiting."

"What do you mean?" the Chief was now curious.

"You seem to know who I am by the way we have spoken. So, you would have to know that I am fairly well off."

"Well…yes, but that still doesn't tell me what you're getting at."

"I have a helicopter on standby should we need it. If one of the medics and a couple of your men would like to fly with Zachary and me, that would be helpful; in case we find survivors." Robert could not swallow the lump in his throat as he said the words. The three remaining had been out in the cold for eight days and the likelihood that they were still alive was minimal, but both Zach and Robert held onto all the faith and hope they could muster that things would turn out in their favor.

"Fine. Get your helicopter here and let's see if the wreckage is there. If it is, Zachary, we owe you more than a debt of gratitude."

"No need, Chief. I just want to find my fiancé alive and hopefully not hurt." He did not believe after being left to the elements this long that she wasn't hurt, but he could always hope.

Within thirty minutes, the helicopter was there. It didn't take them long to get everyone who was going onto the helicopter, including supplies and anything they thought they might need to help the survivors…within an hour of being in the air, Zach shouted, "I see something! Does anyone else see that?" he pointed at what looked like debris.

"I see it," one of the medics who came with the group claimed. "It's small, but it's there."

"The question is," Robert interrupted, "how do we get down there?"

"We need to go back to the station, take a look at that map again, and talk to the chief. They know this terrain. Plus, I noticed a park ranger among the myriad of people who have been searching for survivors or bodies, maybe he can help," one of the other men that went who had been assisting in the search over the past several days, replied.

"There is?" Zach's mouth hung open. "Are they not supposed to know the ins and outs of the park?" It made him sick to think that there was someone who knew the park but did not offer ways to help.

Robert could tell Zach was losing it. He could not blame him. If it had been Belinda, he would go insane. This was his daughter, so it was more horrific for him, but he did not want to let on.

One of the other men came to the park ranger's defense, "He's new, I do not think that he has been shown all the area yet. And, where we saw what we believe to be debris? That's going to be a hard place to get to. They may not even allow us to go down there because the day is getting darker and colder."

Zach gasped, "But if that *is* the plane, they can't be out there another night!"

"There may not be any survivors after this long anyway," the medic said, "but, let's go talk to the higher-ups and see what they think."

It didn't take them long to land and drive back to the base. Knowing that his emotions were on the surface and he did not know what might come out of his mouth, Zach let Robert and the medic do the talking.

"We found what appeared to be debris," Robert said, "the problem is, it looks to be in a place that is extremely hard to reach."

"Where?" the Chief asked.

"Let me see the map," Zach answered, "I can show you." Once he had the map open and a flashlight shining on it, he pointed to a place called *Boulder Ridge*.

The Chief scrubbed his face over his eight-day scruff. "That's a difficult place to reach and there is no way we'll be able to reach it; not tonight. Even during the day, it's a hard trek because of the ridge that overhangs the rock, sunlight doesn't reach it well."

Zach's face was red with rising anger, "You mean to tell me that, even if that is the plane and there are people who need help, they're stuck down there in the freezing cold for another night or more?!?"

The chief dealt with distraught family members on a daily basis, so more than knew how and when to hold his tongue. "Mr. Blaze, I know you're incredibly concerned about your fiancé, but I cannot, in good conscience put more people at risk to go down there tonight. Trust me, at first light, we will send men that rock climb down there because they will more than likely have to scale the ridge to reach the spot where you're talking about."

"I'm sorry, Chief." Zach began to weep. He hadn't shed a tear, except in the night when he was not sleeping. All he could think about was his beautiful, stubborn, tenacious Roxie having to withstand elements she'd never been in. He hoped and prayed she was alive and that she was not alone.

Epilogue

Roxanne split her eyes open. She'd been pinned under the airplane for so long, she could only feel her arms and hands a little until it grew colder at night, and then those limbs were numb. At least she could move them occasionally. Her legs were a different story. Roxie couldn't feel them at all and it frightened her. She was vaguely aware of the two others who kept her as warm as they could, but she was in and out of it so much she couldn't make heads or tails of the situation. Poor Roxanne did not know their names, but listening to them talk about their lives, when she *was* lucid brought comfort to her somehow. At least, they were all together. Her last thought before she passed out again, was: *What happened to the other people who had been on the flight with them?*

"Well, she's out again," Joshua announced with a shaky voice. He had a broken leg and a pretty nasty cut on his own forehead, but he was okay for the most part.

Vivienne was in more pain having broken her right arm in what looked like four different places, one area even had the bone sticking out. She'd also gotten a concussion but knew enough about medicine to keep them all from going to sleep, where possible. About the fourth day, for they had been keeping track by scratching marks on the side of the wreckage, Vivienne figured she was safe to sleep. She'd had no memory loss; who could forget that frightful plane crash anyhow?

"Yes. I'm afraid she may die before we get rescued," Vivienne voiced, quavering concern drenched through her words.

"We don't even know her name," Joshua added in defeat.

"Today is the first day she's been conscious for more than a few minutes at a time and made any sense at all. She doesn't speak loudly, but I asked the poor girl her name and she told me we could call her Roxie. Before now, all she muttered was, "Where's Zach?" Whoever that is." They kept talking and stayed huddled together for warmth, passing through time as it slowly passed.

>> >> >> >>

Zach hadn't slept at all the night before. He insisted he and Robert be at the mobile station at first light, as that's when the chief said they would begin the last search. This being the last one, Zach could not help but wonder if they would find his beloved before it was too late. It was possibly already too late. *No.* He could not let his mind go there.

As if reading the young man's thoughts, Robert disclosed, "I know what you're thinking, Zach (he had gotten used to calling him by his official name, like Roxanne, because it made him feel closer to him) and we cannot go there. If she were dead, I would hope we would feel it or that she would have been thrown from the plane like some of the others, which she was not."

"I know. It's just getting harder and harder to imagine her out here in the wilderness, possibly hurt and alone."

"We can only hope she is not out there alone," Robert replied with confidence, "That's one of the only things that have gotten me through this whole ordeal. We have not been called and told that she is deceased, so we can hang on to the fact that she isn't. Does that make sense?"

They reached the station just as the chief and a bunch of volunteers showed up. The chief worked quickly to organize everyone they would need to go to *Boulder Ridge*. "Robert, you and Zach and the same men who went yesterday, take the helicopter up because if we find any survivors, that will be the only way to get them out. They will have to be airlifted."

"Okay, chief." The men who were experienced in climbing Boulder Ridge were assembled and ready to go through the forest to try to reach those who might still be alive. Zach and Robert, and the two men; one being a medic and the other proficient in CPR, got into the helicopter and went up into the sky. It took them several hours to get to the spot where they thought the plane had gone down. Once they reached the desired area, they waited to see if there was any movement.

One of the volunteers chimed in over the the intercom of the helicopter, "Is there anyone here? Is there anyone alive?"

At first there was no response or movement. Just when they decided to try for a third time, the crewman heard a muffled reply, "We're here; over here!"

Due to the thick brush and trees, it was difficult to tell where the weak voices were coming from. They had yet to find any part of the debris, and had not gone out to look over the bluff. They feared that that might be where the voices were coming from, and if that's the case, getting to them would be dangerous. On a walkie-talkie which was used to communicate with the station as well as the helicopter, they heard, "We hear survivors. We do not know exactly where they are. We will keep looking until we find where the sounds are coming from." The climbers knew they'd been dropped over Boulder Ridge, but they didn't know exactly which part of the cliff they were on.

"Keep us posted," the chief reiterated. "Let us know whether we need to have an ambulance here or whether we need the medical examiner."

"That is a 10-4, Chief. Go ahead and make sure there's an ambulance waiting just in case we have a need for them." The walkie-talkies were three-way so those in the helicopter heard exactly what the chief did.

Zachary could not contain his excitement at the mere thought that his Roxie might be one of the ones yelling for help. He spoke with one of the rock climbers and asked, " Do you have a visual on the survivors yet?"

"Not yet, but I can hear them! We have yet to climb over the boulder to see if they may be on one of the cliffs. Can you see from up there where there might be debris off the cliff closest to us?"

"We can see something that looks like parts of a plane but we can't tell whether there are people down there or not," the helicopter pilot responded over the com.

"It looks like we might have to propel down the boulder, either way," the volunteer said. He had done this many, many times before, but never with the intent on getting people out. He had always been aware he might have to do that someday, and he hoped that today would be a good day for everyone involved with the search.

The other volunteer rock climber was less eager to scale the cliff because he had not had much practice with repelling as the other guy, but he was determined not to let the survivors die, not on his watch. "Are you ready? the first rock climber asked.

"As ready as I'll ever be. I don't have much experience in repelling a cliff like this one so I hope we can work together and bring some people some happiness."

"Don't worry. we've got this! What is your name, by the way, in case we get out of touch?"

"My name is Henry. What's yours?" Henry asked.

"Oh, mine is Jeremiah but you can call me Jerry. I have a feeling by the end of this we will have become good friends. It's kind of weird that we have been together for nearly ten days and we just now learned each other's names. Guess that comes with the territory."

Henry just nodded at that response. They already knew Zachary and Robert because of Robert's money; they were able to do things and get equipment that they would not otherwise have been able to acquire. They knew the medic was a Phlebotomist by trade and his name was Sergeant Jason Kurt from the United States National Guard Reserves; he lived in the area, and Matt Jenkins who volunteered at the hospital in Denver; the same place the Sergeant had practicing rights in.

"Ready, Henry? We need to make certain one of us is up here and the other one propels down so that if something happens, there's a way to get help. Since I have plenty of experience on this cliff, I'll propel down so that you will be able to throw me the rope or whatever I need depending on what I find."

To say that Henry was relieved was an understatement. He was more than happy to allow Jeremiah to go down and check the place out. It took them twenty minutes just to propel down to the first cliffhanger. There was nothing there but a few pieces of the plane. Jerry was good at this stuff but even he was not looking forward to what he might find. He could only have faith that those who had survived, used whatever was in the remnants of the airplane to stay alive. That would be the only reason they were still able to call out, and, for that, he was grateful.

"How are things going?" Robert questioned from the helicopter. They were only able to see what looked like dots as they watched Jeremiah stealthily handle the face of the mountain. They all watched in angst as he reached the second cliff. Luckily for him, the second cliff stuck out more, giving him room to analyze the situation.

"I'm on the second cliff. There are what looks to be two females and a male down here. Give me a moment to speak with them and assess their injuries."

At the mere mention of two females, Zach's spirits rose. "Robert, do you think that could be her?" He'd begun calling his fiancé's father by his first name after spending the last several days with him. They had gotten to know each other quite well during this harrowing time.

"It could be." Robert could not help but feel Zach's excitement. He might have some good news to tell his wife and the Blaze family when he called to report later. As things currently were, he did not have good news, but maybe…just maybe…

The next installment of
the From Brat to Bronco Series:

FROM BRONCO TO BRIDE

From Bronco to Bride

Book Three

HUNTER MARSHALL

FROM BRONCO TO BRAT

Copyright © 2021

From Bride to Bronco

HUNTER MARSHALL

Huntermarshall78@gmail.com

All rights reserved. Except as permitted under the U.S. Copyright Act of 2011, no part of this publication may be reproduced, distributed, or transmitted in any form or by any means, or stored in a database or retrieval system, without the prior written permission of the publisher except in the case of brief quotations embodied in critical articles and reviews.

The characters and events portrayed in this book are fictitious. Any similarity to real persons, living or dead,
is coincidental and not intended by the author.

For more information visit our Facebook Fan Page:
https://www.facebook.com/huntermarshall2015

Cover Design by Jessica Ozment

Formatting by Jessica Ozment

CONNECT WITH
AUTHOR HUNTER MARSHALL

Facebook Fan Page:

https://www.facebook.com/huntermarshall2015

Acknowledgments

I could not have been happier when asked by a reviewer who'd read From Brat to Bronco what was going to happen with Roxie and Zach. They know they are engaged, but does it work out, does something awful happen? So, I decided to make this a trilogy. This is the second book. I do not know who that reader is, but I would like to thank them because I have never written a series before and this makes me stretch farther as an author.

Thank you so much Jessica Tahbonemah for not only creating fantastic covers, as usual but taking my story and making it the greatest story it could be. Thank you for being there whenever I need a listening ear or to rant and rave with. You are truly one of my best friends,

I'd like my best friend to know how much his reading and soaking up my words; begging me to write more so he has more to read has meant to me. He believes that I have several stories to tell and helps me hash out different scenes as I'm working. You are truly one of the best men I know!

My family! Mom and dad especially for getting excited for me whenever I reach a new milestone or publish a new book. They realize this is not just a hobby for me. They know that it's vital to my wellbeing to write. Thank you, momma, for being there to title my books and bounce ideas around with. You will never know how much I appreciate everything you do for me. I have the greatest parents, ya'll! Thanks to my kids for allowing me the time to write. And, for at least acknowledging when I get ecstatic about where I'm at in a story. I have the best kids on the planet. Okay. I might be a tiny bit biased.

Last, but definitely not least, thank you to my readers and fans who take a chance on my work every time they decide to read any of my books. You give me a reason to keep writing. I love hearing what y'all think. You're awesome!

**Hunter Marshall,
2021**

Prologue

"More news coming at you from CNN, your favorite national news source," the reporter recited. *"As of now, it's been nine days since the crash of flight 265 from Los Angeles, which was supposed to have a layover in Denver, but instead, needed to make an emergency landing. The passengers and crew crash landed somewhere within the Rocky Mountain region and, our sources say of the one hundred and fifty passengers, only three are unaccounted for as is the wreckage. We will keep you posted as more information rolls in."*

As Zach and Robert, along with the medic and two other volunteers waited to hear news from Jeremiah about whether anyone was alive on the second cliff or not, Zach did something he hadn't done since he was a child. He began biting his thumbnail. Robert saw how distraught Zach was and patted him on the shoulder, trying to do his best to comfort the young man. He completely understood his behavior, it was his daughter who had gone missing that made him this way.

"When will we hear any news?" Zach shuttered. "I don't know how much more of this waiting I can take. The love of my life is out there, and we have no idea whether she's alive or not."

"Son, I have told you before and I will tell you again, no news could be good news. We will hear something as soon as the rock climbers have news for us. They're doing the best they can under dire circumstances. With the temperatures being as low as they are, we need to be grateful that Jerry is down on a second cliff where the debris actually is."

Just then, Jerry came over the walkie talkie, interrupting their conversation. "I 've found two people alive so far." As the voice cracked over the walkie, everyone who hadn't gone with Jerry cheered at the mention of more survivors. "Vivienne has a broken arm in four places and most likely a concussion, but she is awake and alert. Then, there's Joshua…who has a nasty gash on his forehead. He's going to need to be stitched up so we can treat him for his broken leg. They both seem to be holding their own, under the circumstances."

"That's good to hear," Sergeant Jason Kurt replied.

Zach couldn't stay silent any longer, so he stole the silence following the Sgt.'s comment, "What about the third person? Have you found them yet?"

"We need to get Joshua and Vivienne out of here. Jason, can you repel down and take them up one by one once we get their injuries assessed? We've got to secure their broken bones with splints. I've begun that process, but I sure could use a hand."

"Where is Henry?" Jason asked Jeremiah.
"We thought it best he stayed up top since we had no idea what we were facing." In reality Jerry was afraid Henry couldn't make the distance. In times like that, showing fear was the worst thing a person could do, and Henry was definitely scared.

"Sounds like a plan." Jason turned to Zach who was falling to pieces having not heard Roxie's name as being one of the survivors. "Don't worry, we'll let you know if your girl is down there once we get the other two secured."

"Wait? That means if she's down there, we have to leave her here alone?" The thought of her being scared and alone made Zach break out into a cold sweat.

"No," Jason calmly explained, "Jerry will continue to search through the debris. Unfortunately, all of this is a slow process, and we can only take one injured person at a time but if your fiancé is down there, he'll find her."

Zachary sighed, resigning himself to the fact that he would have to wait even longer than he already had until he knew something about Roxie's whereabouts. It took Jason less than a minute to be ready to repel down to the cliff where the injured passengers were.

Once down there, Jason assessed Vivienne first because her injuries were more severe. It took a lot to get her arm securely splinted so that he could propel up to the helicopter with her and get her to the ambulance, which would transport her to Estes Park Hospital. It was the closest hospital in the area.

It took nearly an hour to repel and secure Vivienne, who was on the way to the hospital. Jason placed a call, alerting EPH that there would be at least one more critically injured person coming in. As soon as that was relayed, he got back in the chopper to get to Joshua, praying the entire time they would find Roxanne McCain. If she was still alive, it would be a slim chance. Joshua and Vivienne showed signs of moderate hypothermia but were still lucid enough to understand simple commands.

As time slipped away, Zach's patience was wearing excessively thin—it had been nine days—NINE DAYS—since he had talked to Roxie. That was a long time in his book because they could not even stand living a couple hours apart and wanted to marry as soon as it was feasible for everyone; and he wondered if he did get the chance to speak with her again, whether she would know him or remember anything.

While the chopper was taking Vivienne to the ambulance, which would transport her to the hospital where she would undergo surgery on her arm, Jerry splinted Joshua, softly talking to him as he did. "Joshua, is there anyone else here?" He figured if he could get an answer, he would know where to look for the third person who he hoped, for Zach and Robert's sakes, was Roxanne.

"Yes," Joshua croaked. Both he and Vivienne were severely dehydrated and although Joshua tried guzzling water when it was given to him, Jerry slowed him down knowing it could make him sick if he drank too much, too fast. "She's over…there…" he needed to take several breaths to continue, "under…the airplane. She's trapped...and we… couldn't...get her...out."

"That's okay, Joshua. Thank you for the information. It's a great help." Just then they heard the whirring of the helicopter blades, "Looks like they're here for you, my friend."

It was a little easier getting Joshua secured and into the helicopter but still took a while. Before Jason left with Joshua. Jerry relayed what Joshua had told him about the other survivor. "I'm going to need some help down here I'm afraid. I don't know her condition or even if she is alive. Joshua did say that she drifted in and out of consciousness, and they gave her sips of water from the little bit they had left whenever she would wake up. But she has not stirred in two days; neither he nor Vivienne could tell whether she has been breathing or not."

"I'll get some help, but I think it best if neither Zach nor Robert come back this time. You know, just in case." Jason had seen many gruesome and heartbreaking scenarios in his line of work as an army medic, and he knew when to allow family in on search parties and when not to.

Jason didn't say anything to Zach or Robert about staying behind until they were ready to go back up for the other person; hopefully, alive. "Zach...Robert, I don't think it's a good idea for the two of you to come for the third person. Now, we know from the other survivors that it is indeed a female. We know she is severely injured, but we do not know whether she is alive. I need the two of you to stay here while I, and a couple of other men, go help Jerry get her out."

Zach wanted so badly to punch Jason in the mouth. *How can he tell me I can't go help get my fiancé out?*

Robert must have sensed his frustration because he stilled the young man with just a hand on his arm. Then he said, "Zach, maybe he's right. We do not have any ideas about how much debris is down there and by Jason's own account, that ledge is not large enough for a lot of people. If they have to sift through more of the wreckage, we would just be in the way."

That didn't make Zach feel any better, but he finally conceded. He jerked his arm away from Robert, raked his hands through his already mussed-up hair, and stormed off. He knew it was childish, but he couldn't help himself. He was angry, sad, depressed and anxious. *That must be her, and she must be okay! Heavenly Father, please let that be her and please let her be alive!* "Fine," Zach came back after he calmed some, "Take whoever you need to, but keep us alerted about what you find," he gulped, trying to swallow the lump in his throat...please?" He was pleading by that point.

"Son, you have my word...once we know anything...we'll let you know. Just so you are aware, she may not have identification on her so we might not have anything to tell you until we figure out who she is."

"I understand and thank you. I appreciate anything you can do." Being left behind gave Zachary too much time to think. He had to stay busy so, because he knew how to break bad news, gently, as he had done more than once in the vet clinic, he asked the chief if he could assist in calling families of the other victims that they hadn't contacted yet. They had a difficult time identifying some and it had been a hard road, but the only passenger they had not found yet was Roxanne and the chief knew that Zach *needed* something to keep him busy.

"Zachary, if you would like to help make calls, that would be fine. We still have several to call," the chief said, "I know you need something to do."

Zach was in the zone, making one heartbreaking call after another. He hated doing it, but there wasn't much else he could do. So, he painstakingly called each number and broke the news to families he did not know but felt for anyway. In a way, he was in the same position except Roxanne's whereabouts were still unknown. Until he was told otherwise, he kept hoping that the last member was her. The woman he went from hating to loving intensely in a matter of months.

Finally, the team came through. "We need a life flight stat," Jason said to the chief called in from his walkie-talkie. "Oh, and will you tell our boy Zach that we got his girl? She's critical, but still alive."

Zach breathed a massive sigh of relief. *How critical is she? Can she still die?* He tried to push those frantic thoughts aside and be grateful they found her, and of all things, found her alive! "Can I go with her to the hospital? Zach begged once the chopper returned.

Robert, knowing she was his daughter, but also knowing she belonged with this young man, conceded, telling Zach he would meet them at the hospital.

Chapter 1

It did not take long for the Life Flight helicopter to arrive or for them to get Roxie to the hospital. She'd been left to the elements for ten long days, and Zach could barely tell it was her. The ring on her left hand let him know it but—she was unconscious, which worried him. The doctors and nurses who were on the flight; Sergeant Jason Kurt included, assured him she was as stable as they could get her without the use of the hospital's facilities.

Before Robert made the twenty-one-minute trip to Estes Park Hospital, he called Gerald, Clara, and Belinda who he was certain were waiting by the phone for any news. Throughout the ordeal he had kept them in the loop as much as he could, "We've found her," he practically shouted into the phone with excitement. He could not hold back the tears he hadn't shed yet, being strong for both Zach, and his wife "They life-flighted her to the closest hospital which is Estes Park. Zachary rode with her in the ambulance and I'm heading there now. Once we hear the extent of her injuries, I'll let you all know." Then he asked to speak to Gerald, "Can you find the best trauma hospital in Tennessee?"

"Sure, but why? Wouldn't they have better hospitals in California?"

"It would, but she needs to be close to home and Los Angeles is no longer that for her. She will not be able to be transported for a while yet, so when I call you back with news, I'll send the jet for all of you."

"You don't need to do that. We can fly coach."

"Nonsense. I own the plane. There's no need for you to do that."

Gerald decided he wouldn't argue with the unyielding generosity of the man who had taken his son and helped search for Roxie, who he had come to love as one of his own. It suddenly hit him that he hadn't remembered to call Stevie! She won't stand around waiting like the rest of them to hear any news, instead, she worked overtime at her job at Tennova Healthcare-Cleveland as the head manager of Housekeeping.

"Thank you," Gerald replied to Robert's statement, "That is kind of you." After a pause he continued, "I need to go so I can call Stevie and let her know Roxie has been found."

"Alright. I'll let you know when I know something different. By the way, would you tell my wife I love her?"

"Certainly." The two fathers hung up with each other. If there was one thing Robert had learned from this whole ordeal with his daughter and spending one-on-one time with Zachary, was that family was the most important thing in a person's life. It certainly wasn't money or prestige. As he drove around, he vowed to give more to those in need. It wasn't like he didn't have the money to spare. He also promised to spend more time enjoying life and his family; work was not as vital as he and Belinda had believed all these years.

"Where is she?" Robert questioned Zach once he arrived at the hospital.

"They're trying to bring her temperature up due to the hyperthermia she may have suffered. In the chopper, Jason put her under aluminum blankets, but it hasn't helped so far. She hasn't woken up either, and her legs and torso were crushed under the plane. They didn't tell you this once they had her?"

Robert felt tears burn his eyes. His baby girl was hurt and hurt badly. "They do not know if she will survive, do they?"

Zach didn't want to acknowledge what he said, but that's exactly what the doctors and nurses told him. "The doctor said it's a possibility. If they can't raise her temperature and get her into surgery to gauge what kind of damage was caused by being trapped for almost ten days, she won't," Zach sobbed into his hands tears that felt like heavy anvils. That was the first time he let himself feel the emotions of maybe having to let go of Roxie for good. It wasn't just crying, though. It was the lip sucking; hyperventilating kind of ugly cry men rarely do. Once he started, he couldn't seem to stop himself.

Several painstaking hours later, the doctor came to speak with them. Robert had not called the others yet, because he wanted to know what they were up against before delivering the devastating news.

"Hello, I'm Dr. Kendall. Roxanne is in stable condition right now, but the next forty-eight hours are critical. She's breathing on her own, but her legs were severely damaged, she suffered quite a bit of frostbite. The good news is that we managed to stop the internal bleeding, for now. Due to the pain she experiences when awake, she was put into a medically induced coma to let her body heal. If there are any other family members who are not here, you might want to get them here, just in case. There is hope, but we need to prepare the family for this going south at any moment. We will do all we can, take solace in that fact."

Robert and Zach sat together, hugging and crying. Zach had never wanted to sit in his mama's lap more than he did at that moment, except maybe when his brother died. He had to call them; get them there to be with him. And, her mom, what would she feel after having lost one baby already? It was no secret Belinda did not like Zachary, but he still felt horrible for her. When he pulled himself together enough, he called his parents while Robert phoned Belinda and regurgitated what the surgeon had told them. They would be on the jet once it arrived at the Cleveland Airport. That gave them a few hours to pack.

Zach knew once he saw his parents, he would let it all out—the anguish, despair, the unknown. But, at that moment, he needed to see his girl. Even if she could not hear him, he needed to let her know he was there for whatever came next. He needed that contact. Zach went in search of the doctor who was taking her case and was surprised to learn it was none other than Sergeant Jason Kurt. "Hello, Sergeant," Zach shook his hand, "I hear you're Roxie's doctor."

"Indeed, I am. I requested her case because she's kind of near and dear to my heart. I look in on Vivienne and Joshua, but the doctors who are assisting their recovery are doing a great job. They both, like Roxie, suffered severe hypothermia and had to have surgery to repair their damage, but it looks as if they will both make a full recovery."

"That's great news! I bet their families were happy to hear that," Zach did his best to sound upbeat, but he just was not feeling it. He knew that, at some point, he would visit the other two survivors. Right now, though, seeing Roxie was utmost on his mind. "Can I see Roxie yet? he blurted out.

"You know she's in a medically induced coma, right?"

"Yes, the surgeon told us. I don't know if she can hear me, but I must see her. I want to talk to her. They do say sometimes those in comas can hear the conversation."

"That is true. We believe that even in the induced state, having loved ones talk with them, touch them, things of that nature can speed up their recovery. Roxanne had much more extensive damage and hypothermia, so right now, we have no idea whether she suffered brain damage."

"We'll deal with that when we know. I just need to see her," Zachary was urgent.
"Okay, but she's in the ICU until we feel it is safe to wake her up. We don't want to cause more
trauma to her body than she has already endured. You may go see her, but for now, let's keep it at ten-minute intervals, and only one person in her room at a time."

Zach wasn't aware Robert had joined them until he saw the two men shake hands. "So, you're the doctor on my daughter's case?"

"As I told Zach, I requested her case. The two of you have been troopers this whole time and I feel like we've gotten to know each other quite well."
"That is true, my friend. That is true." Robert clapped him on the shoulder. Robert was not a hugging kind of person, but he wanted to let

the other man know he was grateful for all that he did during the search, and for what he would do in the coming weeks and months. Robert was not naive enough to think that they would be moving Roxanne anytime soon. Along with not knowing whether she would walk again, no one knew if she suffered any brain damage.

"Jason, can I go see her now?" Zach was chomping at the bit.

"Yes, let's take you to your fiancé." He felt for the poor kid, having been through leaving his own girlfriend, who was now his wife, many times when deployed. Thankfully, he was stateside for a while.

Zach entered the room, but he was not prepared for what he saw. Roxanne had tubes and wires going into her every which way. Her face was so bruised and swollen it showed more purple than her skin color. She was in what looked like a cast, but he could only see her legs as the rest of her body was covered by a thermal blanket they kept warm at all times. He pulled a chair next to the bed and found her hand under the blanket. The tears fell at that moment. "Hey, Darlin,' It's me. You gave us quite a scare, but to be honest, I'm still afraid. The extent of your injuries is unknown until they wake you up, but Sergeant Jason Kurt, who is an army medic, well he's your doctor. After spending time with him, looking for you and all, I think he has your best interest at heart. Darlin,' I wish I could look into your beautiful chocolate brown eyes. I wish you could respond. I miss our usual back and forth conversations, but right now, the best I can hope for is that you hear me. Can you hear me, doll?" His ten minutes went by too fast and then it was Robert's turn.

While Robert was visiting Roxie, Zach called his family, and this time his mom answered, "Hey, momma," he did not want to cry anymore. It was like that was all he did when he was talking to Roxie, but hearing his mom's voice, he could not help it. Through lip-sucking sobs, he croaked, "She looks...dead, mom. What if she doesn't wake up? What am I going to do?"

As she did many times before, Clara softly replied, "Son, you have to have faith and keep praying that all will be well. This is in God's hands now, and nothing we can do will ever change the outcome. Be there for her and with her even during this medically induced coma. She needs you more than ever right now. We will be there as soon as we can, so you and Robert aren't facing this alone. We are just waiting for their jet to arrive as we're at the airport at the current moment."

After speaking with his mom, Zach ambled up to the gift shop to find something he might brighten up Roxanne's room with, but before he did that, he found Jason and asked if it was okay seeing as Jason was her healthcare provider. He found a small bear which looked like something Roxie would enjoy when she woke up. He wished he could get some flowers and balloons, but because she was in the ICU, he couldn't go all out like he wanted. To pass the time while he waited, he bought a book to read, but it barely held his interest.

When Robert finally came out of Roxie's room, he asked Zach if he was hungry. Zach wasn't but knew he had to keep his strength up for Roxie's sake. They decided they each needed a change of scenery, so after making certain Jason had both of their cell phone numbers in case there were any changes, they took a trip up to The Mountain Cafe in Estes Park because they didn't want to be far from Roxie should there be new developments. Mountain Cafe reminded Zach a little of the coffee shop in Tennessee where he and Roxie first met, and where he also asked her on their first date. He didn't think that he was all that hungry, but he ordered a bacon, lettuce, and tomato sandwich with a side tomato soup. He wasn't particularly fond of their tomato soup, but that was one of Roxie's favorites. Robert ordered a chicken-bacon-Ranch salad because he knew, he too, needed to keep his strength up if he was going to be able to help Belinda when she got there to cope with what was going on with their daughter.

As they ate, they discussed everything from the upcoming wedding, and how that would turn out should she be paralyzed, and how they'd deal with Zach's reaction, should she have extensive brain damage to the point where she would need round-the-clock care for the rest of her life. When they were done eating, they went back to the hospital to wait until the others arrived from Tennessee. During that dreaded waiting period, Zachary begged and pleaded with Jason to let him sit with Roxie. He didn't like the idea of her being alone and afraid. He firmly believed not only could she hear them, but she could feel emotions such as fear, not knowing where she was or why. Jason did his best to assure Zachary she felt no pain nor any other emotion while in a coma. That did little to comfort Zach, so Jason allowed him to sit with her until it was time to go pick up his parents and Roxanne's mother, Belinda. The time seemed to go by too fast as Zach reminded Roxie of all the things they had done in their year and a half together. His hope was that she would hear him.

Jason came in too soon to tell him that his parents and his soon-to-be mother-in-law had arrived safely at the Denver Airport and they were ready to be picked up. Zach was correct in knowing he would break down as soon as he saw his mom.

Clara understood how he was doing but asked him how it was going anyway. His response was exactly what she thought it would be; he grabbed onto his mother for dear life and didn't want to let go. "Son, it'll be okay. Whatever lies in store for us and for Roxanne is in God's hands, just as it has been the entire time."

"But Mom, I can't do this. I can't keep wondering if I'm watching and waiting to see whether she will even wake up from the coma or if I'm watching her die slowly. All I can do is sit by her and talk to her, but I don't know if it's doing any good."

Belinda joined the conversation at that point and told Zachary her daughter would be fine because she could not believe that God would take both of her daughters from her. Once everyone's baggage was claimed, it was decided that Belinda needed to go see her daughter. They would wait until later to find a motel; not that any of them would want to stay away from the hospital for extended periods of time anyway. They would have to decide that when the time came, but all of them were certain that someone would be always at the hospital. They would spell each other off since none of them had gotten much sleep over the last ten days.

When they arrived at the hospital, Belinda demanded to speak with the doctor in charge of her daughter's case. When Jason met her, he did not see the hard-nosed woman she portrayed herself as, but rather a grieving mother. He explained to everyone the dire circumstances Roxanne was in and why they had placed her in the medically- induced coma. "Can I see her?" Belinda asked, quietly. It was disconcerting for Zach to hear Belinda sound so frail, for she wasn't the fragile one in the bunch. He was seeing a different side of her and in a way, it frightened him.

"Yes. You can go see her, "Jason wasn't cold to her plight. He took her to Roxanne's room, where he patted her on the shoulder and said, "We are only allowing ten minutes at a time with visitors until we know more about how she is doing. I am so sorry we're having to meet under such difficult circumstances."

Belinda sat by her daughter. She spoke softly to her, praying that Roxanne could hear her. She had never apologized to Roxanne for the way she had held her at arm's length, leaving her with nannies all the time and working when she could have been home with her. She explained about how she was scared to take care of Roxanne, especially when she was smaller for fear she might do something to hurt her. Belinda knew she might have to explain all of that again since there was no guarantee Roxanne could hear any of it, but it felt good to get it out anyway. The ten minutes that were allowed went by far too quickly for Belinda. She had never felt the motherly bond to her daughter more than she did then. She pondered over the many conversations she had with Zach's mother, Clara, during her stay in their home. They spoke about Amelia and the loss of Clara and Gerald's middle child, Bryce, in a four-wheeling accident the year before. They talked about the grieving process and how there was no timetable or even an order to the five stages. Belinda felt a lot better because she had decided she was flawed all these years, although she knew what to tell her clients, believing it of herself was more difficult.

Chapter 2

The day they released both Vivienne and Joshua was a joyous occasion, especially for their families. Zach was happy for them, but at the same time, sad that Roxie was still in the medically induced coma that would allow her body to heal and giving her no sense of pain. There was a little going away party for them since they were leaving only a few days apart from each other. All told, they spent two weeks in the hospital recovering from their own ordeals.

    The next several weeks were long and heart-wrenching for the Blaze and McCain families. Gerald could not stay the whole time because he had furry patients who depended on him. Zach should have been starting his sophomore year at the University of Tennessee-Chattanooga but deferred with the indefinite possibility of Roxanne being hospitalized and he wanted to be there every second. Neither Robert nor Belinda had to rush back to California for patients. Luckily, their colleague and friend, Brendon Harris, had been able to fit the needy clients into his own schedule, freeing up time for them to remain in Colorado with their daughter. Beyond measure, they hoped Dr. Jason Kurt would wake her up; her body was slowly healing, but each day, that was still indefinite. They still did not know whether she had brain damage from the lack of oxygen or whether she would ever walk again due to the severity of her legs being crushed under the plane. Jason kept them appraised of all changes, even if it was only a slight change in her blood pressure. Zachary spent most of his time in her room, although she was still in the ICU, by the sixth week, he was able to sit by her bed daily if he wanted. Belinda and Robert took their turns as they desired, but both thought it vital for Zachary to be there. They perceived that if Roxanne could hear speaking, she was more likely to be most relaxed with the sound of his voice. The times that they had spent with him and his parents had changed their minds quickly about him. He was the man in her world now, where her daddy should have been all those years ago and was not. The doctors had encouraged them to spell each other off so they could get adequate rest, but Zachary refused to leave and his mom, Clara had to pull him away from the room a time or two. She used the logic that Roxie's parents needed quality time with her as well.

At the end of the sixth week, Jason came to them with great news. It was time to wake her up to see where she was mentally and physically. Zachary, Robert, Belinda, and Clara were excited to see what would happen, but at the same time, apprehensive as to what they might find. As Jason woke her slowly, no one was allowed in the room until he read her reactions. "Roxanne, do you know what happened to you?"

Roxanne awoke groggily as if she had been in a dream, and she did not know where she was or who the man was who was talking to her. The only thing she assumed was that he was a doctor due to the white lab coat he wore and the name tag. She vaguely remembered being trapped under the airplane and having two other passengers talking to her and taking care of her as best as they could. She also remembered the voice of the man talking to her now. Her first question was, "Where am I and how did I get here?"

"Do you remember being in an airplane?" Jason question not expecting too much for an answer right off.

Roxanne was more than a bit frightened as she recalled what happened that fateful day for the doctor. Her next question after that was, "What day is it?"

"It is November 24th," Jason replied. "You've been in a medically induced coma for the past six weeks because of the injuries you sustained in the crash and from when you were trapped so you could heal without feeling a lot of pain. Your family and your fiancé have been here day in and day out the entire time waiting and talking with you. Can you recall anything that was said to you during the last six weeks?"

"I honestly thought it was all a dream. I could vaguely hear voices…but couldn't place any of them. Is Zach here right now?"

"He is, as are your parents and your mother-in-law...but I need to ask you a few more questions first."

"Okay."

It didn't seem Roxanne had suffered any brain damage, during her cold days and nights nor was her memory screwed up by any serious means. "I know these are standard questions and you know the answers, but I must ask them anyway. What's your name?"

"I understand, Doc. My name is Roxanne 'Roxie' McCain."

"What's your date of birth?"

"August 21, 1999."

"Very good."

"What's the last thing you remember?"

Roxie didn't skip a beat. "Being trapped under that plane after it crashed with two other people. Going in and out of consciousness when they would give me sips of water. But that's about it."

"That's excellent considering how long you were there. Do you recall being picked up by life flight?"

"No, the next thing I remembered is being here, right now in this moment. Can I see my fiancé, please?"

"In just a few minutes. I have some things to check first and then I will let him in." Jason checked her vitals. Her blood pressure and her heart rate were normal as was her oxygen saturation. He pressed gently on her abdomen and asked if she felt any pain there.

"No."

"That's great!" Then, he moved to her feet, which was the biggest concern for the doctors; whether she would be paraplegic due to her crushed legs or not. They hoped the surgery would have helped but with the extensive damage, he was afraid she'd be wheelchair-bound. He ran a pen over the bottom of her feet. "Can you feel that?"

Roxanne was extremely scared, "No. Why can't I feel my legs? I'm not going to be paralyzed, am I?" She started to cry at the prospect. *What if I can't walk down the aisle at my own wedding? What will Zach think? Will he be turned off by my being crippled?* A million questioned ran through her mind.

"That's a real possibility because of the crushing your legs took. The surgeon did the best he could to repair the damage, but there's still no way to tell until we work with you in physical therapy."

Roxanne began to cry, "I need to see Zach, NOW!" The fear could be heard under her anger as tears streamed down her face.

A few moments later Zach came into the room; he couldn't stop the flow of tears when he saw that his Roxie was awake and talking. He gently gave her a hug and lightly kissed her. Her lips were badly chapped but that was to be expected. He had tried to keep them moistened whenever he was with her so that they wouldn't get worse, but that didn't seem to do much. He took the Chapstick from his pocket and generously applied some to her lips. She was crying and Zach thought he knew why. "Are you in any pain?"

"Yes, but that's not what worries me. Dr. Kurt said that I may be paralyzed from the waist down because of the plane crash. That does not change how you feel about me, does it?" she was serious as the words left her lips.

"How could you even think that? Whether you're wheelchair-bound for the rest of your life or finally able to walk, I'll love you no matter what." He was a bit stern with her because he wanted her to know he meant every word.

Roxie began to feel the pain that Zach had mentioned, mostly in her abdominal area where the surgeon had to go in and stop the internal bleeding. This left her with a long incision that, even six weeks after surgery felt like someone ripped her guts out. "Can you call the nurse and tell her I need something for the pain in my stomach?"

"See this button right here?" Zach motioned to the remote-control looking thing at the side of her bed, "All you have to do is push it."

Roxanne tried reaching over to do just that, but her body was stiff from weeks of no movement. She was sure a lot of what she felt was internal bruising from being under the plane for nearly two weeks.

Zach saw her struggle and it made him sad to know that his fiancé had an extremely long road ahead of her. But he also knew she was stronger than she knew. "Let me go find Dr. Kurt and see what his recommendation is."

Roxie was in so much pain, it was all she could do to nod. Zach hated seeing the tears rolling down her cheeks as she tried to be brave. He knew she was doing her best to withstand the pain. This was the same girl who would not take so much as an Aspirin for a headache unless it was so bad that she was in tears. He hugged her gingerly and went to find Jason. While he was gone, and because she was awake, the family was allowed to go in together, so, this was the first time she had seen her parents' faces since she left from her visit almost two months ago. "Hi, sweetheart," Robert kept swallowing to keep the tears back.

"Hi, daddy. Hello, mother," she was tired and hoped that their visit was short, and that her mother would not be rude or curt.

To her utter astonishment, her mother came over, seizing her up for a huge bear hug. She was not one to show any kind of emotion, but there was no mistaking the tears glistening in Belinda's eyes, "I am so glad to see you're awake! When they could not find you and we had no idea whether you were among the dead or the three missing, it took me back to when we lost your sister. I realized after talking to Clara, a lot, about grief and loss that I have not been the best mother to you; that you were raised by nannies because I thought I was the reason Amelia died and was afraid I would cause harm to you…so, I did the only thing I knew how to do. I worked. The one thing I knew how to do and do well. I'm so sorry for distancing myself from you. The older you got, the easier it was to ignore you and the things going on in your life, but since this ordeal, I have vowed that will change. Even my feelings towards Zachary and Tennessee have changed. Getting to know his parents has been very good for me. I have learned that money is not as important as I made it out to be, and that family is everything."

"Mom," Roxanne had longed to call her that instead of 'mother,' but she was never allowed to. She wasn't afraid of her mother's repercussions for some reason, "I'm going to be okay."

Roxie seemed fine through all the visitors, even Joshua and Vivienne came to see her on their last day of physical therapy; before they went home. "We honestly thought the plane had crushed you so badly that you would not come out alive, I'm glad to see you're awake." Vivienne hugged her, gave Roxie her phone number and told her that if she needed to talk, she would be there.
Jokingly, Roxanne said," I have two headshrinkers that I call parents. I don't know that I would need another but could always use a friend. I'm grateful for your help during the entire situation as well as coming to see me before you left, and giving me your number. I'll be sure and call you to let you know how I'm doing."

Then, it was Joshua's turn to hug Roxanne. "I'm so glad to know you're alive. I know you have many months of therapy ahead of you, but I've no doubt you're tenacious enough and strong enough to get through it. You're an inspiration to, not only myself, but everyone who has watched your story unfold." Joshua left before she could see the tears streaming down his cheeks. He was not a crier but having been in the accident and surviving with not much more than a broken leg, it made him grateful and aware of how fleeting life could be.

As everyone talked, Jason came in to tell them that Roxanne needed her rest. She had all the visitors that he would allow for the next several hours. It was time for more pain medication and along with that, he gave her a sedative to help her sleep. The only people allowed in the room while she was sleeping was either Zachary or one of her parents. It did not take long for the consensus to be decided that Zach should be the one to sit with her. When everyone left the room to go back to the motel, Roxie let out a frustrated cry. She wanted to scream but her body hurt too badly. She had been holding her anger in while there were people there with her, but she knew Zach wouldn't care whether she became unglued or not.

"What's wrong?" he questioned. Zach thought he knew what caused her to outburst, but he also knew she needed to face whatever demons would come in the months ahead.

"This isn't fair!" Roxanne wiped at her tears ferociously as they streamed down her cheeks. "What if I'm stuck in a wheelchair for the rest of my life? What kind of life would we have if that is the case? Would we be able to have kids? Would we be able to lead a normal life? Would you still love me?"

The last inquiry was the main question running through Roxie's mind but the easiest for Zach to answer so, he said, "*Nothing*, not even a wheelchair would change the way I feel about you. I still want a life with you, no matter what that might be. That won't change, no matter what gets thrown at us from here on out. Do you understand me?" That last part might have sounded a little harsh, but Zach needed Roxie to understand true love did not change to suit the circumstances. True love found a way around them.

She answered with a meek, "Yes," just before the sedative kicked in. Zach sounded stronger than he felt. The adoration he had for this woman showed all over his face, especially in his eyes. As he watched her sleep, he could not help but marvel at the human being she was. Not only had she grown up in a house where money or materialistic things were given in place of hugs and affection, but she had moved far away from everything she had ever known to attend a college that she had not wanted to attend in the first place, worked for the first time in her life, but she survived a plane crash that should by all rights have killed her. As she slept, he let the cleansing tears he had held in for hers and everyone else's sakes wash over his cheeks. Sometimes, when someone needed a good cry, it was easier to do it when no one was watching.

Little did he know, Jason had heard what he told Roxie and watched as the young man let out his own anguish so he could be her hero when she awoke again. That young man had impressed him from the first time they met.

Over the next two weeks, Jason slowly got Roxanne moving around more to help the muscles in her upper body, which were stiff, loosen up.

He gave Zach and Roxie's parents exercises to do with her to strengthen her upper body so she would be able to push her own wheelchair when the time came. One particularly bad day, Roxie threw a tantrum while Belinda was helping with her exercises, "This is getting old, and I want to go home! I hate these exercises! I hate the idea of having to be in a wheelchair! And I hate being in the hospital!"

Belinda had never used a stern tone with her daughter but now seemed like a good time to start, "Young lady, you must be grateful for even being alive. I pray you never know the agony of not only losing one child, but also the unknown of possibly losing another. You're lucky to still be with us and I will not hear any more childish tantrums from you here on out. Do I make myself clear?"

Having never heard her mother speak to her in that way, Roxanne was taken by surprise and the only thing she could say was, "Yes, mom." Without another word, she continued the painstaking exercises she needed to learn, so she could get around. Due to the tantrum Roxanne had with her mother, it was decided between Zach, Robert, Belinda, Clara, and her doctor Jason that there would be no putting up with Roxanne acting childish. Zach wasn't sure whether he had what it took to keep her from feeling sorry for herself, but he knew learning to use a wheelchair was vital for her independence and well-being since no one knew for certain whether she would walk again.

The first time Roxanne used a wheelchair, she hated it. She was bound and determined to walk no matter what it took. That is how badly she despised that chair. Zach pushed her around the hospital because it was too cold to go outside. Robert and Belinda decided Roxanne would be moved to a hospital in Tennessee barring any issues from Dr. Jason. By that time, they had been in Colorado for three and a half months. It was time to go home. Although it was not Robert and Belinda's home, they felt they needed to stay near their daughter until she was better, and they knew more about her physical circumstances.

Dr. Jason Kurt had no problem with her being transported to Erlanger North Hospital in Chattanooga Tennessee. He knew some of the staff and doctors there and was certain she would receive excellent care. He was also associated with a physical therapist who worked there and had no doubt that they would take care of the woman who had quickly become his favorite patient. The day before Roxanne was set to fly by helicopter to her new home for the next few months; Estes Park doctors, nurses, as well as other patients, her parents, her in-laws, and Zach decided she needed a going away party. They resolved not to talk about it where she might hear because they wanted it to be a surprise.

"Are you ready to go?" Zach asked Roxie after they had packed everything up.

"I have never been more ready to see Chattanooga, Tennessee than I am at this moment. I'm kind of scared of the helicopter ride, though."

"You've every reason for that, but nothing is going to happen. It's only a two-hour ride and I will be there with you the whole time." Zach steered her wheelchair away from the elevator that would take them to the helipad. He was aware they must be accompanied by a nurse to enter this area, so he told Roxanne they were going to find a nurse. When they arrived in the cafeteria, Roxanne looked at Zach, puzzled. It had a sign out front that stated it was closed for cleaning. "Zachary Blaze, what are you doing? We cannot go in there. Have you not read the sign?"

Zach's response was a huge smile as he turned on the lights. All of a sudden, there was a loud echo of, "Surprise!"

"What is this? Roxie wondered, "How did I not know about this?" She was extremely curious.

"It was planned by many, many people...in secret," Zach kissed her, "There are so many people whose lives' you have touched by your courage and determination that they all wanted to wish you a farewell."

Since the accident, Roxie found she could cry at the drop of a hat. She hardly ever cried before that; she considered herself too upper crust, but this…Roxie couldn't help herself. As the tears dampened her red-hot cheeks, she smiled through it anyway, touched by the kindness of all those she had gotten to know intimately throughout her stay here. "You guys!" she gushed, "You didn't have to do this!"

"We wanted to know how much we love and care for you. We want you to thrive in Tennessee and you have got to keep us posted on how you are doing," Dr. Jason said. He was nearly in tears himself. He had come to know and love both the Blaze and McCain families as if they were his own.

"We will definitely keep you updated," Zach spoke up, "you will, undoubtedly, be invited to our wedding, come spring."

When Zach mentioned their wedding, Roxanne's face fell. She was not sure where they would be by then. She still was not sure she wanted to put him through being married to a cripple. It did not matter what he'd told her after she woke up. Zach spotted her troubling expression but did not want to ruin her party. After some cake and farewells, it was time to go home.

Chapter 3

Due to Roxanne's inability to walk, it was decided that she should stay at the Blazes until she could return to her apartment, but that wasn't the only reason. There were a lot of people who could assist her should she need it nearby. Knowing their daughter was in good hands, once she settled into the spare room that had been Bryce's, Robert and Belinda made the difficult decision to return to California; even though they had originally planned to stay indefinitely. The couple had left their clients long enough and since Roxanne was in better shape the decision was made with everyone involved in that process. The McCains did not want to leave their only daughter if she was not ready for them to go.

"I'll be fine," Roxanne assured them. "You've taken enough time out of your lives in California to be here with me. Two months is a long time to pawn your patience off on other doctors."

Belinda was having an especially difficult time leaving her daughter, although she trusted Clara and Gerald completely, this experience taught her the importance of a family and she felt as if she were leaving too quickly. Once again, Roxanne assured her mother she would be fine; that the Blaze family was their family, and they would care for her in their absence.

Dr. Jason had put in a call to the best doctors in Chattanooga before the family even left Colorado so he would know that Roxie was getting the best care, physical therapy, and memory recall. There were times that she had noticed, while in Colorado, that she could not recall when certain things happened. Her short-term memory was okay, but to recall things in the past was a bit harder. Jason had informed all of the family that it was normal and that, given time, her long-term memory would return. At least that was the hope.

Knowing they would be returning for Christmas and feeling as if they knew the Blaze family well, including Stevie and Jeb, Stevie's boyfriend; the McClain's resolved to return to Los Angeles since they would be coming out on December the fifteenth. They said their goodbyes to their daughter, promising to return in just under two weeks, and flew back to Los Angeles to make sure everything was good there and checked in with their clients.

To say everyone was on pins and needles waiting to hear whether they returned safely, even they were flying in their own jet, was putting it lightly. No one, especially Roxanne breathed relief until Robert called her that night to let them know they were home and safe. Roxie loved her mother, but the newfound motherliness that was Belinda, had been suffocating for Roxie. It was not something she was used to and did not know if it was permanent now that Belinda knew she was okay, or whether it would flit away as it had done several times during her childhood and adolescence. She loved having her mother spend more time with her, but it was getting to be a bit too much. She missed her parents but was glad when it was just her and her other family. Clara tended to be the mother hen that Belinda tried to be, but she knew when Roxanne needed her space too. Although she was in a wheelchair, they did not treat her as a cripple. The only things she needed help with were getting from the chair to the toilet, getting from the chair into the shower, which Clara or Stevie were the only ones that helped her with, and when there was something high up that she could not reach. Other than that, she was pretty much self-sufficient. She was grateful to them for giving her the space she required.

One evening, not long after her parents left, Roxanne and Zach were sitting on the stuffed couch in the den: their favorite place to spend their time alone. The topic of their wedding had only come up once while she was at the hospital in Colorado. It frightened her to bring it up, but she knew she must voice her concerns again just so Zachary knew how she felt and where she was coming from. That night she had replaced her wheelchair for the couch because sitting in it all the time was terribly uncomfortable. They were sitting by candlelight and lights from the Christmas tree Clara demanded to be put up every year just after

Thanksgiving, but because they had all been in Colorado, it did not get put up until just a few days ago. Roxie fidgeted with her hands, which was a telltale sign something was bothering her. Of course, Zach picked up on her cues and asked, "Darlin,' what's goin' on?"

"Nothing," Roxie was not sure she could articulate what she wanted to say without crying, but Zach deserved to know. She hedged for quite some time as they cuddled on the couch and listened to the *Trans Siberian Orchestra.* She didn't want to ruin the tranquil mood that they were in.

Zachary could feel something was clearly wrong, so instead of pussyfooting around the issue, he boldly proclaimed, "I know there's something bugging you and I have a feeling I know what it's about."

"Really, and what would that be?" Roxie was kind of skeptical, but at the same time, not too much. Zach knew her better than she knew herself, at times.

"That chair you believe you'll be confined to and our wedding. Am I close?" Zach arched his brows.

"For the most part. I feel as if I will be a greater burden on you than I am at this moment with your family."

"You heard Jason before we left Colorado; you may never walk again. And, as I have told you before, whether you can or not doesn't matter to me. I love *you*, not just whether you can walk or not."

"I know you want to have kids. What if I can't?" This was the question that stressed her out the most; even more than whether she would walk again.

"Jason and the doctors here have told you the same thing. The internal bleeding was taken care of. The airplane did not damage anything other than your legs, although they expected it might. If you want, my mom can take you to a gynecologist that she knows; and yes, she's a woman. That way, you can have at least that part of your worries put at ease."

"You mean, if we cannot have children of our own, you would still marry me?"

"How can you ask that? Of course, I would. I'm not marrying you for your walking ability nor for your reproductive system. I admit it will be something we will have to get used to, but there are other ways to have children."

"Yes, but you want ones of your own blood, don't you?"

"There are ways to do that without you carrying them, but let's cross that bridge when we get to it. For the time being, let's see if we can get you standing. If not, do not ever think I will love you any less because of a stupid chair, okay?"

Roxie's answer was to bury her face in his neck and sob.

Christmas came and along with it, a visit from Roxanne's parents. She was getting stronger and stronger, to the point that she needed no help when moving around. She was not as self-conscious about being in the chair and did not let it deter her in any way that was not necessary. Robert and Belinda were both astonished at the changes in their daughter from just a few weeks before. She had been working hard to be her best self.

Before Robert and Belinda arrived, it was determined, that although it would be quite cozy, the Blaze's requested that they stay at their home. Where their daughter, Stevie, spent most of her time at Jeb's apartment, she gave her parents' permission to let Belinda and Robert use her room and she would sleep in the den on the pull-out sofa, and she swore she would not peek when 'Santa' came.

They arrived the week before Christmas. A mere ten days after they left Roxanne in the capable hands of her soon-to-be in-laws, fiancé, doctors and physical therapists in Tennessee. Both of Roxie's parents were stunned at how self-sufficient their daughter had become, even being in a wheelchair. There was not much she couldn't do. During the week leading up to Christmas, candies were made, and carols were sung to those less fortunate. Belinda was fascinated by this because she had always been given everything and to see this family she had come to know and love, who did not have as much as they did, made her that much more grateful for them, and what she had.

Christmas morning was full of the traditional blueberry pancakes and homemade maple syrup with eggs, sausage, and bacon. Then the festivities of opening gifts! Once again, the McCain's were overtaken by the generosity of Zach's family. They did not have to purchase gifts for Belinda and Robert, but they did anyway. Not only were Clara and Gerald taking care of their daughter, but they were treated like family as well. As Belinda watched the excitement around her, it reiterated her resolve to be a better mom, wife, and person, as well as a psychologist. She loved her clients like they were family and she vowed to treat them as such. She was aware she was hardened by the trauma's life had thrown at her, but that was something she learned did not have to define her.

Roxanne sat next to Zach, blessed that she was not only alive, but had everyone she loved under the same roof, too; something she never thought would happen. A lot had changed in a year and she looked forward to what the next year would bring. Her parents had surprised her with a car that was built so she could drive herself around. It wasn't her Porsche, which before the plane crash, she regarded as her baby, but this new car would give her that much more independence. It was a cherry red Ford Mustang. Zach promised that after everything settled down, they could take it for a spin.

The day got away faster than anyone expected. After eating a Christmas meal of turkey, ham, mashed potatoes and gravy, Waldorf Salad and cranberry sauce and rolls, everyone thought naps were in order before delving into the leftovers, another Christmas tradition in the Blaze household. It saddened Roxanne that the only family tradition her family possessed was that larger-than-life Christmas Eve party her parents threw. She was pleased they would not be holding one in Tennessee. She was never fond of them anyway, especially since meeting Zach's family and seeing firsthand how close a family could be. She hoped her parents would make more of an effort to spend time with her even after she and Zach were married and still going to school. These were the things that flitted through her mind as she tried shutting off her brain, and she snuggled next to her man who smelled of fresh Christmas tree, chestnut, and wood. He didn't have to wear cologne that day, his natural smell was just as intoxicating, if not more.

The Christmas and New Year's visit from her parents flew too fast for Roxanne. She never wanted more time with them before the accident. In fact, she could not wait to get away from Belinda's pretentious need for material things. The crash and everything since had changed that. She never thought she would look at Belinda as a mom—instead of mother—in the derogatory sense—but Belinda had learned a lot about herself and the traumas she had endured during her childhood and early in hers and Robert's marriage that made her the person she was that she wanted to change, not only for her family's sake but for any grandchildren that she might have.

"You and mom seriously have to leave now?" Roxanne begged her parents to stay another week. She felt as if she was just barely getting to know them. She and Zach had taken them to the airport the day after New Year's so they could open their office the next day.

"We would love to stay, but with the clientele we have been playing catch up with and your impending nuptials, we truly cannot take any more time away; not that we wouldn't love to. We would if we could. I hope you know that." Belinda hugged her daughter. This, and her mom "being real" was still something Roxanne could not comprehend; getting used to her being a mom and not just a mother was different, to say the least.

"We'll see you in a few months unless you are planning to push your wedding date out further since you badly want to walk down the aisle," Robert inserted.

At the mention of their wedding, Roxanne's eyes misted over. Belinda saw it although Roxanne did her level best to hide the tears threatening to spill down her cheeks.

"What's the matter, my girl?" Robert asked.

"Nothing," Roxanne tried hard to hide her feelings. She was one to wear for feelings on her sleeve where everyone could see even when she was trying to hide them. "I got something in my eye," she lied. She did not want to worry her parents more than she already had but she was not sure whether she could tell them how she felt at that moment.

"If you feel the need to keep quiet about it right now, that's fine but someday I hope you can open up to me," Belinda exchanged. Just then, they were made aware that their private plane was ready for takeoff. As

Belinda and Robert walked away, she could not help but wonder what was on her daughter's mind. She knew Roxanne wanted to walk at her wedding, but she was aware that may not be a possibility, but she sensed there was something more to the tears than that.

On the short drive back to Cleveland, Zachary could not leave what happened at the airport unresolved. "What are you thinking, Roxie?"

"I'm okay," Roxanne smiled. Zach knew whoever or whatever was bothering her had to do with their wedding, and he thought, with her inability to walk. He was afraid she would call it off even though he had assured her on many occasions that whether her legs worked or not, would not deter him from wanting to spend eternity with her.

Once they arrived home, Roxanne said she was tired and needed to sleep. Zach didn't know how to handle what was going on with her so he went in search of his father, "Dad, can I talk to you for a minute?"

"Sure, what's up?" Gerald asked curiosity laced his question.

"I think Roxie is still having doubts about my feelings for her. She connects those feelings with whether she gets out of that wheelchair or not. How can I make her understand my feelings have nothing to do with that wheelchair?"

"Son, you have to realize she was raised in a family where feelings were not talked about and were hidden under materialistic things. Yes, she's one to show her feelings now but she wasn't like that when you first met if you recall. You also must realize that a mere four months ago she was walking, and in a blink of an eye, that changed. She's still struggling to come to terms with what the rest of her life is going to look like should she never get out of that chair."

"I know. She doesn't understand my feelings for her do not have anything to do with the chair. She seems to think that one is tied to the other."

"You know she wants to walk at your wedding with her father, correct?"

"Yes."

"And she knows there is a huge possibility that it won't happen."

"I know all that but what can I do to reassure her that I love her no matter what?"

"All I can tell you is to keep loving her every day and help her to be as independent and she can, even in that chair."

The talk with his dad made Zachary feel a little bit better but he still wondered whether he was going to be able to marry the love of his life if she couldn't see how important she was to him. He feared she would call it off. Roxie woke up and seemed to be in better spirits than when she had been before her nap. He knew having to navigate the wheelchair all the time was difficult for her and it took a lot of her strength, both emotionally and physically. He did not want to add to that exhaustion, but he knew they needed to have 'the talk' once and for all.

Later that night after his parents had retired to their room, Zachary and Roxanne could be found in their favorite spot in the den with them lying on the couch, cuddling with their legs entwined. Although Roxanne could not feel her legs, once they returned from Colorado, they came up with a way to snuggle even without her feeling anything in her lower extremities. The first few times they tried this position, it was a flop until Zach learned the best way to position her first. He had to lay her down before him and gingerly wrap his legs with hers. They couldn't do this often because it made Roxie feel awkward about her new way of life, but tonight she had asked him if they could. The night went off without a hitch which seemed to boost Roxie's spirits and, in turn, boosted his. They laid for a bit with soft country music playing in the background, basking in each other's company. It took a bit before Zach could get up the courage to confront the demon plaguing them. Once Roxie was no longer tense, he went for it, "I went to the clinic and talked to my dad after we came home from the airport."

"Oh, what about?" Roxie was already sure of the answer.

"Us. You, the wheelchair. Your feelings about it and your fear about me."

"That's a lot to discuss. What did he say?"

Zach had positioned her so that when this talk took place they were facing each other. "Stuff that I already knew, but I think you don't quite understand the depth of my feelings for you."

"I don't?" Roxie was a bit confused.

"Not when it comes to you and walking at our wedding."

"What did he say about that?"

"I think he understands better than I do why you feel how you do, and he made me see that I need to explain myself better to you."

That shocked Roxanne. She loved Zach's family, but she had never heard either of his parents talk to him so matter-of-factly. "What conclusion have you come to then?"

Silence followed as Zachary chose his next words carefully, "After we have this talk, I don't ever want you to feel like I give a crap about that chair, okay?"

"Okay," Roxie drew out.

"I know you think because you don't walk right now, it makes you less of a person, less of a woman. I'm going to say this—that chair does not make you any less sexy in my eyes, got it?" he grinned his lopsided smile to let her know that, even though he was serious, he wasn't mad at her. "You are you, no matter what. That chair doesn't define who you are, and we will get married whenever you feel comfortable even if we need to push it out another year to give you time to see if you're able to walk down the aisle. That choice doesn't need to be made yet. I just want you to never forget my feelings are about you as a person, not your disability."

The only response that Roxie could give him was a nod as her tears dropped like torpedoes. He would never be able to get what his words meant to her. He'd said essentially the same thing many times before, but he had never told her she was sexy, not since before the accident. She vowed that no matter what she had to do over the next six months, she would walk down that aisle even if it were on crutches. Roxanne also decided she would ask not only her father to walk her down the aisle, but Gerald as well. It was because of the talk that he'd had with Zach that made her feel more loved than she ever had.

Chapter 4

New Year's ended and then the winter semester started for both Roxanne and Zachary. They began their second year during the first week in January. Zach tried to convince Roxie she needed to continue to stay with him and his parents. He did not like the idea of her being alone in her apartment, although she assured him that she was more than capable of taking care of herself, even in a chair.

"Zach, sweetheart, I'll be fine and it's not like you live that far away anyway. Trust me, if I didn't think I could do this, I wouldn't attempt it, but I'm okay."

"Promise you'll call if anything happens, or if you just find yourself too lonesome?" He smiled as he shut the door to her Mustang. Earlier that day, he went with her to make sure all the pertinent stuff was within reaching distance and that her 'gator grabber' as they called the item she got for Christmas that helped her reach things up high, was in working order.

"I will. Remember, tomorrow after school I have therapy and we are trying out the crutches; standing with them at least." From the time they had returned to Tennessee once Roxie was released from Estes Park Hospital in Colorado, she had been adamant to see if she could stand with crutches. She was able to pull herself to a standing position with the bars, but her therapist warned her standing with crutches was much less stable and he worried that she wasn't ready. She had worked hard for the past month to prove that she could do it, so today was that day and she was confident.

Zach was worried she wasn't ready, that Roxie was pushing herself too hard, but he did not want to dampen her spirits. He loved the fact that she fought so hard to be normal, and at the same time, knew where her limitations were in most respects. "I haven't forgotten," he laughed as he kissed her goodnight and left her apartment still troubled about her being there alone. Once he returned home, he called her right away. She seemed to be okay and promised again that she would let him know if anything was amiss.

The next day school went well for them both, although Roxanne got some strange looks from people she had known when she started at the University Tennessee-Chattanooga. It was as if they hadn't heard about the plane crash and the heroics that went into saving her and the two other passengers. Roxanne tried not to let it bother her, but she could not help feeling out of place. She and Zach had ridden together that morning in her new Ford Mustang her parents had bought her for Christmas, decked-out so she was able to drive it without the use of her legs.

"How was your day?" Zach could tell she was hiding something; he was certain she didn't want to make him any more distressed than he already was with the new way of life they were both getting the hang of.

"It was okay," Roxie replied.

"Why the glum face then?" They didn't have any classes together but Robert, being an alumni, had made sure adequate actions were taken to accommodate Roxanne in her classes.

"It's nothing." This was Roxie's answer for everything when she did not feel like answering a question.

"It certainly *is* something," Zach pressed the issue.

"I felt out of place, that's all."

"You sure?"

"People we hung out with when we started here gave me strange looks. It was like they didn't expect that just because I'm now in a wheelchair, I can't be and do what I want. That, somehow, the use of my legs has something to do with my ability to design clothing."

"They haven't had time to get used to it. Once they see that you are still the same, loveable Roxie, it'll change." Zachary wondered if he was giving her false hope. He prayed he wasn't.

Fifteen minutes later, they pulled into the parking lot of the Erlanger Hospital where Roxanne had her physical therapy. "You don't have to come with me if you don't want to. I know you don't believe that I'm ready to use the crutches, but I really want to be married this summer and not put off the wedding any longer."

"You really think that?" He *did* feel like that, but he didn't think he showed it.

"You act like it sometimes. I just don't want to be treated differently or have to put our life together on hold because of this chair."

"I'm terribly sorry if I made you feel that way; that was not my intention at all. Of course, I want to come in with you to see you take this next step in your healing process."

Roxanne had special clothing she wore when doing physical therapy that she kept in her car, although she probably should have been wearing sweatpants the entire time, she did not feel 'dressed' when she was wearing them. She had gotten quite proficient in changing by herself; pulling herself out of the chair and onto the bench in the locker room that was used for those who took part in physical therapy. *Zach would be totally impressed.*

When the physical therapist saw her, he commented on how well she maneuvered her wheelchair as he always did and asked her how her first day of college went. She explained to him the same thing she had explained to Zach, but her physical therapist seemed to understand more than Zach had. "Those people thought they knew you didn't know the person you are inside. All they saw was a spoiled rich kid from Los

Angeles who had everything given to her. Since I've known you, I have learned that there is so much more to you than that. You are a fighter. Otherwise, you would have died on that cliff, or even in the hospital. I hope you know that you not only amazed Dr. Kurt, but you have made incredible strides since you've been here."

Zach listened as the physical therapist gave his fiancé the pep talk and wished he'd have thought to say those things to her. He loved her, but never seeing others in wheelchairs as often as the therapist sometimes, it was hard to know what to say to make her feel better. As he watched her get the crutches clipped around her arms, he did not realize that he was holding his breath until she pulled herself to a standing position from her chair. He let out a sigh of relief and cheered right alongside the therapist when she stood even without his help.

"Holy cow, Roxanne! I'm so amazed at how you were able to pull that off and make it seem as if it were nothing!" her therapist encouraged emphatically.

Zach came over once she was back in the chair and gave her a big hug. He was astonished, "That was totally amazing! You did so well, and I think you're on your way, Darlin'." He couldn't stop grinning as she and the therapist continued working her legs as she lay on the floor.

"Damn, that was tough," Roxie huffed and puffed as the therapist exercised her legs.

"Yeah, but you did it," was his pepped-up response.

"Yes, I did!" Roxanne had never been prouder of herself than she was at that moment. Up until Zach's exuberant response, Roxie was not able to gauge whether he believed in her or not.

"The next several sessions are going to be more important than any we have had to this point," the therapist talked to both Roxie and Zach. Directing his next comment at Zach, he continued, "You have been immensely helpful with getting her upper body strength where it is. Now, because she is determined to walk down that aisle, we need to slowly get her to where she can take steps with the crutches. You up for that, man?"

"Of course, I'm in this one hundred percent."

"You need to stretch her legs twice a day. Now, I know you don't live together yet, but would your parents be willing to help if you need it?" The therapist had met with both the McCains and the Blazes and he had no doubt that Clara and Gerald would help if need be.

"Yeah, my mom and my sister could help," Zach replied.

"Now, since our girl has only been on the crutches once, I do not want her trying to stand up without assistance until she's much stronger on her legs," the therapist firmly stated.

"Trust me, I have no intention of allowing her to stand up without support," Zach replied.

Roxie and Zach were so ecstatic she was able to stand with the crutches, they could not hold back their excitement any longer and asked his family if they wanted to go to dinner with them that night. They did not tell any of them; not Stevie and Jeb, nor Gerald and Clara, what the occasion was. They met at the FEED CO Table and Tavern. None of them drank alcohol except Jeb, but even he had cut back trying to prove to the Blazes that he loved Stevie and would do whatever he had to do to prove that to them.

While waiting for their drinks, it was Stevie who broke the silence, "So, what is such great news that we had to come all the way to Chattanooga for?"

Zach chuckled and replied," Stevie you spend more time in Chattanooga at Jeb's apartment than anyone else and the two of us are going to school here and the others own business, so I don't get what you mean by 'coming all the way to Chattanooga.'"

Everyone laughed at that point. Zach looked over at Roxie and motioned her to tell them her big news. She bit her lip, trying not to cry; not because she was sad, but they were tears of joy. Clearing her throat, she said, "Well. As you all know, I'm determined to walk at our wedding this summer." They all nodded. "Today, I stood up with my crutches. No bars, just crutches!" That received a round of applause from the entire table. To Roxanne's embarrassment, there were many looks from the other nearby guests. She wasn't the kind to like calling attention to herself, not since the accident, but she smiled anyway because she knew she deserved every accomplishment she conquered.

When she arrived home, and since her parents were two hours behind her; it was only seven o'clock in the evening in Los Angeles, she could not wait to tell her parents. This was a new feeling for her, because up until recently, she didn't think she mattered much to them, most of all, her mother. She dialed her dad's number first because even though her relationship with Belinda was getting better, Roxanne had always been closer to Robert. He was more into playing with her when she was little and was always telling her stories about Amelia and why she was in heaven. So, as she got older, even the dynamics with her father changed. He seemed more caught up in his job just as her mother had been her whole life. On what seemed like the thousandth ring, Robert finally picked up, "Hey, my girl. How are you?"

"I'm doing really good, actually. Listen, are you at home? I have something I want to tell both you and mother (that would be a difficult habit to break; calling Belinda either by her name or mother—Roxanne was never allowed until recently to call her just 'mom') and it would be easiest to tell you both at once"

"Good news, I expect," Robert responded. "I have one more client coming in at seven-thirty, then I'll be home. Your mother had a migraine, so she stayed home today. I hope she's resting. How about if I call you at nine o'clock unless that's too late."

"No. That's fine. I won't crawl into bed before midnight or later anyway. You know homework and college life."

"Yes, I remember. I may be older but I'm not *that* old—all-nighters and procrastination seem to be the norm with college students regardless of age," Robert laughed, "Hey, my seven-thirty just arrived so I will call you as soon as I get home."

"Sounds good. I love you, daddy."

"I love you too, sweetheart." That was another change in both Roxanne's parents. Her entire life she spent doing everything in her power to make them love her; and tell her as such. What got her was it took her facing death and them facing losing their only child to learn that children, no matter how old they are, nor their circumstances, needed to hear those words, and often. Thankfully, Zach's family had shown her love and acceptance from the first time they met her. They gave her the affection and the words of affirmation she needed from her own parents.

As promised, Robert called at eleven o'clock Tennessee time. He put the phone on speaker so that Belinda could hear as well. "So, what's the good news?" Anticipation could be heard in Robert's voice. Both Belinda and Robert knew pregnancy was not the news because both she and Zachary had made a vow to wait until they were married to start a family. It was known that Roxanne wasn't certain she could carry a baby even though all her doctors and even Clara's gynecologist assured her that, physically there should not be anything stopping her, but it continued to frighten Roxanne—just the mere thought gave her panic attacks, so they knew that was not it.

"I stood up on my crutches today! It was difficult and painful, but I did it!" Roxanne felt like a little girl at Christmas.

"Congratulations," both of her parents replied. There was an air of foreboding in their voices.

"What's wrong?" Roxanne questioned.

"We just worry that with school and therapy, you are putting too much strain on yourself," Belinda spoke up.

"Trust me. I won't do anything dangerous. I know my body and know when and where my limitations lie. I promise you both. I will not do anything stupid."

"That is good to hear," Robert injected into the conversation, "we certainly don't want you to overdo yourself and perhaps have a relapse. We do understand why you want to learn to walk again. You want to walk down the aisle, not wheel down it. We want you to know that it doesn't matter to either of us whichever way you choose."

"Your father is right," Belinda added, "No matter what, we are both here for you. Please, please do not overextend yourself."

"I won't mom." Roxanne liked the sound of that. It sounded more personal and loving. "Well, I have classes tomorrow, so I better hang up," she said.

"Yes, you need your rest," Belinda replied in support, "I love you, Roxanne. Do you know how much?"

"I'm learning…mom. It's still interesting to hear you say it since it wasn't said to me when I was younger except by my nannies and the rest of the staff."

"I know that, and I'm very sorry for never being there for you when you needed me most."

"Mom, we have talked about this. We will move forward from here. That's all we can do. Good night—I love you both. I'll keep you up-to-date on any new developments."

"Good night, sweetheart," they replied in unison, "We look forward to more great news," the uneasiness evident in her father's voice.

Roxanne laid in bed until far into the early morning. For some reason, sleep thwarted her at every turn. There was a part of her that understood where her parents were coming from but there was another part that wished they showed more enthusiasm no matter how scared they were. Still, she couldn't stop the grin that formed whenever she thought about her accomplishment earlier that day. She knew though, that if she did not get at least a little sleep she would be no good at school the next day.

Over the next several days, when they weren't doing homework or projects for school, Roxie was pushing herself to practice standing with her crutches: never without Zach spotting her as per her therapist's orders. Every week, Roxie had physical therapy and every time she saw the therapist, she begged him to let her try taking steps, but each visit he told her not to rush. He was optimistic that she would be able to take a few steps eventually, but she would most likely always need her wheelchair as a backup in case her legs got tired.

Zachary worked quite a bit at the clinic and Gerald asked Roxie to come back as the receptionist. He had never hired another one because he felt she would be back. For Roxie, it was a nice surprise, but she felt guilty taking money from them. She told Zach but he reassured her that his parents insisted on paying her since she was an employee. Her favorite thing to do when times were slow at the clinic was to hold and pet all the animals who had surgery or who were sick. The Blazes had taught her that animals needed as much care and support as people; sometimes more than people since they could not voice what was wrong or how they were feeling. Before meeting Zachary, Roxie was not an animal person. Being Belinda's daughter, she had looked at animals as filthy, when in fact, they were cleaner than people in many respects but that had changed over the last year and a half.

Chapter 5

The first time Roxanne took a step with her crutches was the greatest moment of her life, besides meeting Zachary, of course. She was in therapy and the therapist, out of the blue, said, "You ready to take those steps you've been bugging me about for weeks?"

"You're serious?" Roxie squealed and could not contain her excitement and she could see that Zach felt it too.

"Yes, I'm serious," was the response.

"You've got this, Darlin,'" Zach encouraged, watching from his favorite chair. He'd become accustomed to coming with her after it was clear she could stand with crutches. She was not only spunky, but she was stubborn as all get out.

Roxanne was able to take three steps that day and had to call Jason Kurt, the first doctor who she saw when she came out of her coma. She'd learned too, that he was extremely instrumental in finding and getting her out from under the airplane. Jason who, when Roxanne was released from Estes Park was not sure if she would ever be able to use her legs again, was almost as enthused as everyone else when they found out. Even her parents were more excited for her this time.

As the months flew by with school, work, learning to take steps and planning their July wedding, both Zachary and Roxanne were very busy.

Roxie decided upon using the wedding dress that she had picked up in Los Angeles before the plane crash. Thankfully, she had chosen to leave it at her parents' house, so it was still intact. She called her parents and had them send it to her in case any new adjustments needed to be made to accommodate her wheelchair. Both she and Zach began feeling the pressure as the semester and finals ended. Roxanne was surprised at how well she did on the general education finals. She would begin Fashion Design in the fall.

On one of the rare evenings that Roxie went over to Zach's house; they preferred to stay at the apartment that would be theirs, not just hers once they were married, they were sitting on the couch in the den talking about their honeymoon. Roxie knew they could go anywhere their hearts desired because her parents planned to pay for the two weeks, they were planning on taking off work for their adventure. "Are you okay with Mom and Dad paying for the honeymoon?" Roxanne asked Zach.

Zach wasn't going to lie; he felt uncomfortable with that. Although Belinda and Robert, as well as his parents, told them that it was customary for the bride's family to pay for the wedding and the groom's family to pay for the honeymoon; they were doing it a little backward. The Blazes were paying for the wedding, Zach felt the honeymoon was his responsibility but knew with school and the little he made at the family business, it did not lend him the opportunity to do what he wanted. So, he said, "You know I have a hard time allowing either of our parents to pay for anything, but I understand why. It's just difficult having your parents pay for, not only our honeymoon but the reception in Los Angeles as well."

'I know, but this *has* to be one of those times you must not let your pride get in the way. My parents *want* to do this for us."

"I know that too. That's why I'm trying not to let it take over."

"You know I love you, right?" Roxie asked gingerly.

"Of course. Why would you even ask that?" Zach was puzzled.

"Because I don't want you to feel like my parents are taking anything away from us by paying for the stuff they are. When you first asked me to marry you and even before the crash and everything that's gone on since, there would have been no way I would have guessed my parents would do as much as they are."

"It's a guy thing, I guess." Zach shrugged as if it were no big deal, trying to hide his true feelings, but knew Roxie could see them, regardless.

"A guy thing?" Roxie furrowed her brow, "What does that mean?"

"It's just that I was raised to do whatever it takes to take care of my own, and Darlin,' if you haven't figured it out yet, you're my own."

Roxie's stomach immediately produced butterflies. Not just because he called her a pet name other than the Roxie one he had given her, but the way his deep voice called her *his own* made her cheeks that much hotter.

"Honey, I think your cheeks are on fire," Zach teased.

Swatting his bicep, Roxie buried her face in his chest until the warmth went down, "Don't make fun," came the muffled reply.

"Oh, I'm not. I think it's cute when I can make you blush that hard," he gave her his askew grin she had grown to love so much.

"Back to the subject...where do you think we should go on our honeymoon? I mean, how many all-expense-paid trips are we going to get?" Roxanne asked.

She has a point. "Hmm...should we stay stateside or go to a different country?"

"I was thinking maybe the Bahamas or Cancun. Hawaii even?" Roxanne added her input.
"Oooohhh. The Bahamas. I like that one." The pride in him had vanished and in Zach's eyes, excitement took its place.

"I'm glad to see some enthusiasm," Roxanne told him. She worried that he'd never warm to the idea of a honeymoon he did not pay for.

"It's growing on me, I'll admit. What about Jamaica?"

"That could be fun too, but remember, we don't just have to worry about my chair but my crutches as well."

"I know, Baby. Trust me, I've got you." That led to a hot and heavy make out session being caught by Stevie as she came home.

"Boo!" Stevie scared the crap out of both Roxie and Zach causing them to jump.

"Stevie!" Zach warned, "*That* wasn't the slightest bit funny." Next to him, his fiancé wasn't the least bit perturbed. She was laughing hysterically right alongside his sister. "Oh, I see how it is," he teased.

"Yup! Girls gotta stick together. Especially ones that are just as good as sisters," Stevie replied.

Hearing her soon-to-be sister-in-law call her *sister* made Roxie smile. Her entire life, Roxie felt like part of herself was missing; and in a way, it was when her twin died. Now, she felt a part of something much bigger than herself and loved the Blaze family. Soon, they would be hers. Glancing at her watch, Roxie pipped up, "I didn't realize it was so late. I better get home so I'm not bleary-eyed for the new semester tomorrow," she could not believe in three short months, she would be Mrs. Roxie Blaze. It felt good to say that, even if only in her head.

"Yes. And soon after this semester is over, we'll be husband and wife," Zach gushed.

Roxie couldn't help the giddy feeling she got when she thought about how close they were or the feelings of foreboding at the thought that it almost did not happen. "Your mom is helping me address invitations this weekend," Roxie reminded him as he helped her to her car. She pretty much only used the crutches now, unless she was overly tired or overdid it, she tried not to do that too much because she only had three months. Three months to prove to her physical therapist she would not need the crutches when she walked down the aisle; not when she had both her "dads" walking with her.

As she drove home, got into the apartment and got ready for bed, she recalled the day that she had asked Gerald if he would walk with her and her father down the aisle. She remembered the tears brimming in his eyes as he answered. She never thought he would say no but was relieved just the same when he didn't.

Saturday found Roxie at Zach's house earlier than usual. He and his dad were tuxedo hunting, which left her and Clara alone to address envelopes to those who would be coming to the wedding ceremony and reception in Tennessee. There were only twenty-five people invited to the actual ceremony because Zach and Roxie wanted to keep it small and intimate, but they still had to address the envelopes and invites to the reception in Tennessee and the ones for the huge party Belinda had insisted on having in Los Angeles in August. One month after Roxie and Zach married. That left seven hundred envelopes to address and stamp. Not only that, but remembering what card went where. "This is going to take all day and then some," Roxie concluded.

"It won't take as long as you think," Clara smiled as she brought out two stamps; with her Tennessee address on them, "I figured we didn't have to kill ourselves off," Clara laughed.

"Good thinking," Roxie sighed in relief. "Too bad we don't have stamps for all the addresses on this list my mom sent."

"We'll get as much done as we can today. I figure, if we get the ones for the ceremony and reception here finished, and start on the ones for your mom, that's good. I don't want you to get too tired."

The day went on and before Roxie knew it, they had made great strides on the list of names, even some Belinda sent. "Woohoo! I'm pooped! Clara declared, "We have worked our butts off. Should we call it a day and watch a movie or something?" They had not even stopped to eat anything except the bagels and cream cheese that Roxie brought that morning.

"Yes, we have," Roxie said, "Are you hungry?

I'm starving since my bagel disappeared several hours ago. My stomach is telling me it needs food."

"How about we order Chinese? I don't know when the boys are going to be home, but we might as well get enough for everyone because you know as soon as we order just for us, they'll show up and of course, be hungry," Clara giggled like a schoolgirl as she hadn't done for many years.

"It sounds like a great plan to me," Roxie replied. Clara ordered while Roxie explained to her what she liked, which wasn't much different than Zach's taste.

Once the order was placed, the girls went into the den because that was the closest television and Roxie had, once again, overdone herself. She began getting tired several hours before but didn't want Clara to know because they were on a roll and she didn't want to ruin that for them. It felt good to get out of her wheelchair and into Gerald's recliner. The same coveted recliner of every person in the house, but Roxie seemed to be the only one who could sweet talk her way into sitting in it. Some might've thought it was because of her disability, but she had charmed her way into the chair long before the plane crash.

When she was settled, Clara asked what she wanted to watch. "Should we do comedy or romcom?"

"Well. The boys aren't here, so bring on the romcoms!" Roxie proclaimed as they both laughed.

The food arrived just as the movie started. Clara made quick work of dishing up food just as the previews ended. They weren't even twenty minutes into their fun when they heard, "Hey! Is that Chinese I smell?" being hollered from the back door.

In unison, Roxie and Clara yelled back a resounding, "No!" Laughter and glee followed as they were caught red handed with their mouths full of delicious food.

"YOU!" Zachary pointed an accusing finger at his fiancé, "You put my mom up to this, didn't you? You know what I like, and you just had to go and order it, huh?"

Roxie couldn't stop laughing as she spewed fried rice in Zach's face. Once she regained her bearings, she replied innocently, "I would never…" Then she said, "If you hadn't made me laugh, you wouldn't have gotten a face full of rice either."

Gerald joined the party, and while the boys got their plates filled, the movie was paused. They then spent the next hour and a half watching *She's Out of Control* with Tony Danza in it. Zach had seen it before, but Gerald had not, and he couldn't help but comment on what it was like for him when Stevie started dating, although she was not near as homely looking as the main character.

It wasn't extremely late, so they decided to watch another movie with some caramel popcorn; a recipe that Clara had handed down to her by her grandmother. Due to overdoing it for the day, Roxanne was pretty much ordered to stay in the chair. *I couldn't get out even if I wanted to,* she thought. Zach decided to help his mom while Gerald cleaned up from supper. This time, they only thought it fair that they let the men choose the movie. Both women shook their heads when they saw *Robocop* as the movie of choice but knew they couldn't complain since Gerald and Zach had graciously watched their chick flick and even laughed at some of the funny parts. By the time it was over, it was after one o'clock in the morning, so it was decided that although Roxie only lived a few minutes away, Zach, nor his parents felt comfortable with her driving home after the long day she had.

It didn't take long for the day to catch up to Roxie. It was a good thing it was the weekend, and she didn't have classes until Tuesday. This semester her classes were only on Tuesday and Thursday. That left her with the availability to work Monday, Wednesday and Friday. It wasn't until Zachary came in and kissed her softly awake that she realized she had slept in until almost noon. "Why didn't you come to wake me up?" She wanted to be mad, but he was just too damned good looking to stay pissed at for long.

"I came in and checked on you, but you were snoring so softly and looked so beautiful I didn't have the heart to wake you. Mom and dad decided on brunch and it's ready. Let's get you to the table and then I'll take you home so you can shower and rest."

"I think I've rested enough, and we still have a lot of invitations to address. Are you going to help with that today? We could take the boxes to my apartment and work on them there. The sooner we get them done, the happier my mom will be. She's remarkably calmer than I thought she would be throughout this whole process though."

"We can do that if you feel up to it," Zach replied. He was not looking forward to writing names and addresses all day but knew Roxie wasn't able to do them alone. As they headed to the kitchen, Roxie was insistent on using her crutches when Zach would have felt more comfortable if she used her chair. She was determined to only use the chair when it was absolutely necessary, which meant that she had to hide when she hurt badly. What she was not aware of was that, whenever Zachary was with her, he could tell, but he wasn't going to stop her from bettering herself. He was already made aware from both her doctors and physical therapist that she wouldn't ever be without the chair. Her legs had been crushed so badly that there would always be pain whenever she was on her feet. She experienced pain as well even when in the wheelchair, but she wasn't going to let this disability that she was left with stop her from living her dream.

They made quick work of brunch consisting of homemade waffles, strawberries, and whipped cream. As soon as they were done, Zach and Roxie went to her apartment. While she was in the shower, Zachary could see that there were a few things that needed cleaning. Because it was challenging for Roxanne to reach the stuff on the floor, and due to school, which took a lot out of her with homework and everything, not to mention their wedding plans, which he would admit he was not much help with, she wore herself out daily. She did not have the time or energy to clean up. Roxie was not a filthy person by any means, so Zach did the dishes, picked up items on the floor and vacuumed.

"Zachary Blaze, what in the world are you doing?" Roxanne had finished her shower and made it into the kitchen as he was finishing up the dishes.

"Damn it, you caught me," the sheepish sideways grin gave him away.

"You don't need to be cleaning for me," Roxie pretended to be angry but in reality, she was grateful for it. She had pondered on how she would clean the place up. As usual, it was her godsend to the rescue, again, "Thank you, though. I wondered how I was going to get this place clean. One other thing that makes this chair a crapshoot."

Zachary kissed her, loving the strawberry shampoo and body wash she used, "You're more than welcome, Darlin.' Whatever I can do to lighten your load, I will; no matter what it is."

"What did I do to ever deserve you?" tears glistened in Roxie's eyes.

"Almost knocked me down?" Zachary smiled.

"You're never going to allow me to live that one down, are you?" Roxie countered.

"Nope," was the response as they spread their wedding invitations and address stamps across the table. As they worked, neither could believe how close they were to becoming husband and wife.

.

Chapter 6

The spring semester came to a close, and with it a thrill that, in just six weeks, Zachary and Roxanne would become Mr. and Mrs. Zachary Blaze. He guessed that she would want to keep her maiden name; maybe even hyphenate the two so that she didn't lose the hype that went with her name, but she surprised him one day by telling him she wanted only his. "Are you sure?" he questioned. They had both finished their last final of their sophomore year and were at Peggy's, the coffee shop where they first got to know each other; the same place where Zach had asked her on their first date and the same place where he had proposed a year and a half before.

"Yes. I want nothing more than that: if the last several months have taught me anything, it's that life can change in a fleeting moment and I don't want to waste any of our time together." She kissed him then, with more passion than she ever had.

"I'm so glad to hear that. I was worried you would want to keep your maiden name, which I understood, but I was raised that when you're married, the woman takes the man's name and, for me, that would be the biggest gift that I could ever give you."

After finals, Roxie and Zach finished the invitations for the party Roxie's parents were throwing a month after their honeymoon. They still had not decided where they wanted to go being that Roxie had been to several awesome places and Zach had been nowhere. The farthest he had ever gone was Los Angeles with her their first Christmas together. It had taken a lot of pushing and prodding from both Roxie and Zach's parents to make him get on that plane. He wasn't fond of being in the air, but he was grateful that he had the chance to see Los Angeles and the places where Roxie grew up.

"Where do you think we should go?" Roxie asked Zach.

"I still like the sound of Jamaica, but we can go wherever you want as long as we're together. The Bahamas would be awesome, too. We can spend our days on the warm beaches and our nights in our hotel room," Zach wriggled his eyes at her which made her blush.

"You're so bad," Roxie giggled. In truth, she was scared she wouldn't be able to perform the way that she knew she was supposed to, due to the fact that her legs didn't work the way that they used to.

Zack saw the concerned look on her face and asked, "You aren't still worried about that particular thing, are you?"

"Wouldn't you be?"

"You remember what the doctors told us, don't you?"

"I do, but that doesn't make me worry any less." This subject always caused Roxanne to cry. The fear of the unknown ate at her all the time, but she hated bringing Zach into her issue constantly. Deep down, she knew he would love her whether they were able to make love or not. She just hoped and prayed that the doctors had not gotten their hopes up for nothing.

"Please don't worry about our sex life. We will figure that part out as we go. Even if we could never have sex, I would still want you."

"But a man has to have his *needs* met," Roxanne argued.

"That is true, but I wouldn't be the first nor the last man to live without a conventional love life."

"You could get an escort or prostitute to do the things that I can't. It would be a hard pill to swallow but I would do it if it meant that you were taken care of."

Zachary could not believe his ears. His fiancé was essentially giving him permission to use other women for his gratification. He couldn't believe she would consider that something like that would cross his mind. But he understood why she would think that at this point. "How could you even think that I would even go there?"

"I don't know. I just know that I don't like this; the uncertainty of the damage, the internal injuries caused that I might not have the ability to satisfy you."

"As long as I have you, the rest of it doesn't matter. Don't get me wrong; I cannot wait for our wedding night. If we can't do what normal couples do, we'll work around that." They had spent the last six months talking about the subject until Zachary wanted to puke. But he never let on to Roxanne that he was getting tired of saying the same thing to her repeatedly. That having her as his wife was much more important than sex; there were more ways to be intimate than that.

"Okay," Roxanne said, "I know you must be tired of listening to me babble about my fears but I'm grateful you're here and you listen. I will try for the next six weeks not to bring it up again and we will plan to have a peaceful time before we get married."

They still had a lot to do for the ceremony. They decided they wanted to fix up the barn at Zach's house and have the wedding and reception there with the reception spilling out onto the lawn. There weren't going to be as many people in Tennessee as there would be in Los Angeles, but they wanted to make it a beautiful wedding anyhow. "Now that the semester's over, we need to think about the barn and how we want it to look. My parents said they would pay for us to paint it and for the decorations on the inside and we have a caterer to set up the tables and chairs that spill out onto the lawn.

"That sounds like a good idea. You do know that I'm not going to be able to help you paint, right?"

"Yes, Darlin,' I'm completely aware of that. Why don't you and my mom go pick out the centerpieces for the tables and the decorations for the barn while Dad and I work on painting the barn? I think dark red on the outside would look really good and if we just cleaned up the wood on the inside and made it look rustic, it will be the vision we want."

Once again, Roxanne and Clara had an excellent time deciding on the western themed centerpieces that would go on each table as well as the little wooden bowls that would contain snacks and wedding favors for each guest. It surprised Clara how well Roxanne handled all the stress of the wedding. She thought, for sure, that being the entitled person she was, she would want a more high-end reception then Clara and Gerald could afford. She was also amazed at how well Roxie managed getting around in her wheelchair for the couple of hours they were in town. "Do you think the boys have even started painting the barn?" Clara asked Roxie.

"Honestly, I bet they're watching sports as we speak and haven't even begun the priming process. Have you received any RSVPs from any guests yet? I wonder how many people will show up. I realize none of these are people that know me so I hope that even in this chair I can make a good impression on your family and friends who I've yet to meet."

"Are you worried about that? Sweetheart, you've been such a blessing to not just our son but to our family as well and I'm certain that anyone who is worth their salt will love you just as we do. You have changed so much in the time we've known you, and you have made Zachary very happy and that is all I can ask for as his mother."

When they finally arrived home, the primer had been put on the barn and the boys were most definitely sitting in the den yelling at the television. Roxy believed that was the only reason either of them watched sports to begin with. It gave them an excuse to be cavemen. Neither Clara nor Roxie made themselves known but watched from a distance as the yelling continued. They almost expected to see their men beating on their chests like gorillas. The embarrassment and red faces that greeted them should have been one for the books. "How long have you two ladies been standing there?" Gerald tried scolding but all he could do was laugh at the looks on his wife's and his soon to be daughter-in-law's faces.

"Oh, we've been here watching the two of you make fools of yourselves for about ten minutes," Clara responded through spurts of laughter. "We actually made a bet about how far y'all got with the barn and whether you would both be sitting here doing exactly what we predicted."

"It looks like the two of you will be making dinner for us tonight. It's up to you what you do with it, but we will not be the ones in charge of that this evening, "Roxie giggled, "but please, not pizza again."

"Damn, that's exactly what we were thinking," Zachary teased.

"Since we have to wait for the primer to dry, we can't paint until tomorrow, why don't we all get cleaned up and go out for a nice dinner; possibly a movie?" Gerald requested.

"We have a few hours yet. Why not allow Roxie to rest up a bit before we do that? I think I wore the poor girl out with the shopping we got done today but we did get the centerpieces and wedding favors for the tables, "Clara replied.

Although Roxie didn't say anything, everyone could see the relief washing over her face at the prospect of taking a nap. She wondered if she would ever get used to all the exertion she needed to move her wheelchair or use her crutches. She doubted it. She glanced at Zach who gave her a knowing look and a waggle of his eyebrows. She knew he would love nothing more than to lay down with her while she slept. Something he didn't think he ever told her was that watching her sleep was one of his favorite things to do. "It sounds like a plan," Zach interrupted, "Why don't you and dad spend some much-needed time together and Roxie and I'll nap in here since this seems to work well for her."

It did not take long for Roxie to fall asleep, even though Zach had let her pick a movie to watch. He figured she wouldn't last long once she laid down. He could see the tired weariness in her eyes even as she laughed right alongside his mom.

A few hours later, the foursome was at one of the higher-end restaurants in Chattanooga. The men thought they had all busted their butts to work toward a beautiful wedding and they concluded that the women needed it perhaps even more than they did. They chatted back and forth as they waited for their drinks to arrive and their food order taken. "Well…" Gerald commented, "there's no turning back now."

"Why would they want to at this point anyway?" Clara asked, "They have both earned this with everything that was thrown at them this past year."

"Yes, they do. And we could not ask for a better daughter-in-law than Roxie." When they had first met her, Gerald was not okay with his son dating a spoiled rich kid. Then, as they got to know the 'real' Roxanne, it had not taken her long to worm her way into their hearts. They had met her parents at the scariest time in any of their lives and he still wondered if Belinda and Robert would have been that down-to-earth and pleasant had the plane crash not taken place. From Zach's first meeting with them, he gathered they were snobs—no wonder Roxie had felt entitled all the time when they first met, but he learned people change, especially when faced with something as difficult as the unknown. Gerald and Clara understood. They had been there two years before when they had lost Bryce in that horrible four-wheeling accident. As Zach—and then his parents— got to know Robert and Belinda who had already lost Roxie's twin sister, Amelia, they supposed that had Belinda and Robert lost Roxie as well, it would have torn them completely to pieces, where when Bryce had died it brought the Blazes closer together.

"Do you realize mom and dad, that we are on a double date? I never thought I would be doing this with my parents, but it is kind of fun," Zach brought to their attention.

Clara spoke first, "I never really thought about it, but I guess we are. And it's fun just being able to talk and relax with my son and his fiancé, whom I have grown to love as my own daughter."

Roxanne spoke at that moment, trying not to cry, "I am incredibly grateful that, even when you all thought me a spoiled, rich, brat you gave me a chance anyway. I don't know any other family that would've taken in a person who acted as I did and helped her to see who she really was."

By the time Roxy was done speaking their food had arrived and they continued talking as they ate; mostly, about the wedding but some about the happenings that were going on at the clinic. "You're still planning to work for us throughout the summer other than the two weeks that you and Zach are taking off for the party in Los Angeles, correct?" Gerald asked her.

"Of course, but aren't you and Clara coming to Los Angeles as well? My parents have bought a plane ticket for the two of you if you would like to go."

Clara and Gerald had never really talked about going to the reception and they didn't know if they could leave the vet clinic closed for that long, but it would be fun to see how the other half lives. "We will have to see if we can get one of my colleagues to run the clinic while we're gone or we can just come for the weekend of the reception," Gerald replied.

"Your parents didn't have to buy the plane tickets for us. We could've afforded tickets on our own.

"These are not just any plain old economy class plane tickets though," Roxie said, "They're flying you first class since the airplane that we own is broken down and Dad didn't know whether it would be fixed before then."

Two weeks before the wedding, everything was falling into place. The barn was painted, and all set up except for the tables and chairs that would be brought in by the caterers. Roxanne asked her parents to be there, although they would be seeing her two weeks after their honeymoon. One evening, she and Zach were at their apartment where they had begun moving his things in and as they were finishing for the night they were sitting on her couch and talking about the honeymoon. They needed to make a decision as to where they wanted to go so that her parents could purchase tickets. The more they talked about it, the more Jamaica seemed to be the honeymoon of choice. Neither of them had been there and Roxie wanted to make sure they went somewhere that she had never been so she could experience another culture right alongside Zach. "So, Jamaica it is then," she said, "Do you think we ought to let my parents know sooner than later?"

"Hmm…possibly," Zach chuckled, "I think we've haggled this one to death, don't you?"

"Possibly." Roxanne giggled. She then called her parents to let them know what their honeymoon plans were. Robert, who took the call, scolded them for waiting so long to let him and Belinda know what they chose. "We're sorry, daddy. It took longer to decide because we couldn't choose between the Bahamas and Jamaica."

"They are both excellent choices," Robert softened his words. Sometimes, because of how self-sufficient Roxanne had become, even with walking difficulties, he forgot how close he and Belinda had come in losing her. "Thank you for letting us know. We'll bring the tickets when we arrive next week."

"Okay, daddy. I can't wait to see you and mother."

"Bye, sweetheart." And, with that, the call ended.

"Everything okay?" Zach couldn't help but notice the worry lining her forehead.

"Yes, everything is fine. Daddy was just a bit perturbed that we didn't give them an answer sooner, that's all. They will bring the tickets when they come next week."

"Okay." Zach wasn't certain that was the only thing bothering her, but he let the matter drop.

"Now all we've do is put them together we have a few hours yet. Why not allow Roxie to rest up a bit before we do that? I think I wore the poor girl out with the shopping we got done today but we did get the centerpieces and wedding favors for the tables. Now all we have to do is put them together."

Over the next week, they finished moving the rest of Zach's things in, minus the essentials he would need since he wouldn't be staying there until their wedding night.

On June twenty-sixth, Belinda and Robert arrived to assist in putting the finishing touches on the wedding. They insisted on staying at a motel as it was just the two of them on Roxanne's side of the family and they didn't want to put either the Blaze family or Roxanne out. Roxanne had only told her father and father-in-law that she would be walking down the aisle with no crutches. It was supposed to be a surprise for the rest of the guests, and Zach. A lot of Zachary's family lived in other states but were either driving or flying in for the wedding including his Grandma and Grandpa Blaze who had yet to meet Roxie. They would arrive a couple of days early to spend some time with the family. They didn't get out much anymore, but they couldn't miss their grandson's wedding and couldn't wait to meet the girl that stole his heart.

The day they arrived; Zach couldn't help but feel like the little boy who would stay summers at their home in Kentucky. Unfortunately, Clara's parents had passed away when she was eighteen, but she was certain they would be proud of that young adult their grandson had become and she had no doubt that Bryce was in heaven, spending time with them and watching over his family. She often wondered whether Bryce had been with Roxanne and the other survivors before they were located.

Zack saw his grandparents and wanted to run to them like he had when he was a little boy, but they were both frail now and he knew that he couldn't. Once he helped them with their luggage into the house, he gave them both a big hug and introduced them to the love of his life, and her parents. His grandparents immediately fell in love with the girl who stole their grandson's heart. "Isn't she just beautiful," Grandma Blaze marveled. It didn't seem to bother her, or Grandpa Blaze that Roxie was in a wheelchair. It might've been because they had heard about the accident and her miraculous recovery as it was going on.

Roxie, of course, blushed at the compliment. She was thankful they gave her the benefit of the doubt even though they knew she came from money. Zach's grandparents were not ones to make snap judgments about other people until they knew them well. Until that time, they loved them as if they had known them all their lives. They even treated Robert and Belinda as if they were already family. "Where's Stevie?" Grandma Blaze asked, "Is she still dating that boy?" She didn't like Jeb that much and was not afraid to say so. Neither her nor Grandpa Blaze had seen him since Bryce's funeral and, at that time, he had not won any brownie points with them.

"Yes, she is still dating him, and they should be here in a few minutes," Clara replied. "He's changed a lot since you met him. I think watching everything that happened with Roxie messed him up bad. He doesn't smoke pot anymore nor does he drink as much; definitely not around us."

"That is good to hear," Grandpa Blaze, who sat quietly and listened until that point, said.

The rest of that week was spent making sure the wedding would be pulled off without a hitch.

Chapter 7

Zachary and Roxanne's wedding day had finally arrived. To say they were both a tad nervous was putting it mildly. They spent the twenty-four hours prior, apart, as the superstition went that it was bad luck for the bride and groom to see each other before their nuptials. That was extremely hard for Zachary, but he did it anyway because Roxanne wanted everything traditional. She stayed with her parents in their motel and that would be where she would get ready and then she, her parents, Stevie and Clara would go to the Blaze's together.

    The day dragged on for Zach and Roxie as they waited for the six o'clock moment when they would see each other once again and become husband and wife. Before too long, however, it was time for the wedding march. As Zach waited, somewhat impatiently for a glimpse of his Roxie, he was taken aback when he saw her with Gerald on one side and Robert on the other walking toward him, slowly. His mouth fell open, along with many of the guests, as they watched her go to him without crutches. *She's going to fall.* That was the first thought that entered Zach's mind but when he saw the smile spreading across her face, he couldn't deny this was what she had always wanted. When he realized that neither his father nor Robert were going to allow her to fall, he focused on the gorgeous woman in front of him. Once he could peel his eyes from her, he noticed her wheelchair waiting for her next to Stevie who was her maid of honor. He was grateful that they had thought ahead and knew she couldn't stand for long periods of time. There were whispers all throughout the barn about how beautiful his bride was. He could not have said it better himself.

"Dearly beloved, we are gathered here today to join Zachary Bradley Blaze and Roxanne Leigh McCain as husband and wife," the mayor recited by heart. "If there's anyone who wishes that these two not be wed, speak now or forever hold your peace." Zach let out a sigh of relief when no one came forward. The mayor continued, "These two have opted to write their own vows, so I will allow them to say them now."

Zach went first, "Roxie, the first time I saw you, I admit, there were some mixed feelings. You were spoiled and entitled, and you weren't afraid to let everyone know it. Then our Algebra professor that first semester threw us together to help each other. I thought he was, for sure, off his rocker, but as we spent time together, helping each other, I learned there was more to you than the spoiled brat that you let people see. I'm so glad I didn't allow that to stand in my way and that you agreed to our first date. Otherwise, I don't think we would be standing here today. I want you to know how much I admire and love you. The last several months have been hell for you as you survived the plane crash, went through paralysis and learned to walk again just so you could be walked down the aisle by your father, and mine. I love you. I love your laugh, I love your smile, I love the way you get my jokes and even if you don't, give me a courtesy laugh anyway. I love that you have stretched me beyond my comfort zone and helped me see there are parts of this world that I would have missed had it not been for you. I will take care of you and love you for eternity if you'll have me."

Roxanne couldn't stem the flow of tears as she listened to her cowboy tell her what she already knew. Then it was her turn, and it was difficult to say while trying not to cry, "Zach, you are my rock, my hero and my best friend. I know that at first, I was a huge pest, but I was used to getting what I wanted anytime I wanted it and I was determined to have you whether you wanted me or not," this elicited laughter from the guests, "since our first date, I've known we have something special and that we're connected in a way that only soulmates can be connected. Thank you for loving me regardless of my spoiled battiness and in spite of my disability. I love you more than there are stars in the sky and cannot wait to see what our life together will be like."

"What beautiful vows," the mayor included. "Now, Zach. Do you take Roxie to be your lawfully wedded wife, to have and to hold from this day forward, in sickness and in health, for better or for worse, from this day forward?"

Zach looked into the chocolate brown eyes he had grown to love and did not hesitate, "I do."

"Roxie, do you take Zach to be your lawfully wedded husband, to have and to hold from this day forward, in sickness and in health, for better or for worse, from this day forward?"

Through teary eyes, Roxie proclaimed, "I do." Then they exchanged their respective rings.

"By the power vested in me, and by the state of Tennessee, you are now husband and wife. You may kiss your bride. After what seemed like the most passionate kiss the two had ever managed, the mayor continued, "May I present to you, Mr. and Mrs. Zachary and Roxanne Blaze!" A whole bunch of catcalls and whistles went up as they were formally presented to the small crowd.

By the time the reception was over Roxie was exhausted, even spending the entire time in her chair. She wasn't ignorant enough to think she could stand for any length of time after walking down the aisle, but it felt good to see the jaw drop on her husband's face. They were able to visit a bit with the doctor who had a huge hand in her rescue and recovery, Sgt. Jason Kurt. He could not believe how well Roxie looked and was amazed at how she was able to stand, much less walk down the aisle. He was glad he could make it and had even brought Vivienne and Joshua with him; the other two survivors from the crash. Roxie was so worn out that they left before everyone else. They didn't see the point in renting a motel when they had never stayed in the apartment together.

Their wedding night would be one for the books. Zach was aware of Roxanne's pain and gently helped her take the bobby-pins from her hair and gingerly pulled her out of her dress and into the shower. Since it was a walk-in shower, she could sit on the bench while he stood behind her, washing her hair and lathering a loofa sponge with the strawberry goodness he loved so much, and helped her get the grime of the day off. Once she was cleaned up, she stayed put while he took his shower. Instead of putting her back in her chair, he wrapped a towel around her, and carried her into the bedroom and laid her on the bed. He lovingly dried her hair and took a dry towel and dried her body. He tried not to allow the heat between them make her move any faster than she could, but it was hard. Roxanne couldn't wait any longer as she pulled him down, towel and all for a passionate, burning kiss; one that they had never dared try before for fear of going too far. "Rox," he growled, "Do you know what you are doing to me?"

Innocently, she replied, "I do, and I've waited a long time for this," she giggled. That giggle sent him clean over the edge.

To each other's bliss, they made meaningful, steamy love, well into the night. At about three o'clock in the morning, he asked, "Are you okay?"

Roxie's response was a contented sigh. She worried so much about how they would make this work when her legs were so mangled, but that didn't matter. The night was perfect. That didn't stop her from asking, "Was I okay?" This wasn't her first time having sex, but it was her first time making love.

"You're kidding, right? That was amazing! Neither of us are new to sex but both of us are new to lovemaking with disabilities involved. I didn't want you to know but I wondered how we would make this work and it seems that we have figured it out. We are truly soulmates and I love you."

"Honestly, I thought I would disappoint you."

He took her hand and put it up to his racing heart, "You feel that? Does that feel like a disappointment to you?

"No"

"Never think that you will ever be a disappointment to me, promise?"

Roxie cried a lot it seemed, since the accident. And, that moment was no different, "Promise."

Zachary wiped her tears with the pad of his thumb. "Are you hungry?"

"It's after three in the morning! You're serious?"

"What can I say, making love to you makes a man ravenous," Zach laughed.

"I'm hungry, alright. But not for food." Roxie rolled on her side and kissed his neck.

"Ah, woman, you're killing me," Zach sighed. Like Roxie, he wasn't new to sex either, but this? This was on a whole different level. He was glad they had decided to wait. It seemed more intimate somehow.

Finally, at five o'clock, after no sleep, Zach went to the kitchen and made a simple breakfast of eggs, sausage and toast and served his wife in bed. "I could get used to this," she smiled. Even being sleep deprived, she was the most beautiful woman he had ever seen. "All I can say is I'm happy that we don't leave until tomorrow for Jamaica.

"Me too. We can stay in bed all day and sleep between…" Zach waggled his eyebrows at her and grinned his lopsided smile.

"You, my dear husband, are wicked," the glazed look in her eyes told Zach everything he needed to know.

"I love the way you say that word," Zach commented.

Continuing to tease him, Roxy said, "What word? I?" She batted her eyelashes at him.

"You minx—you know exactly what word I'm talking about."

"Yes, I do, but this is more fun," she snickered. They spent the rest of the day sleeping and spending time in each other's loving arms, making sure that Roxie did not overdo it.

The next morning at seven o'clock, found them at the Nashville airport, awaiting their flight to Jamaica. Roxie had not been on an airplane since that fateful evening when she was coming home from Los Angeles. Zach worried she might have some anxiety, so a few days before the wedding he made an appointment for her with her doctor to get something to help with that. To his amazement, the doctor didn't even hesitate to give Roxie her prescriptions that she would need to help make her flight less anxious.

"Are you scared?" Zach asked his wife.

"A little, but you're with me so I'm going to try and not think about what might happen."

"That's a good way to look at it, but even still, I think you need to take the medication the doctor gave you. This cannot be easy for you."

"It's not, but I can't wait to experience Jamaica with you."

It wasn't too long before their flight was called for boarding. Roxie did her best to squash her angst, but Zach saw right through it. Once they were seated and, in the air, Roxie let out a sigh of relief. They had made it that far. An hour into their flight, Roxie nodded off, her head resting on Zach's shoulder. He watched her sleep while listening to the movie they had playing on the screen. He was more interested in memorizing his wife's face as she slept than watching anything on tv. She'd agreed to taking medication just before the plane taxied down the runway.

Roxanne's next recognition was Zach nudging her awake. They had landed at the airport in Jamaica, and it was time to deboard the airplane. "I slept that whole time?" she asked amazed and also relieved.

"Darlin,' it was only about a three-hour flight. And yes, you zonked the entire ride. Part of it could've been from the anxiety meds, but we were up awfully late over the last few days," he gave her his famous flirty smile.

Roxie turned around so she could see his face even though she heard the flirtatiousness in his voice and she could even hear the smile, it made her heart skip a beat when she could see it; knowing *she* caused that look and smoldering in his eyes. *She* was the reason. "What am I going to do with you?" she shook her head and grinned. They hailed a cab and had gotten checked into their hotel room in record time. It helped that Robert called and set everything up just as soon as the newlyweds told him where they wanted to go. Having connections didn't hurt either.

The two weeks that the newlyweds spent in Jamaica, although blissful, were far too short to see all the sights they wanted and go to, they wanted to visit all of the places they were told about. Before long, they were on an airplane headed to Los Angeles for the reception there.

Zachary was not looking forward to the extremely large reception his in-laws put together for all their friends and colleagues. He was a small-town boy and Los Angeles was too much for him, but he couldn't let his mother-in-law down so he swallowed and dealt with the hundreds of people he didn't know who had come to the country club Robert and Belinda belonged to, to pay homage to the couple. Most were just curious about the cowboy who Roxanne had chosen as her spouse. They never thought she would marry; she was too selfish after all.

As they sat in tuxedos and the extravagant black, lacy dress that Roxanne's mother demanded she buy since she allowed her to wear *her* choice of a wedding dress, Zach could not help but think that if Roxie had not been born and bred into such high fashion, she may have turned out differently; more like the girl he knew and loved. The one that, at that moment, was doing the best she could to prove to the snobs that she had known her whole life she was no longer the spoiled brat that she was raised to be. She and Zach both tried their best to talk with these people who were bound and determined to prove that Roxanne had not changed at all. Eventually, Zach couldn't take it anymore. Luckily for those who were trying to discredit his wife, Clara and Gerald were there to douse his temperament, otherwise, those people who *thought* they knew Roxie would get a taste of what he would allow, and that was not much when it came to his Roxie.

They decided, since Zach's parents were in Los Angeles, they wanted to take them to Disneyland. Even though there weren't many rides Roxie could go on because of her disability, they both wanted Clara and Gerald to experience the thrill of the scarier rides. They watched together, as terror crossed Clara's face on more than one ride. Both laughed because Zachary had those same expressions when Roxie had brought him to this same place many months before. Things were different then, but at the same time, they seemed better now. Neither Zach nor Roxie would let either of Zach's parents off the hook about going on the roller coasters. The same ones that had caused him intense fear. "I did it," he said, "And if I can, you two can as well."

Roxie decided to sweeten the pot just to see if they would take Zach up on his challenge. "If you both go on Space Mountain, we will pay for you to see the opera tomorrow night before we go back to Tennessee."

Zach knew his mom would never let a bet like that go so, without even consulting her husband, she grabbed his hand, much like a gleeful schoolgirl and ran for the line toward the horrendous roller coaster. After handing over their tickets. Clara turned to her son and daughter-in-law and replied, "Get ready to eat your heart out!" The dread that crossed Gerald's face was priceless.

"Dear," he gulped, "Are you sure about this?"

"For the opera? Damn skippy." Zach laughed at his mom; she never swore and if anyone else heard her they could tell she was not from California. When they got off the roller coaster, Gerald's face was three shades of green. He looked like he was going to puke at any moment. "We did it. Now y'all owe us opera tickets."

"Just as I promised," Roxie said. "That's a great last night in L.A., don't you think?"

"What're the two of you going to do?" Clara wondered. She should have known better than to ask that. She rolled her eyes at her son's crooked grin.

Chapter 8

The opera was everything Clara had hoped it would be. Belinda had even let her borrow one of her ball gowns; one did not go to the opera in a normal dress. The burgundy, sleeveless gown which flared out at the bottom was elegant, yet simple. Much like Clara, herself. When they arrived at the opera house, everything was big. Bigger than Clara was used to, that was for sure. She took in the sights of it all as their tickets were punched so if they needed to, they could go in and out. Their seats were box seats; she was sure that Robert had used his clout at Roxie's request in order to get those. She was grateful for this once in a lifetime opportunity. She could not help but smile at the thought of the terrifying feat she and Gerald endured to get them. Her daughter-in-law never ceased to amaze her.

While the Blazes were at the opera, Zachary and Roxanne spent some time with Belinda and Robert, since when they returned to Tennessee they didn't know when they would see them again. They spent the evening doing their best to teach Roxie's parents how to play Pinochle; a game that Zach had taught Roxie when they were just beginning to get serious. They had been at her apartment, and after studying for finals for what felt like forever, Zachary asked her if she had ever heard of the game.

"Of course not. Does that sound even remotely like something that someone such as myself would have heard of, much less, played?" That was the turning point in the way Zach dealt with her. He had no qualms about telling her when her hoity-toitiness was showing. She had learned to play the game that night and they'd played many times with Clara and Gerald after that. It took a while for Belinda to catch on but once she did, there was no stopping her. They played far into the night, eating popcorn, drinking Mountain Dew and Pepsi with Roxie's parents telling Zach of the trouble Roxie got into as a child. It saddened Belinda that most of the stories were relayed to them by the nanny for they were always busy at work.

"You didn't!" was Zach's response to Roxie's first attempt at baking at the ripe old age of three.

"I did," she giggled, "The nanny was so mad at me. I'd done what I'd seen her do on numerous occasions. I didn't think I was doing anything wrong."

"In her defense, "Robert intervened, "She, at least, made everything on the counter. Never mind that she spilled the eggs, flour and sugar everywhere, thinking herself big enough to bake all by her lonesome."

"I have a question, my darlin,' what in the world were you trying to make?"

"Cookies, of course," Roxanne defended herself.

"With just eggs, milk and flour?" Zach was rolling with laughter and almost fell off his chair.

"Hey! I *was* only three!" It felt good being able to share stories from her childhood with Zach. It almost felt like her parents had been around.

"What about the time she was six and 'did the laundry'?" Robert asked.

"No, daddy! Please do not tell him that one. Please!"

"Oh, come on!" Zachary complained, "It's only fair after all the stories my parents have told you. And *that* was from the beginning too! Not after we got married, so please, tell away. I have to have something to tell our kids." He grinned her favorite smile and she forgot for a moment how embarrassing her antics as a child were.

"She thought she would help the maid with the housework, one day. She was good at that as a kid. Loved being around the staff and helping wherever she could. That time though, she thought she was big stuff and did what she had watched the maid do many times before. It was not difficult for her to put her three favorite stuffed animals; a brown cocker spaniel named Squishy, an orange tabby named Meow and a white cotton-tailed bunny named Cotton in the washer as we had a front load one. But then the little stinker climbed up on the washer, got the detergent down, climbed back down and dumped a whole bunch of the powder into the washer and slammed the door," Belinda grinned at the memory of the nanny who had told her. That day though, she was madder than a pit bull. Luckily, the mess was cleaned up by the time she'd heard the story.

"What happened next?" Zach chuckled.

"Well, "Robert continued where Belinda had left off, "there were so many bubbles, Roxanne figured she could take a bubble bath."

"Where was the nanny?" Zach couldn't help laughing.

"She thought Roxanne was in the nursery. Well, the toy room." Belinda inserted. "I will tell you, she thought she was going to be fired that day."

"She barely got me cleaned up by the time mom and daddy came home," Roxanne decided to join in the fun even though it was a story about her, and it was embarrassing to let her new husband know that she'd been full of shenanigans when she was little. Thankfully, they had not gotten to her teenage years yet. "It took the butler, the nanny and the maid to get rid of all the suds and they'd barely finished before my mom came home from work. Dad was out of town on a business trip."

"How did you talk yourself out of that?" Zachary asked Roxie.

"What makes you think I had to?" she asked with mock hurt on her face.

"I know you better than that. You've been talking yourself out of, and sometimes into stuff your entire life. It worked on me and I'm sure it worked on your nanny and maid, too." The twinkle in Zach's eye was noticed by everyone at the table.

"She tried blaming the maid," Belinda admitted, "she always did stuff like that if she thought she was going to be in trouble."

Feigning innocence, Roxie gasped, "I would never…" but couldn't help the chuckle that erupted at the rolling of her husband's eyes. "Hey, don't you roll your eyes," she teased as Zach grinned at her.

"What are you going to do about it?" he taunted.

"You'll get yours," she teased back.

"Ohh, you're so scary!"

"You two act like a couple of teenagers, not a married couple." Robert was amused.

"Sometimes we have to, "Roxie defended them, but smiled all the while she spoke.

"I think it's time we retire for the night," Belinda laughed, "This has been a lot of fun, but I am exhausted," glancing at her husband, she asked, "Are you coming, Robert?"

Without missing a beat, he replied, "Yes, dear." They both bid the newlyweds goodnight and went upstairs where their bedroom was.

It was about two o'clock in the morning when Clara and Gerald returned from the opera. Clara was tired, but on cloud nine at the same time. She could not hold in her enthusiasm as the adrenaline coursed through her veins. As Gerald observed his wife, she was much like the young woman she had been when they'd married all those years ago. No one would have guessed all the heartache this fantastically gorgeous woman he was proud to call his wife had endured in the last twenty years they had been married. He watched her all through the opera, like a kid at the candy store for the first time. Gerald never would have taken a chance on that roller coaster, not in a million years but when he witnessed the yearning in his wife's eyes at the mere mention of tickets to the opera, well, he knew he would endure that, and whatever else he needed to to see the glee that crossed her face. And, then to watch her at the opera and the feelings it stirred in him, he would have done anything for her. "Are you tired, my dear?" he asked as he kissed the top of Clara's head.

"Hmm," Clara's eyes were already drifting closed as the limo took them back to Robert and Belinda's mansion, "A little."

"You had a good time, didn't you?"

"Yes, and you?"

"I would do whatever was necessary to see the excitement on your face I saw tonight."

"It *was* a once in a lifetime chance, wasn't it?"

"I think we could arrange a trip to New York City to see one again. I rather enjoyed myself, although I'm just a lowly veterinarian."

"My sweet, you don't seriously think of yourself like that, do you? I hope not. You're so much more than that. More than no amount of money could buy."

They were a little surprised to find Roxie and Zach had waited up for them. They walked in on the newlyweds watching *Eight Seconds,* a movie that had always been on Zachary's most favorite, but until now, could not get Roxie to watch it. That was, he thought, because it was a heart-wrenching movie, and she did not like him to see her vulnerable. It was difficult enough for her to still need his assistance with walking and getting in her wheelchair some days when the pain was too much. She had learned to be independent and, for the most part, was just that, but there were days…

"You finally got her to watch it, huh?" Gerald asked as he helped Clara off with her coat.

"Yup... You guys have a good time?" Zach questioned. He could tell by the tired, yet happy look on his mom's face, that they had had a splendid evening.

"It was wonderful!" Clara's excitement was still evident, "I would ride a million rollercoasters to be able to experience that again."

"I told you, didn't I?" Roxie inserted, "There is nothing like a good opera."

"Except maybe a good rodeo," Zach razzed his young wife. He had yet to go to an opera, but she had accompanied him to a rodeo a time or two since moving to Tennessee.

"You just wait, my dear son. She'll get you to an opera yet," Clara said, "In fact, your dad and I are talking about catching one in New York. Maybe the four of us could go. Then, you can see what we mean."

"You mean it?" Roxie asked Gerald.

"I mean it," was the reply.

"That would be so much fun!"

"Well...we see that your parents have already gone to bed. I'm tired and we have a long day ahead, getting home," Clara responded.

"Yeah, I'm tired too," Roxie reciprocated, "It *is* four in the morning Tennessee time, and we leave at noon to go to the airport." Her parents had insisted that they fly first class since Gerald and Clara did not want the private jet to linger at the Chattanooga Airport, which would mean they would be responsible for it—it had been fixed in the two weeks the Blazes had been in L. A.

Saying goodbye to her parents was harder on Roxie than she expected. She was just getting to know them as adults, as people, and not just as the ones who called themselves her parental figures. She was never more grateful for their ability to travel when and where they wanted as she was the day they left to go back to Tennessee. Tears flowed as she gave both of her parents a hug and a kiss on the cheek, something her mother would never have allowed before, but had learned a few things since the accident several months before.

Both Blaze couples were grateful by the time they reached their respective homes with the taxi dropping off Zach and Roxie at their apartment first. Both newlyweds were exhausted but ecstatic that every part of the wedding was done, and they could look forward to their future together. School started again for them both in a few weeks and, although Roxie was not as interested in school as she once was but knew she needed something to keep her busy and her mind off the one thing that still niggled at the back of her mind; school could help with that. She and Zach had discussed starting a family fairly soon after their wedding but there continued to be that worry for Roxie that she wouldn't have the inability to carry a baby, even though several different doctors had told her there was no reason why she could not. Unbeknownst to her husband, Roxie had talked with Stevie and Jeb a bit about being a surrogate in case she was unable. Stevie has been ecstatic at the prospect of being able to give this gift to her brother and sister-in-law. Roxie wasn't sure how Zachary would react and was almost afraid to talk to him about it since they'd only been married a couple of months.

A few days after they returned from Los Angeles, Zach and Roxie had to ready themselves for the busy semester ahead. It was nice to be able to go to the bookstore and get their needed items together. Due to her inability to walk excessive amounts, it was decided, after much discussion, that Roxie would use her wheelchair during school hours unless Zach was with her. They didn't have many classes near each other and that worried Zach a little because he knew his wife was stubborn enough to try and walk to classes by herself.

It was definitely different for both of them on the day classes started, as they got ready together and left together from their apartment when they were used to one of them picking the other up. "This is nice, isn't it?" Roxie asked as Zach wheeled her out to the car, leaving her crutches at home so she would not be tempted to try walking alone

"What?" Zach questioned.

"Being able to be together all of the time. I loved getting ready with you this morning. Don't get me wrong, picking you up wasn't bad, but I like this much better."

"Me too," Zach replied as he deposited her in the passenger seat of his truck. It had been decided, that because they both worked at the vet clinic, he would drive most days because he couldn't drive her car being that it had been specifically made for her. On the days she had to wait an hour for him to get out of his last class, which was only two days a week, they took separate cars. Roxie did not mind letting her husband drive. She relished sitting next to him on the seat of the truck, and for a little while, at least, she could forget she now had a disability she would have to live with for the rest of her life.

Epilogue

Roxie got pregnant a year after they were married but lost the baby. The doctors couldn't tell them why because as they said, she was perfectly healthy other than the use of her legs. The couple was heartbroken. Roxie suffered from depression even before the miscarriage, but after, it was so much worse. She didn't go to school or really want to do anything. Zachary didn't know what to do or how to handle the situation. He knew she couldn't miss much more school, or she would get suspended, at the very least.

Three weeks after the miscarriage he'd finally had enough of watching her wallow. Taking care not to hurt her anymore and she was already hurting, one Monday morning he opened the blinds before she was up and said, "Good morning,' Darlin." He hoped his pet name for her would at least get her in the shower, "It's time to get up and get ready for school. You missed a lot, and although your teachers are understanding, you can't miss much more without running the risk of being suspended. I don't want to see that happen, so let's get up." He patted her on the bottom, as she stirred.

"I don't care if I ever set foot inside that school again. That's not important to me anymore."

Taking a harsher tone than he liked, he urgently said, "Baby, I know this is a setback, but you heard the doctor; we will be able to have a baby one way or another. He doesn't know why this happened, but it happens even to people that are not paraplegic. Let's get out of bed and get to school. Now!"

Zack had never spoken to her like that before and she was sure she would be grateful for it one day but at that moment she wanted to slap him, but she did as he said and allowed him to assist her out of bed. She had to admit that taking a shower felt nice and almost made her feel human again.

Once they were at school, Roxie could put the miscarriage to the back of her mind, but it was always there. She wasn't even able to know whether it was a boy or girl and when she imagined him/her she could see her brown eyes and Zach's curly, brown hair or his green eyes with her straight as a bone dark hair. Paying attention in class was difficult, but she made it through her first day without any real mishaps. After school, she and Zach rode together to work where her in-laws were grateful to see her face even though there was sadness there.

The doctor said they could try again as soon as Roxie felt ready, but she was afraid to. She couldn't handle going through another miscarriage; just the thought of such an ordeal made her more anxious than she already was. So, one night, four months after her ordeal, she decided to talk to Zach about the surrogacy idea. "Hey, sweets, can I talk to you about something?"

Zach was studying but could tell by her tone that it was relatively important, "Sure," he replied as he closed his books, giving Roxie his undivided attention.

"Do you remember before we got married, not long after the accident when I was concerned about my ability to carry a baby?"

"Yes," worry etched Zach's brow.

"I talked at length with Stevie about being our surrogate should it come to that."

Zach wanted to be angry and hurt that she had gone behind his back, but he also knew that was something she needed to do on her own, as a woman. He was curious as to his sister's response, so he asked, "What was the verdict?"

"She and Jeb both seemed excited about it. The thing is, it'll cost us a lot of money and I'm apprehensive to broach the subject with my parents because I really wanted us to do things on our own. You know what I mean?"

He went over to where Roxie was seated on the couch, picked her up since she was as light as a feather and set her on his lap. Once Roxie was seated and Zach's arms securely wrapped around her, he continued, "To be honest, I'm a little hurt that you would ask my sister without talking to me first but I do understand why you did it and I think your parents would be glad to help with the cost if it means your peace of mind and that we have a baby."

Roxie began crying, swiping at the tears furiously as they rolled down her cheeks, "How did I ever get so lucky?" She kissed him, then added, "I should have had you come with me but when I first mentioned the idea to Stevie, it was just she and I and, I thought that it might be kind of awkward if you were there."

"That makes sense, I guess, so what you're trying to tell me is that you don't want to try getting pregnant again yourself? Is it because you're scared that you might miscarry again or is it because at least this way you know that the chances are higher that we will have a baby sooner than later?"

"A little of both, I think."

"Well how about we both talk to my sister and Jed and maybe my parents, then we will approach your parents."

"That sounds like a good plan." The relief was evident on Roxie's face.

One year later…

The past year has been a roller coaster full of appointments, school, more doctors' appointments and finally the birth of triplets to Zach and Roxie Blaze. Stevie had no problems carrying the babies. To say they were surprised at triplets was an understatement but that just meant more for the grandmas to spoil. The day they were born was hard, but at the same time, amazing for Roxie. She wished she had a better feeling about herself carrying a baby full term, but she didn't. Being able to be in the room with her husband and mother-in-law was a great experience, though. The babies only had to stay in the hospital for two weeks as they gained weight and learned to suck from a bottle. It was a lot less time than anyone thought since they were taken via cesarean, and were born six weeks early, but all three were healthy and thriving.

As Roxie sat holding Daxton Lee, and Ronneigh Grace while Zach was changing Alanna Rose's diaper, she could not believe how blessed she was. She would forever be indebted to Stevie for giving her and Zach the greatest gift anyone could give. She had already been spoiling them as much as she could at their tiny age and Roxie was not about to begrudge her of that.

The last few years had been difficult, but they'd made it through, and for Roxie, she had come full circle…From Brat to Bronco.

The End

About the Author

Hunter Marshall is a cowboy, jean wearing, country music and rock lovin' cowgirl who loves books and jewelry. She was born three months too early with a disability and wasn't supposed to be able to walk, talk, see, hear or have any semblance of a normal life. Her mother, however, knew she was more than a disability. She made sure Hunter did everything she was capable of to reach her full potential.

Coming from a big family, it was either keep up or get left in the dust. It was because of her love of reading and writing that Hunter knew, even at an early age, she was destined to be a writer. Hunter began reading at the age of four and writing as soon as she could spell, filling up folder and folder with short stories and keeping a journal which, she still does.

Hunter went on to graduate high school much to the awe and amazement of the doctors' who told her parents she would never amount to anything. She did the exact opposite, going on to get married and have children. She then succeeded in getting a degree in Social Work which she uses to write her books.

Hunter lives in Idaho with her two kids, husband and the newest member of the family, a Maltese named Oakley who has become her writing 'helper.' She has one published novel, Wake Up! Based on a true story of abuse and betrayal, has written for an anthology, A Christmas Wish, and is currently working on a couple surprise projects.

Hunter loves hearing from her reader.
Shoot her a message or an email!

Important Links

Facebook:
www.facebook.com/huntermarshall2015

Twitter:
www.twitter.com/writermom2015

Instagram:
www.instagram.com/huntermarshall78

Amazon: Amazon.com/author/huntermarshall

Book Bub:

https://www.bookbub.com/profile/hunter-marshall-be731da9-120c-4dc0-8e7b-533f6684ee8b

Email:
Huntermarshall78@gmail.com

Made in the USA
Middletown, DE
06 March 2023